Up Periscope!
and Other Stories

Up Periscope!
and Other Stories

Alec Hudson

with a Foreword by
Captain Edward L. Beach, USN (Ret.)

Naval Institute Press
Annapolis, Maryland

© 1938, 1939, 1940, 1941 by Wilfred Jay Holmes
Introduction © 1992
by the United States Naval Institute
Annapolis, Maryland. All rights reserved.

The stories in this collection were originally published in the *Saturday Evening Post* in 1938, 1939, 1940, and 1941. They were later published in two collections by the Macmillan Company—the first, in 1942, entitled *Rendezvous*, and the second, in 1945, entitled *Open Fire!*

The Naval Institute Press edition is a facsimile of a special edition published by The Readers Club, Inc., in 1943 entitled *Rendezvous and Other Long and Short Stories about Our Navy in Action*.

Library of Congress Cataloging-in-Publication Data

Hudson, Alec, 1900–
    [Rendezvous and other long and short stories about our Navy in action]
    Up periscope! and other stories / Alec Hudson ; with a foreword by Edward L. Beach.
        p.   cm.
    Facsim. ed. of: Rendezvous and other long and short stories about our Navy in action. Readers Club, 1943.
    ISBN 1-55750-377-X
    1. World War, 1939–1945—Naval operations, American—Fiction.
    2. United States—History, Naval—20th century—Fiction. 3. War stories, American. I. Title.
    PS3515.U2213R46   1992
    813'.54—dc20   92-3744
                                                          CIP

Printed in the United States of America on acid-free paper ∞

9 8 7 6 5 4 3 2
First printing

FOREWORD

ALEC HUDSON WAS the pen name of a U.S. Navy submarine skipper who was forced through physical disability to retire from active duty nearly six years prior to our entry into World War II. His naval career curtailed, he became a professor of engineering at the University of Hawaii and vicariously continued his service to our Navy by writing stories about it. The first of these appeared in the late 1930s.

I was then a midshipman at the U.S. Naval Academy in Annapolis and, as I recall, there came a letter from my father to the effect that this particular author simply had to be the genuine article, that "Alec Hudson" was undoubtedly the pen name of a professional naval officer. Dad, already a retired captain when I was a child, had written a total of thirteen published books about the Navy, and I intended to follow in his footsteps. The *Saturday Evening Post* of those years carried some of Alec Hudson's work, and it was through this medium that I first began to know him as an author. The reinforcement of Father's own naval-cum-literary career played no small part in confirming my own determination to write about the Navy from the point of view of someone who served in it and respected it. Clearly, Alec Hudson knew the Navy, and loved it. In the literary sense he was a continuation of the man who had given me life and purpose.

A number of years later I discovered that Alec Hudson was, in real life, CDR W. Jay "Jasper" Holmes, USN (Ret.), and in due course, with some trepidation, I began a small and rather infrequent correspondence with him. My first letter was critical, for I thought I had detected an inconsistency in one of his stories. He answered immediately, a habit he continued to observe in subsequent years. It was tremendously exciting for me to receive his replies, and at some point it struck home with force that he had responded thoughtfully to every single letter I had written. That, too, has had its effect on me, and I've tried to follow his example.

v

Around this time World War II intervened, and Alec Hudson disappeared for the duration. I guessed what had happened, partly at least. He had, before the beginning of the war at that, returned to active duty. What I didn't know was that he had become an intelligence officer at Pearl Harbor and, after the attack on the Day of Infamy, had taken on himself the particular and personal dedication to see to the destruction of every ship that had participated in it. During the war, from time to time, commanders of submarines would receive by messenger, without explanation, a bottle of fine whiskey. Little by little the word got around that one of the ships sunk on a recent patrol had carried special significance for someone. In this way Jasper Holmes never left our submarines. It was through him that we would sometimes receive orders to be somewhere at a certain time—and on occasion there was a bottle of booze at the end of the trail.

That Alec Hudson was a pen name caused me some problems, however, for when I began to write about the Navy, after the war, I had to sort out whether or not I wanted to use a pseudonym myself. Once or twice I was on the verge of writing to ask Holmes for his rationalization for this, but thought better of it. It was too private a thing, I felt. I cherished our bi- or tri-annual exchanges too much to risk them; and besides, it was the sort of thing that one should handle for one's self. I did, in fact, once use a pen name, one time only; but in the end I decided not to because Father had not.

There is a special quality in Alec Hudson's writings that I found fascinating when I first noted it, and still do. He went into long introspective dissertations on how things worked as he knew them, and even though some of them differed from what I was trained in, one knew instinctively that he was accurate for the time about which he wrote. This is how it was back then. This is how he expected to function, and how his training led him to believe his weapons would perform. Not once, in any of his stories, did a gun, or torpedo, or bomb fail to function as it was supposed to.

His descriptions of torpedo attacks are good examples of this. Reading them now one knows that our torpedoes never performed that well, and never could have because of the failure of both builders and testers. What actually comes across is that CDR Jasper Holmes, USN, was simply describing the faith he had in the Navy and in his weapons, the faith he had every right to have. Thus Alec Hudson, besides being a top-notch writer about our Navy, is among many other things a perfect mirror of the past. This was how the Navy was in 1939, when I graduated from Annapolis, just before the war that we'd been unknowingly preparing for throughout our naval history. This was how we all expected things to be. Alec Hudson was describing them as he had been taught they should be.

That they were, in reality, not that way at all is of little consequence insofar as his stories were concerned, but it is of enormous consequence to the postwar Navy of today. He made the picture of our Navy sing. My father and I loved his stories. But when it came to things that he had to take on faith, like the performance of the weapons our country gave us to fight the war with, the picture he painted then illustrates nothing so much to us now as how fatuously wrong most of our prewar concepts actually were. Thus, even here he does us a service.

Until 7 December 1941, we were, all of us, living in a fool's paradise. The sad thing is that so many with responsibilities in these areas actually knew in their hearts that things were not as they seemed, that too many test results were faked ("gun-decked") because failed tests were unacceptable, whatever the reason, and that someone up the line wanted it all glossed over so long as he was in charge. When the war came, as everyone really knew it would, not one single individual was made to assume personal responsibility for the egregious incapability of practically every weapon we had. Whatever failures can be laid to our Pearl Harbor commanders, they were unimportant compared to the colossal and continued failures of our Naval Bureau of Ordnance.

It should be noted that despite being a dyed-in-the-wool submariner, Alec Hudson did not write only about submarines. One of his stories is about an old four-stack destroyer, similar to one that I served in for two years and still look back upon with great nostalgia. Everything Alec Hudson's destroyer did was authentically possible, if a bit high on the heroics, and students of the short campaign of our Asiatic Fleet at the beginning of the war will get some idea of what we thought those ships could do. But the fact is they could do nothing. They were totally outclassed. We lost nearly every one, because it was the enemy that had prepared well, not we ourselves. Training does no good if your tools never work right, and that was our real situation.

Although it took the reality of all-out war to tear the veil from our eyes, Alec Hudson told how it was supposed to be with such dramatic intensity that through his tales we see and feel still today what the Navy saw and felt in those days, even though it was all in his imagination. His stories leave us with the emotional determination that these things, this fool's paradise that was the legacy of our prewar Navy, will never, *ever*, be our postwar Navy's legacy to those who follow in *our* footsteps!

—Edward L. Beach
Captain, USN (Ret.)

CONTENTS

Up Periscope!
and Other Stories

RENDEZVOUS

I WASN'T any too well pleased with the assignment. A submarine can expect to be sent out on a fairly wide variety of missions, and lots of them will yield only hard labor and long periods of nerve-racking strain. After a while you come to realize that opportunities to do something effective are few and far between. If chance or fine staff work puts your ship in a position to make an attack, you are in for some intense action for a few minutes. It's more than likely, though, that you will spend a good many weeks at sea, submerged all day and frantically charging batteries all night, without seeing a thing of interest. Then, if you relax your vigilance one iota, disaster is quite certain to pile on top of you without much warning.

You learn to take the best with the worst, the danger and excitement with the plain drudgery, but you should at least have the assurance that your ship will be properly used. A good ship deserves the opportunity of developing her full military effectiveness. The worst of this was that I had been maneuvered into such a position that I couldn't very well grumble about it.

When the force commander asked me to go with him to a conference with the patrol-wing commander and the chief of staff from the Big Flag, I had a premonition that I was going to be put on the spot. There wasn't any apparent reason why he should have picked on me to tag along. Looking back, I can see that I was framed, and I'll bet even money that the only impromptu lines spoken at that conference were my own. As soon as the chief of staff commenced talking, I could read the handwriting on the bulkhead as plain as could be.

Captain Tolliver, the chief of staff, was a blunt man, and he didn't waste words. We had rather reliable information that

1

the enemy was preparing a big expedition at the port of Basoko. Things like that are hard to conceal. They are bound to get out in spite of the tightest censorship. He didn't have all the details, but everything pointed to something important afoot. If the enemy ever got to sea with a well-organized expedition, there were plenty of vulnerable spots he could head for and very little we could do in defense. Basoko was a good three thousand miles away and there wasn't anything we could throw into that area but some light forces to harass him a little. It was an open-and-shut case for some heavy bombing at the port of embarkation while the troops and the transports were concentrated and wide open for it.

At that point the patrol-wing commander came down with the obvious information that it was too far away for his bombers to carry a heavy load of bombs. There was nothing new in that, but we spread out the charts to have another look. I think we all had a good mental picture of the sea area involved, but when I looked at the chart, it seemed to me that Moab, the name of a tiny group of barren rocks, stood out as though it had been printed in red. Its strategic location, less than a thousand miles off the enemy coast, must have been just as apparent to everyone.

"If we could arrange to fuel our planes there," the patrol-wing commander announced, pointing to Moab, "we might be able to do something interesting at Basoko."

That was pretty apparent, too, but the difficulties in the way were so well known that no one bothered to recount them. Moab was two thousand miles away from any effective support. The way was flanked by innumerable islands on which the enemy had a host of patrol craft, planes and submarines. Even if the Battle Fleet had been immediately available, which it wasn't, two thousand miles was a long way to send it to support a raid. To risk the big ships out there, the enemy bases would have to be reduced one by one, and that meant a long campaign. No one had the guts to court disaster by accepting a fleet action two thousand miles from a repair base, with injured ships running that gantlet to get back to a dry dock. A carrier with strong cruiser protection might make a touch-and-go operation of it. But it was risky, and we had too few carriers to gamble them in that fashion.

No one spoke for a few seconds, and I knew that the patrol-wing commander's remark was my cue.

"We could throw some submarines out there and fuel your planes," I volunteered.

From the looks on the faces bent over the chart desk, I knew that everyone was glad that I hadn't muffed my lines. I think that, except for my part in it, everything had been carefully rehearsed.

My force commander had the grace to say, "I had mentioned to them the discussions we have had about the feasibility of such an operation."

I grinned. In my next reincarnation I hope I have sufficient wisdom to keep my mouth shut about things that aren't my own particular business. It used to be that every time I talked myself into a tight spot I would firmly resolve to hold my tongue in the future. I have broken those resolutions so often that I've given up trying any more. This expedition wasn't going to be any more grueling and certainly no more hazardous than any of the operations the rest of the submarines were being called on to undertake. The point was that we should have all the work and all the risks the others were taking, but even if the expedition was spectacularly successful, our part in it would be comparatively minor.

I had spent a good many years training myself and my crew how to handle the ship in a torpedo attack. Together we had risked the ship and our collective necks in countless practice approaches. I thought we were pretty good at it. The Neptune had been designed and built and her crew had been trained for one primary purpose. To reach her full military effectiveness she ought to be used to accomplish that purpose. As a combat submarine she was a superb weapon. As a tanker for aviation gasoline she might do in a pinch, but she would be pretty inefficient at it, and all the training we had gone through would be so much wasted effort.

I didn't voice any of these ideas. Long ago, when there wasn't the remotest chance of undertaking such an expedition, I had been over it all with the force commander. When the problem had been purely academic, I had done most of the arguing on the other side. Now my arguments were coming home to roost.

The bombing of the expeditionary forces was a neat little operation and likely to have far-reaching results. As the wing commander stated, it couldn't be done without refueling en route. No surface ship had the remotest chance of getting in. A submarine was the logical type of ship to undertake it. I had been the proponent of some such scheme in the piping times of peace. I had made all the preliminary investigations for carrying out that kind of a mission. So I was the logical man to pick on to try it. I would rather have had a task assignment with some chance of developing the full power of my ship. Wet-nursing a squadron of planes with a cargo of gasoline wasn't going to do that. But war is like football in some ways. Not everybody can carry the ball. The spectators have their eyes on the ball carrier and he is apt to skim off an undue share of the rewards, but he wouldn't get far without a sturdy line to support him. My main trouble was that I fancied my ship as a ball carrier, and the coaches were giving me a line position to play.

"How long will it take you to get ready and get out there?" the chief of staff asked sharply.

I stepped off the distance on the chart with the dividers and made some rapid mental calculations. We would be sure to encounter at least a few enemy patrols. How long they would delay us by keeping us submerged was anybody's guess. If they kept up down for protracted periods, it would be slow going. The distance we could make submerged was negligible, and when we surfaced after a long run underwater, we would have to use at least a portion of our engine power charging batteries.

I made a reasonable allowance for everything and answered, "Twelve days to two weeks, sir."

"From now?" he asked.

I hadn't figured it so. It would take us at least a day to get ready. We should have to get the reserve fuel tanks ready to take gasoline, and there would be quite a bit of gear to assemble. But Captain Tolliver wasn't the man to permit any dallying.

"Yes, sir," I answered, "from now, if I have every help in getting ready."

"You'll have everything there is to be had," he answered, "and I'll give you ten days."

I reached for my cap. "I guess I'd better be on my way then," I remarked.

"Just a minute," the patrol-wing commander interrupted. "There must be something you will require from us."

"Yes, sir, there will be," I replied. "I suggest that we carry your bombs. That way the planes can carry a reserve fuel supply on the outward trip. Then if it happens that we don't make our rendezvous, they might have enough fuel to get back. We can put the bombs aboard the planes at Moab and top off the planes with fuel before they take off to attack."

"A very good suggestion," he replied. "We start the bombs coming over to you in the morning."

"I can let you have two other submarines," the force commander spoke up. "I wish it could be more, but I haven't them available. When word of the raid finally breaks, we can expect some kind of activity around the enemy's bases. I want to establish submarine patrols there to see if we can't take advantage of it. Two submarines should be able to take care of the refueling. If I give you three, it will provide for certain —er—contingencies. Which ships would you prefer?"

I liked his way of putting it. Two submarines could accomplish all that had to be done, but contingencies certainly should be allowed for in every operation. If he sent three, two could reasonably be expected to get through.

"I'll take the Dryad and the Unicorn," I answered. If he was going to let me have my choice, I was going to take only the best. I knew that Needham in the Dryad and Howard in the Unicorn wouldn't let any grass grow under their feet. They wouldn't hold us up getting ready, and they would get through if anybody could.

"That suits me," he answered. "I'll order them to report to you for instructions."

"It's all settled then," the chief of staff decided. "I'll have the operation order in your hands within the hour, but these will be its main points: Striking force: Patrol Squadron Two."

The patrol commander nodded in agreement.

"Refueling group: Neptune, Dryad and Unicorn, with you, Lieutenant Commander Evans, in tactical command," he went on, looking at me. "The refueling group will depart for Moab as soon as it can be made ready. Take diverging routes to insure that you all won't be held up by counter submarine activities. On the ninth day after your departure —let me see; that will be the morning of the eighteenth— you will occupy Moab with your refueling group. The striking force will leave on the evening of the seventeenth with reserve fuel, but no bombs. They will make a night flight to Moab and contact the refueling group. Then they will refuel and arm, and take off for the attack on the night of the eighteenth. After they have completed their attack, they will return to Moab for refueling, leaving as soon as ready. When the last plane is refueled, the refueling group will return here by the shortest possible route. Is it agreed?"

We all agreed and I left with the force commander in a hurry. I had a long night's work ahead of me and no time to lose.

I found Needham and Howard more enthusiastic about

the whole program than I was. My instructions to them were simple: Get ready to go as soon as possible. We would all shove off at about the same time, but we would proceed independently. There was no need to tell them what to do en route. No one knew what difficulties we were likely to encounter and they were at least as competent as I was to handle the unexpected. We would all carry our tubes loaded with torpedoes, but the reload torpedoes we would have to put ashore to make storage space for the bombs. On only one thing did I have any specific orders. If they arrived at Moab before the eighteenth, they were to lay low and operate off the island submerged until an hour after sunrise on the designated morning. I assigned areas for each in the vicinity of Moab to take care of that contingency, so we should make no unexpected submerged encounters with one another.

Toward evening I found everything going along all right. Bill Green, my executive officer, had everything well in hand, so I decided I would skin home for an hour to have dinner with my wife and kids. I couldn't tell her where I was going, but I could let her know that we should be gone for two or three weeks. By the old and efficient grapevine interwife communication system she would let the wives of my officers know everything she knew before the ships had cleared the harbor. In times past I had often been annoyed by the speed with which the word got around by that system. There was no reason why I shouldn't use it to advantage when the opportunity offered itself. It would save a lot of anxiety if the women knew we were going to be gone for some time.

When I pulled up into the driveway at home, Bob Watkins, who has the house next door, stuck his head over the hedge.

"Going out for a little trip, Joe?" he asked.

"Why, yes, Bob," I answered evasively, "we are going out for a little while again."

It wasn't an expedition to be discussed even with a brother officer. None of my people knew any more than had to be told them to get the necessary work done. They must have known, from the preparations we were making, that we were going out to refuel planes, but none of them would know our destination until we were safely out at sea.

"I'll be seeing you when you get there," Bob grinned.

"That's right," I remembered; "you are flying a plane in Squadron Two now, aren't you?"

"None other," he replied.

"Well, happy landings," I called over the hedge to him as I turned and went into the house.

The next day was filled with the feverish activity of preparations. We had to unload our spare torpedoes and take aboard the heavy bombs for the patrol squadron. We did it while we were loading gasoline into our reserve fuel tanks and taking on supplies for a month's operation. It was with misgivings that I saw the reload torpedoes go ashore. How well-founded those misgivings were I was to find out before I got back again to that harbor.

Toward evening we completed our preparations and we all shoved off together. As soon as we cleared the harbor, the three ships parted company. I got my officers together and laid out the operation order and the charts to show them all where we were going and what it was intended that we should accomplish. It wasn't much of a surprise to anyone. Our preparations had more or less disclosed the purpose of our operation, and for once scuttle-butt rumor had been most accurate. Bill Green, I think, correctly portrayed the common attitude when he remarked that it wasn't going to be a pleasure cruise, but that the planes would have all the excitement. I thought so, too, but both Bill Green and I were wrong.

By dawn the next morning the others were out of sight, pursuing their own independent ways to the rendezvous. Of course we maintained radio silence. The chief of staff had assigned us a radio frequency, but it was understood that we should listen only and not transmit, except in the direst emergency. I didn't know how the others were faring, but we had an easy run out for the first few days and we made good time. We had to stay buttoned up and rigged for a quick dive every minute, day and night, doubling up the watch to keep both diving and cruising stations continuously manned. You get used to that after a while, although lots of captains, and I guess I'm one of them, develop hair-trigger tempers after two or three days of it.

The fourth night out we were due to pass pretty close to one of the enemy's island bases. It was there, if anywhere, that we should encounter enemy patrols, and I figured on passing during the hours of darkness. Because of the good weather and our good luck so far, we were a little ahead of schedule, but I kept going right along, hoping that with a good night's run I should leave the danger far astern by dawn the next morning. We were all alert, of course, and expecting anything, but luck turned to the enemy about that time, and we got a little more than we expected.

It was two o'clock in the afternoon. The sun was high in a brassy sky and the sea was smooth as glass, unbroken except for the broad white wake that led directly from our stern back to the horizon. It may have been that I heard the beat of a plane's motors over the throb of our Diesels, but I wasn't directly conscious of it. The sun bearing was the dangerous bearing and I was keeping a pretty good watch on it. Anyhow, by the merest chance I slipped the ray filter over my binoculars and looked directly toward the sun. There was a plane coming right in at us, the sun on his tail, and bearing down as fast as he could come. He must have had the luck to pick us up when he was right between us and the sun, for up till then we hadn't seen a thing.

We went down fast. The lookouts and the quartermaster went down the hatch in a mad scramble, and my feet were right on their necks as I dropped down and closed the hatch. We weren't any too soon. The periscope was just going under when the bombs exploded. They hadn't missed us by many feet. The explosion shook us from stem to stern and the whole ship quivered and vibrated as though it was about to fall apart. I took her down to eighty feet, and after a few minutes in the eternal silence down there we were able to collect our shattered nerves. It had been a close thing, too close to risk repeating soon again.

After an hour of cruising at eighty feet, I about decided that I could risk coming up to periscope depth and having a look. I know now that I should have gone deeper, much deeper. The sun was still high and the water was clear as crystal. The plane must have been able to catch an occasional glimpse of our shadow under the water. It's one of those things you learn from experience if you live through the experience.

Just as I had about decided that the worst was over, the listener reported the sounds of screws. The surface patrol was coming in, and it wasn't long before we knew they were coming in straight and fast. The beat of the screws grew louder every minute.

The course of the surface patrol toward us was altogether too direct to be explained by luck alone. It became quite apparent to me that the airplane patrol had somehow been able to track us on our course underwater. It was very probable that the bombing we had undergone had opened up our seams enough for oil leakage to show a slick. It was still more probable that I wasn't deep enough to prevent the plane from getting an occasional glimpse of our hull whenever it happened to get the light just right. The conditions were ideal for aircraft observation. I decided to go down to two hundred feet.

It was not an easy decision to make. At two hundred feet the sea pressure was more than six tons on every square foot of our hull surface. The detonation of depth charges close aboard would be much harder on the already severely strained hull plates, but there didn't seem to be any other reasonable course of action I could take.

The depth charges weren't long in coming, and the enemy

wasn't at all stingy in the way he handed them out. We were scarcely down to two hundred feet when they got the first barrage off. They seemed to be ahead of us and astern and on all sides. We were proceeding through a forest of explosions. Then one must have gone off right over the top of us. The conning-tower hatch lifted off the seat from the force of the wave of detonations. All of us and everything in the conning tower got a brief shower of salt water under high pressure before the tremendous pressure of the sea slammed the hatch back down on the gasket again.

I opened my mouth to order the conning tower abandoned, but it was all over before I could speak. Then I noticed that we were coming up at a sharp angle, coming up fast, the numbers ticking off under the depth-gauge needle like the floor numbers on the telltale of a descending elevator. We were up at a hundred and fifty, then a hundred, before there was any apparent reduction in the angle.

The diving officer yelled up from the control room below that the stern planes were jammed. I backed both motors full speed, but it seemed that nothing would stop her from shooting to the surface and certain destruction.

At sixty feet, the diving officer got control. I went ahead again on the motors. Then we started for the bottom, and the bottom was two thousand fathoms down. We went on down, diving to three hundred feet before we leveled off. Then the diving officer got control again, in the nick of time, before the pressure of the sea squeezed us into a mass of wreckage. He planed her up to two hundred feet and I slowed down again to silent running.

The patrol above laid down another pattern of depth charges around us. A few more light bulbs were broken in their sockets. Leaks were reported from both forward and aft. It commenced to look as though the Neptune had encountered the contingency against which the force commander had laid his plans.

After the first attack, things weren't quite so bad. At our

greater depth the plane probably could no longer follow us, and as the sun sank lower toward the horizon the light conditions became less and less favorable for him. Nevertheless, the patrols kept doggedly on our trail. They were following us with listening devices, and they must have been pretty good at it, because it seemed there never was a time that we were out of the sound of an enemy's propellers. Every now and then they would shower down with another batch of depth charges. Some of them were far away, indicating that the patrols had picked up a false scent, but altogether too often they were uncomfortably close aboard. I counted forty-three depth charges that afternoon, and there were lots of times when I was too busy to count.

It got to be rather wearing on the nerves. I noticed that routine operations were no longer carried out with the old snap, and the depth control was particularly ragged. Everybody seemed distracted, feeling that the next attack would be the last. I sent Bill Green on a tour through the ship to estimate the damage we had sustained. His report was not too encouraging, but none of the leaks was immediately dangerous. Up forward it was merely annoying, but back in the engine room the water was slowly getting deeper in the bilges. If it rose high enough to short out the motors, we should be in a bad way. We didn't dare pump bilges, for fear that the oil mixed with the engine-room bilge water would betray our location. In fact, there wasn't much we could do except bear it as best we could, and that in itself was the hardest on our nerves. We would all have welcomed action, even disastrous, desperate, suicidal action.

It couldn't last forever. One way or the other, it had to end. At six-twelve the sun set, and by seven it would be completely dark. Fortunately, there was no moon. The hours wore on. We could always hear at least one patrol vessel, but by sunset they seemed to have lost any direct contact. From the periodic way in which they came and went, I figured they had set up a systematic patrol, steaming back and forth at eight knots, covering the whole area around us.

A little after seven o'clock I decided I had as good an opportunity to break away as I was likely to get. A patrol had passed astern of us a short time before, but the sound of her propellers was rapidly receding in the distance. I brought the Neptune up to periscope depth.

The periscope eyepiece was like a mirror of black glass. Not a single ray of light penetrated it. I came on up to the surface, and as quickly as we could, I got under way on the engines.

I knew we should have to dodge enemy patrols. We hadn't been out of touch with them for five hours. I took only two men up to the bridge to act as lookouts. The quartermaster steered from the conning tower and Bill Green stood by down there to carry out my orders. The tubes were ready for firing, but we were mainly interested in getting away as quickly as we could. All our engines were on the screws, and the luminous wake stood out behind us like a white scar on the onyx surface of the sea.

We got along pretty well for half an hour. Then my starboard lookout reported that he thought he could see the gleam of an occasional white patch on the surface of the sea just abaft the starboard beam. I looked and for a while I thought it was his imagination or the disturbance caused by a playful porpoise.

"There it is again, sir," he reported, pointing off into the darkness.

It was unmistakable now. The lazy, rolling bow wave of a surface vessel forging ahead at slow speed. We had cut directly across the bow of one of the patrols, not more than five hundred yards ahead of her.

For a split second I hoped only that she wouldn't pick up the white streak of our wake. Then I realized that in a minute or so she would be in an ideal position for me to attack with the stern tubes.

"Stern tubes ready for firing!" I called down to Bill Green. "Stand by for a quick dive! Patrol vessel coming in from starboard! Speed eight! Track angle ninety degrees!"

I could clearly make out the bulk of her hull now. It was a destroyer, leisurely hunting through the area on her slow-speed patrol. Without her knowing it, the hunter had now become the hunted.

"Stern tubes ready for firing, sir!" Green reported from the conning tower. "Your firing bearing is one six four!"

I glanced below and could just make out the white moon on his face as he stood in the black void under the conning-tower hatch, looking up, the firing key in his hand. She was coming on the cross wires.

"Fire Five!"

"Number Five Tube fired," Green reported softly, as though he was afraid the enemy might overhear him.

"Fire Six!"

"Number Six Tube fired, sir."

"Stand by for a dive." If we missed and the target remained unaware of our presence, I would keep going on the surface to gain as much distance as I could, but I might have to go down in a hurry. I could see the faint phosphorescent path of the torpedoes. Then there was a burst of flame and a column of water stabbing upward a good forty feet in the air. The roar of a mighty explosion rolled out over the surface of the quiet sea. The destroyer was suddenly blown apart.

"Take her down!" I yelled to Green. "Down to a hundred feet!"

I had nothing to fear from that destroyer, but her consorts would come piling in toward the explosion. We went down. The periscope was of course useless in the blackness of the night, and I went deep to pass under any of the patrol craft that might pass my way.

A minute or two later the listener reported the sound of propellers. Breathlessly we waited a depth-charge attack like the one we had experienced in the afternoon. It didn't come.

Our unexpected attack had temporarily disrupted the patrols. The sound of the screws seemed to indicate that they were searching for survivors back where one of their number had gone down.

After half an hour I thought I could risk it on the surface again. I had to put as much distance as I could between me and the enemy base before dawn. We came up again. I knew that the patrol vessels weren't more than a mile or two away, so I was pretty cautious.

When I got on the bridge again, we lay there stopped and still, a dark blot on the black surface of the sea. The low-pressure air sobbed and whined about its business of freeing the ballast tanks of water. I could see nothing. I called down the hatch to put all engines on the screws. As I stood erect again, the blinding glare of a searchlight suddenly bloomed in the black void astern. For a second I stood transfixed. I felt naked in the flood of light. Even as I started to shout the order to dive again, the beam of light swept on.

With the light full on me I felt that the ship behind it was right on top of us. As the beam swept away I could see that the enemy was at least two miles away. They were evidently searching the water for survivors of the ship I had sunk, and somehow I had escaped detection.

That was the last encounter with the enemy we had that night, but it wasn't the last of our troubles. Less than an hour after we got under way, ticking off the miles between us and the scene of those awful experiences, the engine room reported that they had burned out three bearings on the port after engine.

A little investigation made it certain that the depth-charge attack we had been through had thrown some of our machinery out of line.

Fortunately, we had three engines left in good running order. I could keep one on the battery charge and with the two others still make twelve knots. When the battery charge was finished, I could step up the speed to fourteen or fifteen knots. That would bring me to the rendezvous in time, but there was no telling when we should need that other engine. I didn't have to tell the men in the engine room that. They knew it. Repairs were under way before the casualty could be reported to me.

The next thirty hours were a nightmare of work for everyone. The engine had to be partly dismantled, the bad bearings rolled out, the new ones scraped, fitted and installed. The electricians had a myriad of grounds to clean up, caused by the water that rained in from the leaks the depth charges had developed. The stern plane mechanism had to be overhauled. The leaks had to be patched up as best we could, and through it all we had to keep plugging away toward the rendezvous, all stations manned and ready to dive again on an instant's notice.

In thirty hours we were shipshape again, with the greatest danger far behind us. But I shall never forget that time. Men came off watch to go to work again on repairs, and quit work to go on watch in an unending sequence. When it was over, they dropped beside their tools and slept on the deck where they dropped. I had had one brief moment of exalting, satisfying revenge and success. These men hadn't seen it. They had only been told about it. Their lot had been only grinding toil and a nightmare of uncertainty and danger. They had understood it would be like this. Long years of training had left them no illusions about the glory and glamour of war. Amateurs might have mistaken ideas about war, but not these men. That is why, in twenty years of association, I have yet to meet a professional in any navy who doesn't anticipate war with a numb dread.

It required those thirty hours of unceasing labor to erase the effects of what we had been through, but after it was over I felt we were in first-class shape again. We had to leave a little play in the bearings that been wiped. I was a little skittish about running that engine at full power, but that was a small matter. I could see no trace of an oil slick astern. I was grateful for that. Our after torpedoes had been expended. We had no reloads because of the bombs we carried in the spare-torpedo racks. That bothered me very little. We still had four torpedoes in the tubes forward. Catching the destroyer as I did had been a freak contact. I felt there was very little likelihood that we should again encounter enemy surface ships. If we did, the forward torpedoes would be ample. The empty tubes aft were the least of my worries. Perhaps if I could have foreseen what was to happen, I should have been more concerned.

We made Moab all right, made it with hours to spare, early in the morning of the seventeenth. If I had arrived any earlier, I should simply have had to lay to, waiting for daylight. Moab is nothing but three pinnacles of rock, connected by a partly submerged reef, unlighted, uninhabited and altogether too unpleasant a landfall to have made during darkness. As soon as I picked up the tall central peak, we went down to periscope depth and I ran on in toward the island at two knots' speed.

There was no telling what I should find in there and I had to be cautious. If there was going to be any surprise, I wanted to be on the surprising end. We had all day to close in and make our observations. I saw nothing of the other submarines, which was as it should be. They had orders to stay submerged during daylight hours until the morning of the eighteenth. I stuck to my own area and I expected them to stick to theirs.

The chart showed deep water right up to the reef, so I continued to stand in until I was only a mile or two off the southern entrance. About two o'clock in the afternoon a destroyer stood down from the northward and went right on in to the anchorage inside the half circle of rocks as though she owned the place. I had a bad few minutes trying to figure out what I should do if she insisted on staying. With the planes due to arrive in the morning, we couldn't very well ignore her. However, she came out again in about an hour. It seemed to be just a routine inspection trip, but it gave me plenty to worry about. If she had arrived just twenty-four hours later she would have stuck her thin gray nose right into the little party we had scheduled.

We surfaced during the night, of course, and laid in a good battery charge. Through the periscope I had examined the anchorage as best I could, but there were several blind angles that I couldn't see into from seaward. It was altogether possible that the bay might be defended in some fashion. The destroyer might have made her call for the purpose of mining the entrance, in preparation for just such an expedition as ours. There were a good many possibilities to consider.

I didn't dare try to communicate with the Dryad and the Unicorn. If there was any enemy in the vicinity, a flashing light would disclose our presence. If Needham and Howard were here, though, I could count on their instant acceptance of any situation that might face us in the morning. Come what might, we should have to fight whatever we found inside the reef at dawn. The planes would be coming in early in the morning.

Before sunrise I submerged and maneuvered in close to the entrance. When I had secured what I considered a good position and it became light enough for us to see clearly, I brought the Neptune to the surface with a rush.

We manned the deck gun, and with the torpedo tubes ready, I steamed on up to the break in the reef, depending on the suddenness of my appearance at least to find out what I was up against before any effective counter-measure could be taken. From the entrance I could see into all the corners of the little bay, and I certainly was glad to find the anchorage empty except for myriads of sea birds.

As soon as I was sure that there were no hostile ships inside, I hauled out away from the reef a little way and got the motor launch into the water. The boat went on in through the entrance ahead of us, with the navigator and a man from the deck force to heave the hand lead.

Our chart was based on old surveys and the information

we had was pretty scanty. There were lots of navigational dangers, probably many more than appeared on the chart. But the water was unbelievably clear, and even in the slanting rays of the morning light we had no difficulty making out the passage through the reef. There was even a chance that mines could be seen from the boat if any had been planted in the entrance.

While we were engaged in this maneuver the Dryad appeared, and the Unicorn was not far behind her. I signaled for them to maintain their patrol stations outside until the planes commenced to arrive. The Neptune, I figured, would have to follow the boat on in to scout out the way for the others, but there was no need of us all sticking our necks into what might prove to be a nasty trap. If the submarines were caught inside, they wouldn't dare dive, for fear of getting hung up on some pinnacle of rock. For that matter, diving wouldn't do much good. There was barely enough water to get a submarine under and the Coast Pilot said that the bottom was white sand. A submerged submarine would be almost as visible to a plane as one would on the surface. Outside there was plenty of sea room, and deep water in which to dive. If any surface vessels came snooping around, I could count on Needham and Howard to make it interesting for them.

From a position high on the A frame, I conned her gingerly in and found an anchorage close to the tallest rock pinnacle. As soon as the hook was down I called my best signalman and set him ashore on that rock. From its peak he could get a good view of the whole of the surrounding ocean, and he had orders to let us know the minute anything appeared over the horizon.

It was a nasty assignment, and we both knew it. He was equipped with a breaker of water, blankets and a supply of food, because he would have to spend at least one night on an island that looked as though it wouldn't offer shelter to a mountain goat. If we had to cut and run for it, he would have a chance to play Robinson Crusoe for an indefinite period, if nothing more unpleasant happened to him. He left without displaying a single qualm. Sometimes it takes as much guts to face a situation as it does to play it through.

The navigator continued his examination of the bay in the boat. I hung on to the anchorage because I didn't like to leave his boat completely unsupported, but I felt pretty uneasy all the time we stayed there. We didn't relax much, but the submarines had made the rendezvous. We were ready and waiting for the planes.

For nine days we had been out of touch with the world. We only knew that if the expedition had been canceled, the radio would have opened up and recalled us. Our submerged operations left loopholes in that arrangement, but we could only assume, from the lack of that message, that the plan was going forward. For the planes to find that tiny dot in the vast expanse of water was going to call for some plain and fancy navigation. We were afraid to use the radio to guide them.

It was nine o'clock before they started coming in. We could hear them long before they could be seen. Then there was a tiny dot high up in the blue, dropping down, coming in, getting bigger and bigger every second, until the first plane landed on the water and taxied into the bay. We learned later that they had spread out on a scouting line at sunrise, covering a hundred-mile front, sweeping high above the sea, looking for the rocks of Moab. Even then they had missed it on the first sweep. The squadron commander had had to re-form his scouting line, reverse his course and sweep back again. Then they found it. Now they were coming in, one at a time, with a crescendo of sound that sent the sea birds whirling and screaming above the rocks that had been theirs for centuries.

It gave me a thrill to see those planes drop down out of the sky in such a marvelous display of power and skill and assurance. For eight days we had plodded along on and under the sea, harassed and ever vigilant, escaping destruction by the narrowest margin. Only yesterday afternoon they had taken off to skim over that same weary distance in a night. With our humble aid, the might of the fleet would make itself felt three thousand miles from its base.

Nearly an hour elapsed before they were all in, but we commenced immediately to fuel and arm the first arrivals. The Dryad and Unicorn came on in. Each of us could handle two of them at once, and in a very short time we had the gasoline hose over, topping off their fuel tanks, and the gunner's mates were fitting the heavy bombs to the racks. The plane crews were tired and a little cramped from their long flight, and enjoyed stretching out their legs on our decks.

My cook had anticipated a hungry crowd, and as each plane came alongside he spread before them a feast of hot roast beef, topped off with ice cream for dessert. It's strange that cooks don't play a more important part in the literature of the sea. A good cook, at sea, is more precious than fine gold. They make or break the morale of any outfit, and I know, for myself, that I am more fussy about the qualifications of a new cook than I am about a new junior officer.

Bob Watkins was the pilot of one of the planes I refueled. He was as chipper as ever. He brought me news that everything was well back home, excepting that Sally was having the usual trouble with her arithmetic. I wished him luck for the coming night's operation, but he seemed to have every confidence that he was going to be all right.

The refueling was finished in the early afternoon. As soon as the last gasoline lines were in, the submarines left the bay to take up their patrol stations outside. The planes remained at anchor inside. We had figured on a surprise night attack on the expeditionary force, with the planes returning for an early-morning refueling. It had to be timed just right. While they were waiting the proper time for the take-off, the planes were more vulnerable than I cared to think about, but there was no help for it.

The afternoon passed uneventfully, and an hour before sunset they commenced taking off. In a very short while they were all disappearing over the horizon in formation. The anchorage settled down again to peaceful quiet and the sea birds slipped back into their ordered existence as though nothing had happened.

We patrolled the surface all night, listening in vain for some news of the planes. Something must be happening, but we had no way of finding out what it was. We had to submerge to meet the dawn, but as soon as the sun was up we were able to surface again. Everything was quiet at Moab, and a half hour after sunrise the planes started coming back.

As soon as the first planes had landed we began getting them ready for the return journey. Naturally, our first anxiety was to discover how they had made out, but it wasn't until the second section came in that we got the complete story.

They had made Basoko right on schedule. The first section went over and unloaded their bombs, keeping up at a reasonably high altitude. The raid apparently came as a complete surprise and the first section was in and out before any serious antiaircraft offensive developed. The second section followed right behind the first. There hadn't been time for interceptor planes to get up to meet them, but there was a fair concentration of antiaircraft fire from the ground. In spite of this, they came in at a low altitude. Fires set by high-explosive and incendiary bombs from the first section were already lighting the scene and they could pick out individual targets in the harbor. The transports were tied up, close packed, to the docks. The bombs had literally torn the whole expedition apart.

If anything like effective defense had been organized, the second section would have committed suicide, but the raid had caught the enemy practically flat-footed. Five of the six planes came back out, following the section leader. The sixth had gone down in flames. Twelve big bombers had gone in, deposited their bombs with machinelike precision and eleven of them had come out.

Unfortunately, the single plane shot down hadn't been the

only casualty. Most of the planes of the second section showed some effect of the barrage of fire through which they had flown. Halfway back to Moab one of these planes had signaled that it could no longer keep up. It had to make a forced landing. The entire section stood by, dropping flares to illuminate the ocean surface, until it was safely down. After that there was nothing they could do to help. The section leader had reluctantly brought the remainder of the section in, leaving the disabled plane afloat, trying frantically to make emergency repairs.

It wasn't altogether an unexpected situation. I had been doing a lot of thinking about what I would do if such a thing occurred. It didn't help much when I realized that Bob Watkins was the pilot of that plane down at sea. If the weather continued as calm as it had been and if he could make emergency repairs, he might be able to get into the air again, but any way you looked at it, he was in a bad spot.

I hastily conferred with the commander of the patrol squadron and we agreed on a plan of action. We hurried along the refueling and about noon the planes took off for the return trip. I was now free of my concern for them. The Dryad and the Unicorn I dispatched immediately to the scene of the forced landing. It was a rather futile action. Two days would elapse before they could possibly arrive, and even then the disabled plane would be almost impossible to find in that great expanse of blue water. But it was the least I could do, and sometimes a man must play the hand that has been dealt him and hope for the breaks of luck.

As soon as the anchorage was clear, I opened up with the radio. We were certain to have hostile ships down on our necks soon anyway, and with the radio I could hope to guide Bob in if he succeeded in taking off again. The tiny dot of Moab would be impossible for a single plane to find without direction finding. I resolved that I would hold the bay until all hope was gone or until I was forced out by enemy action.

About two o'clock we heard the motors of an approaching

plane. We couldn't be sure, of course, as to its identity, so I manned my deck gun and the bridge machine guns and rigged for a quick dive. If the incoming plane proved to be enemy I should have to get out into water where I could dive deep enough to keep the shadow of our hull from being seen from the air. The anxiety was all over in a minute. We couldn't mistake him as he dropped down. It was our missing bird coming home to roost.

In a twinkling he had landed and taxied alongside. Bob Watkins, looking none the worse for wear, stuck his head out of the cockpit and yelled, "Five gallons of gas and a quart of oil, Joe, and make it snappy!"

I was so glad to see him that I could have heaved a monkey wrench at him.

"Where have you been all morning?" I asked in exasperation.

My deck force was already putting the gas hoses aboard. We had a couple of thousand gallons of gasoline to get into her and no telling how long we had to do it in.

"We had a flat tire coming over," he answered in the same bantering tone. "I had to pull up to the side of the road for a while. Then I must have taken the wrong turn at the little red schoolhouse, because I couldn't find your place, though it was right there on the chart as big as life. When you piped up with your radio, we picked up a bearing and came on in."

Simple as that. His crew looked tired and worn. He had been flying most of the night and part of the day. For a couple of hours he had been down at sea, helpless in the path of anything that might come along. All morning he had been lost, frantically searching for a microscopic dot in a great sea of water, with the gas running lower every minute. His nonchalance only increased my irritation.

"You had better ride back with me," I suggested. "It's a long hard trip back for a patched-up plane, and if you are forced down again, you can float around till hell freezes over before anybody could get to you."

"Not on your life, Joe," he replied. "A week in that jammed-up, cast-iron sewer pipe of yours and I'd be a candidate for the nut factory. Fill her up and let's get started."

I could appreciate his desire to bring his own ship back, and besides, with good luck, he would be safe at home in the morning. The emergency repairs looked all right to me. If he made the first thousand miles, he could count on the assistance of the whole fleet to bring him in. We had been pumping gas into her while we were arguing. We both appreciated that we had no time to lose. If the enemy hadn't had Moab on their list for a search, the radio would be certain to steer them to us. A few hours might be all the leeway we'd have.

Two hours after he had landed he was waving good-by and taking off again. I had pulled in my signalman off the rock and by radio recalled the Dryad and the Unicorn from the search. My anchor was up before the gas hoses were in and I followed him right out of the entrance of the bay. It wasn't long before he was out of sight and we had our nose headed back on the long grind home.

Bob hadn't been off the water more than half an hour when the control-room messenger came bouncing up the bridge ladder with a message in his hand.

"Heavy cruiser and two destroyers course zero one zero, speed two five."

We hadn't got out any too soon. I'd bet dollars to doughnuts that cruiser was coming in to investigate Moab, and if she was, I was sitting pretty to be more than chief plane tender for the expedition. I rang up full speed and changed course to the westward to try to run ahead of him. With the cruiser coming in at twenty-five knots, I should have to get in almost right ahead of him before I was forced down. If I didn't he would sail right by me on the rim of the horizon, and I shouldn't be able to close to torpedo range with my slow submerged speed.

Jim Gant, one of my machinist's mates, popped up the

hatch, ostensibly to get a breath of fresh air and smoke a cigarette, but really to look the situation over.

"What's the chances, captain?" he asked.

"Fair," I answered, "if we get a few breaks and if he holds his course for a while. He's got plenty of speed to get away and he'll probably put his planes up now for scouts. If they force us down before I can run in ahead of him, he will have a better than even chance of getting by outside of torpedo range."

The gunner's mate joined Gant on the bridge. "Mind if I go down on deck and check over the gun, captain?" the gunner's mate asked.

"All right, but make it snappy," I replied. "We might have to dive any minute."

"Can I go along with the gunner, captain?" Gant requested.

I nodded assent. The news of an impending attack had spread through the ship like wildfire. It inspired me to see how the crew was taking it. A depth-charge attack like the one we had been through had been known to ruin the morale of a submarine crew, but these men were made of sterner stuff. And the situation was different now. Before, we had been intent on getting way, and we had struck back like a cornered animal trying to escape from a trap. We were going in now with an offensive mission. The big cruiser was our quarry, worthy of all the chance we should have to take. The screen might depth-charge us again, but now we were carrying the ball. The crew, I could feel, had confidence in me, and my confidence in them was firmly based on the experience of hundreds of practice attacks like the one coming up. We were through playing a passive part on the edge of big operations.

There was no need of my issuing a multitude of orders to put the men on their toes. All through the ship, people like Gant and the gunner's mate were making last-minute checks on everything. When I needed them they would be there and ready.

It wouldn't do to voice my misgivings, but I knew I was going into attack under a handicap. I had fired my stern-tube torpedoes. We still carried plenty of punch in the bow tubes, but we had lost the sting we had carried in our tail. Like a boxer, I should always have to keep faced toward the enemy. I could angle my torpedoes to cover a fairly wide range of tactical situations, but if the cruiser ever got astern of me the game would be up. With a fast and mobile target, zigzagging at high speed, just that was likely to happen, and the cruiser would be gone and away before I could turn to a firing position.

The men were back from the deck almost immediately. They knew, and I knew, that the gun was all right, but they had to have a last look-see.

"Any chance of using the gun, captain?" Gant asked.

"None whatever if I can help it," I replied. "Not against all that gun power bearing down on us."

He grimaced. His pet gripe was that God and a lot of arduous training had made him one of the best gun pointers in the whole fleet while Fate had decreed that he should serve in a submarine where the gun was entirely secondary to the torpedo armament. Most of his time he spent ministering to the needs of temperamental high-speed Diesels, but the gun was his real love and I was always sure of good shooting when he was in the gun pointer's seat.

The two men went down the ladder. The messenger passed them in the conning tower with another message. "Speed two five, course three four five."

I cursed. Bob Watkins, the fool, was trailing the cruiser. It was his business to get away over the horizon while the going was good. He had apparently caught the cruiser unprepared, not ready to catapult her planes, but a very little time would rectify that error for the enemy. She would have two planes in the air by now and our patrol plane would have a fight on her hands, two planes to one, any minute. Fortunately, we knew the enemy's observation planes were no faster than our patrol bombers, but the enemy planes were smaller and more maneuverable, and two to one was heavy odds for a patched-up plane.

Bob didn't have any bombs on board. The only thing that he could do was to trail and report. He could easily stay out of the cruiser's gun range, and while he was there he would keep the enemy's planes busy, so they wouldn't be out in the advance to force me down too soon. And I was grateful for the information he was sending in. I acted on it now. A quick glance at the chart showed me that the cruiser had changed course directly toward Moab. She was evidently zigzagging and probably suspected the presence of submarines. But I figured she was on her base course now, and I headed right down toward her last reported position. Nevertheless, I could not help being worried about Bob and the two planes I was sure would be after him.

Sure enough, not more than seven minutes after the last message I got another: "One down and one to go. Course zero zero five."

I interpreted that to mean that he had had his first brush with the cruiser's planes and shot down one of them. The enemy had also changed course again, but I stuck to my estimate that "three four five" was about his base course, and I continued boring right in.

A minute or two after that we picked up the cruiser's masts on the horizon. I couldn't see enough to judge our position with respect to him very clearly, but I estimated we were a little on his port bow. I didn't dare run in any farther on the surface. The enemy was undoubtedly alert and looking for trouble. Whether or not he suspected our use of submarines to supply the raiding planes, he was evidently taking all submarine precautions, zigzagging and with an antisubmarine screen out. If he sighted me now, I shouldn't get within miles of him.

But thanks to Bob Watkins' contact reports and his luring

the cruiser's planes out of the forward area, we had gained a favorable position. Down we went.

The height of the periscope cut down my horizon and I couldn't see anything but ocean for a while. It was three or four minutes before he came pushing up over the rim. It doesn't take long at twenty-five knots. I could see that I was out about fifteen degrees on his port bow and the range was twelve or fourteen thousand yards. I changed course then to pull over ahead of him, although I suspected that he would zigzag any minute.

By the time I could see enough of his upper works to make a decent estimate, he made a left zig. It put me dead ahead of him, and the range was ten thousand yards, as I made out. I decided I'd run right down at him and let subsequent events determine how I could attack. The screening destroyers would soon be getting close enough so that there would be danger of my being sighted, so I lowered my periscope.

"Take her down to a hundred feet," I ordered. Bob Watkins would probably be giving the cruiser's remaining plane plenty to think about. I knew he was well enough grounded in submarine tactics to keep his adversary out of the forward area if he could. But events don't always shape up the way you expect them to. The sun's angle wasn't so favorable to the plane as it had been on that memorable day on the way out, but the water was just as clear. If the enemy plane chanced to fly directly overhead, he would be able to see plainly the shadow of my hull if I didn't go down deep. The inconvenience of running deep and planing up only when I wanted to make an observation didn't outweigh the hazard of a run at periscope depth. In war you have to take plenty of chances without adding any unnecessary ones.

I ran down for seven minutes. Then I brought her up to periscope depth again, slowed down, and very gingerly ran up the periscope for another look. Something would have to happen pretty soon now. The cruiser was still headed right at

me. The range was four thousand yards. There was a destroyer out on either bow and about a thousand yards in advance,
and the three of them were coming down at a fast clip.

They had me in rather a tight spot. If both the cruiser and
I held on to our present courses, the cruiser would run right
over me. If I fired from dead ahead of her, of course she
would present an impossibly narrow target. With a flip of the
rudder she would be able to evade the torpedoes and I should
have practically no chance of getting away after I fired. If I
had had my stern tubes loaded, I could have pulled out to
one side to get into position for firing. With only bow tubes,
that wasn't a very promising maneuver.

It was about time for him to zig again. If I tried running
out to one side at a sharp enough angle to permit me to fire
angle shots from the bow tubes, a change of course toward
me would send him right over me again. If he changed course
away from me, he would then pass under my stern and just
leave me there futilely gnashing my teeth. The screen was
rapidly boxing me in and restricting my choice of action.

"Down periscope! Two knots!"

I decided to hold on one more minute. The range was decreasing more than eight hundred yards a minute. If I got in
to three thousand and I was still dead ahead, I'd have to do
something pretty snappy to retrieve the situation, and the
destroyers would be right in my way. The palms of my hands
commenced to sweat. The fire-control assistants stood ready
and alert. There wasn't anything they could do. I couldn't
tell them what to do. I didn't know yet myself. A submarine
skipper is awfully alone in such a situation. Everybody knew
that I was in a tight spot. It was getting tighter with every
tick of the stop watch.

I knelt on the deck with the control button for the periscope motor in my right hand, one eye on the stop watch my
fire-control assistant held for me to see. I didn't dare trust
my sense of time. Each second seemed an hour. As the
eyepiece cleared the deck I squatted lower to look. Hoisting

the periscope up in short jerks I kept my eye glued to the instrument. The instant I could see I stopped the periscope. We were making dead slow speed. If we were sighted now we should be in a fearful predicament. Not only would the enemy have ample opportunity to avoid but his destroyers would be in an ideal position to attack. We should be lucky to get out of it with a whole skin.

It was difficult to restrain my impatience. Everything depended upon what had happened since I last looked. If the cruiser had changed course or if she was changing now, I should be sitting pretty. If I was still dead ahead of him I should have to take drastic and immediate action. By the time I did any turning I should be right under his forefoot. About the best I should be able to do would be to dive deep, let him pass over me and chalk it up as a badly fumbled approach.

As the periscope broke water my heart sank. I could see the cruiser's flaring bows headed at me, her masts still right in line. I could see the creamy white roller on either bow. The screen was rapidly boxing me in. Yet as I looked I could see his wicked stem swing around to starboard. He was changing course. Fascinated, I watched until he steadied on the new course.

"Angle on the bow twenty port! Range thirty-two hundred! Speed twenty-five! Down periscope! Starboard motor ahead full! Port motor stop! Left twenty degree rudder!"

I had him now. He had played right into my hands.

"What's the course for a hundred and ten track? Bow tubes ready for firing! Straight bow shot!" It was like calling signals in a football game, and like a football team, each man knew exactly what was expected of him.

"Pick up the destroyer on the starboard bow with the listening gear! Keep the bearings coming in! . . . Take her down to a hundred feet!"

Their port screen would pass right over us. Until that destroyer had gone by, that would be my chief worry. If they were alert and expecting it, they might even be able to see our hull through the water as they passed overhead.

"Destroyer bearing three zero!" the listener reported. "Bearing four five! Bearing five zero!"

The bearing was changing as we swung to the new course. Nevertheless, a glance at the compass showed me that his true bearing was holding constant. I watched the depth gauge as we gained the depth that would let him pass safely over us.

"I can hear him all around the dial, captain."

Then we didn't need the listening gear to hear his screws. He sounded like a subway train as he passed right over our stern. I could put the screen out of my mind. With him safely over us, it would be all over before he ever found out what was up. He would have to turn through at least a hundred and eighty degrees to head for us. It would take him nearly three minutes to do it, and by that time I'd have my torpedoes all launched and be sneaking off at a hundred feet. We were coming in on the firing course.

"All stop! Forty-five feet! Stand by the tubes!"

I gave her time to lose her way and watched the depth gauge as the diving officer brought her smartly up.

"Up periscope!"

I didn't waste a glance at the destroyer. My eyes were on the cruiser. Down she came, all unaware that anything was amiss. I was well inside the screen. The range was only six hundred yards. I adjusted my periscope to the right offset angle. Behind me there was dead silence. "Fire one!"

What a load off my mind. I felt an icy calm as I got off all four of my torpedoes in rapid succession. I was almost certain of a hit.

Suddenly I could see white smoke puff from the cruiser's antiaircraft battery. She wasn't firing at me. I could plainly see the men at the guns. I swung my periscope around to look at the destroyer.

She gave me the shock of my life, because she wasn't at

all where she should have been. She was up on my beam about seven hundred yards away and turning—turning fast under full rudder. She was turning in toward the cruiser with her inboard afterdeck rail nearly under water. Every now and then a deck fitting or her rail aft would strike the top of a swell and send a cloud of spray over her fantail. She seemed to be lying on her side with her deck canted toward me. It must have been difficult enough to keep upright on that careening deck, but she, too, was firing.

A glance told me that the completion of her turn would bring her very close to my position. Moreover, she would pass almost exactly through the same water in which my torpedoes were traveling. She had but to follow the torpedo track and she would end up right over me in a position to depth-charge the hell out of us. She must have commenced her turn as soon as she passed over us. Why? I suppose I'll never know. Some chance maneuver, perhaps. Certainly we hadn't been sighted, or the cruiser would have made an effort to dodge.

"Down periscope!" I shouted. "Take her down to a hundred feet!"

As the periscope was coming down I saw what they were shooting at. It was Bob Watkins in the patrol plane. He was coming down on the destroyer in the closest thing to a dive he could get out of his heavy plane. All his guns were spouting flame. With a plane as maneuverable as an ice truck, he was making a strafing attack on a destroyer, facing the gun-fire of three ships, at an altitude that wouldn't much more than clear the destroyer's masts.

Before the periscope was down we heard the multiple thuds of the torpedoes getting home on the cruiser. I had almost forgotten them myself. The enemy was so preoccupied with the plane that I'll bet the explosion was their first inkling that a submarine was present. Bob's maneuver had done that much. Besides, if his strafing got home on the destroyer's bridge, she would be out of control at least long enough for me to get safely away. It was magnificent, but it wasn't war. The fool, the utter fool! There wasn't a prayer that he could get away with it.

I got down to a hundred feet and the depth charges that I had been expecting never came—not close, at any rate. We heard a series of muffled explosions some distance away. They may have been depth charges or they may have been the cruiser's boilers going up. I came around to the reverse of the cruiser's course as soon as I was down at a hundred feet, and I stayed down there for a good ten minutes after I had fired. After delivering a successful attack, my job was to get my ship out of there safely, and my curiosity could wait. Play them safe and I'd have a ship under my feet to sink another cruiser someday.

Everything had been quiet for some time before I ventured to plane up and have a look. The listener reported that he couldn't hear the cruiser's propellers, but the destroyers were buzzing away back there where we had left them. I had no trouble picking them up as soon as the periscope broke water. The cruiser was slowly turning over to starboard, and it wouldn't be long before she was finished. The destroyers were standing by, picking up the survivors out of the water. That was all right with me and I wasn't going to interfere. For safety I took a sweep around the horizon before I went back down to a hundred feet.

I think I should have missed the patrol plane if it hadn't been for the enemy plane diving down at her. Bob Watkins had been shot down, but somehow he had made a couple of miles before he had set his plane down on the water. As the low swell lifted her I could see her stretched out on the water like a wounded bird, and that damned observation plane was diving down on her, ripping her up and down with machine-gun bullets as she lay helpless in the water.

I guess I must have lost my temper. Machine-gunning that helpless plane seemed so much like wanton murder. As long as there was any possibility of his doing them any damage

they had every right to dish out any punishment they could
to him. But the patrol plane was obviously permanently out
of action. There wasn't even the excuse of preventing salvage.
Any time the destroyers got around to it, they could steam
over and pick up the plane crew as prisoners of war. They
could sink the plane then, too, if Watkins hadn't already at-
tended to it. The enemy had simply gone berserk at the
thought that Bob had outfought and outflown two planes and
helped lead the cruiser into a death trap. They were out to
wipe him out in retaliation, but cold-blooded murder couldn't
undo what he had done.

"Take her down to a hundred feet! All ahead, full speed!"

It was going to take me twelve or fifteen minutes at my
best speed to get over to the plane. Never did I feel so frus-
trated by our slow submerged speed. But I kept her down
deep, so the observation plane wouldn't see us, and plugged
along as fast as I could go.

When I figured I was about there I slowed down and came
up for another look. We were pretty close aboard. I could
see that they had abandoned the plane and were in their little
rubber boat, paddling away from it as fast as they could.
Even as I looked, the observation plane came in on another
attack. The after gun of the patrol plane was still manned
and firing at him as he came, so he didn't come in too close.

"Stand by for battle surface! Get the machine guns ready
to go up and repel strafing attack! Deck force stand by to
secure plane's crew!"

I hadn't told anybody what was going on. They may have
been surprised, but that didn't slow them down any. I remember Gant passing by me to take his ready position beneath the gun-access hatch. He grinned at me as though he
was remembering that I had told him we wouldn't use the gun.

I ran up the periscope and maneuvered in submerged until
I had a position between the boat and the plane.

"Surface!"

The diving officer brought her up with a rush. I turned

from the periscope and dashed up the ladder to the conning tower. I could see the water level at the conning-tower eye ports.

"Open the hatch!"

I heaved up on the bridge and the machine guns were right behind me. The water was still running off the deck, but the first of the gun's crew was already at the gun, casting off the breech cover.

"Target is the destroyer on the starboard bow!"

The gunnery officer, just coming on the bridge behind the machine gunners, would have to fight that battle. I had other things on my mind. I reached over and gave the wheel a flip to see if I had steering control on the bridge, and the quartermaster was behind me to take the wheel from my hands.

"All stop! Come right handsomely and lay her bow alongside the boat!"

"All motors stopped," he reported back as calmly as though we were coming alongside the pier back home. "Coming right handsomely."

The gun got off the first shot just as I got the boat alongside. The plane crew scrambled up the deck and my own men hurried them along to the gun-access hatch.

"The skipper is in the ship!" they shouted at me. "The skipper is in the ship!" I can still picture one man who stood with feet wide apart on the deck, resisting the efforts of my people to hurry him below. "The skipper is still in the ship!" he kept yelling at me.

"O.K.!" I answered. "I'll get him!" And then he went below without any further argument.

I was going to get him, but not without a lot more trouble. The roar of the observation plane's motors increased to a screaming crescendo. The machine guns on my own bridge opened up. I jumped down beside the quartermaster, pushed the motor-annunciator handles up to standard ahead and just pointed to the plane. He understood. The cruiser's plane was coming over in a dive, spraying machine-gun bullets out of everything he had, but the quartermaster never batted an eye.

I turned away from the quartermaster and crouched down on the port side of the bridge to keep out of the way of my forward machine gunner. The plane was coming in over the starboard bow. As she flattened out her dive, commencing to pull up, I noticed that my after machine gunner was unable to bring his gun to bear because the periscope shears were between him and the plane. He crouched behind his gun, ready and waiting until the course of the plane would bring her down along the port side. As she swept over the deck from starboard to port, he let her have it. I expect I'll never again see as fine a wing shot. The plane never pulled out of the dive. She seemed to waver for an instant and then continued her dive right into the sea, like a kingfisher coming down on his prey. I never thought that I should be bloodthirsty enough to enjoy seeing men die like that.

The sudden cessation of noise was a physical sensation.

"Rig in the bow planes!" I shouted down to the control room. "Get the machine guns below!"

The first salvo from the destroyer arrived. They were away over, but it wouldn't take them long to spot on. I was abruptly aware that it was too quiet. Our gun had ceased firing. Leaning over the bridge, I could see that there was a lot of confusion at the gun.

I heard the gunnery officer shout, "Let the deck force get the wounded men below! Resume fire! Range three five double oh! Scale five three!"

And then I had to turn back to my immediate job. We had our bow almost alongside the plane's after cockpit. I stopped the motors. There was a man standing up in the cockpit, and I shouted for him to jump into the water and swim for us. He waved his arm and shouted something in return, and I let the submarine come on in to bring her bow alongside with a healthy crash.

The man in the cockpit made the difficult scramble to our

deck, pausing whenever he could get a foothold to help Bob Watkins, who followed behind. Then I could see why he hadn't jumped, for Bob had the use of only one arm and he would have had a hard time making it alone.

The instant their feet touched the deck, I commenced backing down.

"Put one shell into the plane," I shouted to the gun's crew, "and then get below!"

The gun swung round and plowed a raking shot right up the fuselage of the plane, from so close a range that the gun blast blew in the plane's thin structure. If anyone was going to have souvenirs of that plane, they would be in mighty small pieces.

A salvo landed short and close aboard. The shell fragments whistled through the air and crashed through the super-structure plates. I saw the last of the gun crew making for the gun-access hatch. I dropped down to the conning tower. The diving alarm wailed. As the hatch closed behind me we took a shell somewhere up forward. I could only hope that it hadn't found the strength hull, because we were on our way down, with the motors full speed ahead and the rudder hard right.

It was nearly three minutes before the destroyers were over us. We were at a hundred and fifty feet then, running dead slow and silently. The first depth charges were quite a distance away, but they dropped one too close aboard for comfort.

The deck plates seemed to lift right off the deck. The whole ship quivered and shook, and the diving officer had a frantic time trying to regain control of the darkness as all the lights went out.

After that we drew away from them. As soon as things seemed quiet enough, I turned over the control room to the executive officer and went up into the forward battery to see how the wounded were faring.

Poor Jim Gant lay stretched out on the bunk. He had spent

six years or more becoming a crackerjack gun pointer, in addition to his other many duties. His gun had been in action less than a minute. He had fired five rounds at an enemy, and now he was dead.

Three others of the crew were badly wounded. The pharmacist's mate was busy doing what he could for them, and Bob Watkins was waiting his turn to have his wound dressed. A machine-gun bullet had plowed through his right shoulder. The bleeding had all but stopped and he was in no immediate danger.

"What happened?" I asked him.

"One of their high-explosive shells just ripped the port engine out of the plane and blew a big hole in the wing. I had to set her down quick," he answered. "Then that lousy observation plane came down on us and ripped us up the back with machine-gun bullets. I got the crew out in the emergency life raft, and the gunner and I stayed behind to get the bomb sight and the code books over the side. We manned the after machine gun to make him keep his distance. He came over twice more before you came along, and the second time he nicked me on the shoulder."

"Before that," I insisted. "How come you tried to take on three ships at once with nothing but machine-gun fire?"

"Oh, that," he replied. "Well, you see, while I was playing ring-around-a-rosy with the observation plane, I happened to get right over you when you came to periscope depth in the wake of the destroyer. My bombardier picked you up right away. The destroyer was already turning in toward you as fast as he could, and I thought maybe you'd been sighted, or soon would be. I know how much you hate to be disturbed when you get all set to fire torpedoes, so I came on in to give them something else to think about."

"You ought to get a court!" I retorted angrily. "Anybody who takes a patrol plane into an unsupported strafing attack against two destroyers and a cruiser is an unmitigated fool!"

"How about a guy who will take a submarine into a surface

engagement with two destroyers just to rescue the crew of one cracked-up plane?" he countered.

"That's different, Bob," I answered.

There was a distant rumble of another depth charge.

"It won't be if those depth charges get any closer," he contended.

UP PERISCOPE!

WELL, I'm a little older and wiser, but certainly no richer, than I was the day I walked down the gangplank of the S-52 at Pearl Harbor, no longer the commanding officer, but merely a Lieutenant, U. S. N., Retired. Fifteen years of commissioned service, the promise of a successful career in the only profession I gave a damn about—and then, finished! Because I couldn't hear a silly watch tick.

I guess I was a fool to get too close to the muzzle of the gun when we fired that last time. But you know how it is during a battle practice. You get so intent on watching the fall of shot and conning the ship that you forget where you are. I honestly wasn't aware of much difference in my hearing. I suppose it came on gradually. Anyway, I walked in for my annual physical examination in a hurry to get it over, and came out in a hurry no longer. My left ear was deaf as a post, and they were of the opinion that it always would be.

So the mills started grinding in the manner laid down in the book. The Survey Board confirmed the opinion of the Examining Board, and the Retiring Board was courteous and sympathetic after the manner of men who might one day find themselves in the same predicament. But there was no help for it. A tin ear was a tin ear, and even I could agree that the bridge of a submarine was probably no place for a man who was uncertain whether a foghorn was on the port or the starboard bow.

"Upon receipt of these orders and when directed by Commander of Submarine Division 21, you will consider yourself relieved of command of the S-52 and of all active duty. You will proceed to your home. . . . The bureau regrets your naval career has been thus interrupted." Regrets! Regrets!

I packed my gear and moved out to the old Moana Hotel. There had been no silly sentimentality so far. It had been a near thing when my quartermaster handed me the commission pennant as I stepped ashore, and I knew that the elation of my second officer with his new orders to command was tempered with sympathy that he yet might find occasion to express, to the embarrassment of us both. Oh, I had managed so far, but I wanted no delegation of sympathy and I had a great desire to be alone. So I hired me a room and sat with my feet on the window sill all afternoon, looking out to sea.

About dinnertime I wandered disconsolately down to the bar. There weren't many there—a few tourists, a plantation manager in from one of the other islands, and a couple of well-dressed Orientals. I stood at the bar and toasted my lost career in silence, when in walked Tony Larsen, off the Louisville, just in that afternoon. Tony hadn't heard of my retirement and he had to be told all about it. Tony had had a couple someplace before he got to the Moana, and his sympathy knew no bounds. He has a voice suited to the quarter-deck, and everyone within a block was fully informed about the matter. "It was a damned shame. . . . One of the Navy's most valuable officers." The Navy seems to have weathered the blow.

The boy had just taken away my lunch tray the next day when the office called and said there was a Mr. Lee to see me. I knew no Mr. Lee, but I told them to send him up. If I hadn't met Tony in the bar, and if he hadn't talked so loudly, I might never have met Mr. Lee. But here was Mr. Lee, a rather undersized Chinaman with the most gracious manners, and apparently with all the time in the world to discuss nothing in particular.

From my retirement and my present plans, or lack of plans, we got on the subject of my China cruise and Shanghai. He had just come back from China, and had been in Shanghai when the bombs had been dropped on Wing On's Department Store. We had mutual regret about the Palace Hotel bar, but, after the manner of Chinese, his emotions were under good control. I could sense that he wanted to feel me out on my views about China and Japan. Well, they were simply explained. My sympathies were definitely with China, but I also felt that even if something should be done about it, it was not up to the United States or its Navy to do it. It seemed rather pointless. I felt that Mr. Lee had something on his mind, but he left without unburdening it.

The next week I had a note from him, asking me to have lunch with him and some friends at Yook Hee's on Hotel Street. Chinese gentlemen usually don't start cultivating freshly retired naval officers for no reason. My curiosity was aroused. A luncheon would commit me to nothing. Anyway I like Chinese food, and Yook Hee served the best. A Chinaman's guest in a good Chinese restaurant is in a gourmet's paradise.

Mr. Lee's friends were three in number, older men and wearing conventional Chinese gowns. It was not until after a dozen dishes, and we were all leaning back sipping hot jasmine tea to ease that distended feeling about the middle, that they came to the point. They wanted me to take command of a Chinese submarine for operations against the Japanese at the mouth of the Yangtze River. They had made a quick check of my antecedents, and they seemed to be sure that they had the man they wanted. They meant business and their proposition was definite and complete. A thousand dollars in U. S. currency deposited each month to my credit in any bank I might elect, my expenses paid from the day I signed on, and a bonus of fifty thousand dollars for any major Japanese ship that I might sink. This was startling in its unexpectedness and in its completeness, and I asked for a week to decide. They were in a hurry, but the week was granted and I was pledged to absolute secrecy.

Now, there were many things to be considered. Although I was retired, I was still a part of the Navy of the United States. They held loose strings on me that could very easily be tightened, and if the Navy ever got wind of what was up, I could expect not only hearty disapproval but immediate action. Even if I succeeded in getting away with it, the least that could happen would be dismissal in disgrace if the matter leaked out later. Although my retired pay was meager, it would keep me from want if I couldn't find work to do. However, I felt that secrecy could be managed. I had no immediate family, nor indeed anyone who would be inclined to check closely on my whereabouts. I had contempt for the usual mercenary, but, on the other hand, my sympathies were firmly with China. The market for slightly used submarine officers was at low ebb. Then, too, I suppose I had a good deal of subconscious resentment at being so peremptorily shelved in the middle of a career that I, at least, had thought to be rather promising. Given a periscope and a deck beneath my feet, I could prove to myself that I was still as good as the best.

On the other hand, wherever the boat might be, or whatever her antecedents, the prospects that she would be even fairly modern and in fighting trim were poor. One does not pick up a first-class submarine in the dime store. The junk yard of some second or third class naval power was a more likely place. The crew would present many and varied problems. I had been too long in the boats not to be aware that it takes more than one man successfully to operate a submarine, particularly under war conditions.

The commanding officer of a submarine is a bigger factor in her success than is any officer or man in any other type of ship that floats. He alone sees the enemy and he alone makes the estimates upon which the success or failure of the attack depends. But the well-trained crew of a submarine is a team. The captain calls the signals and carries the ball, but the un-

timely failure of even the least member of the crew may mean
disaster. That China could supply men with the necessary intelligence and fortitude to make up a first-class submarine
crew, I had no doubt. But time and facilities for their training were too much to expect. The precipitation of brave but
untrained men into a dangerous and complicated situation is
the type of wasteful murder to which pacifist nations are pe-
culiarly addicted. Yet, strategically, the concept of submarine
operation at the mouth of the Yangtze was very sound, and if
the project could be kept a dead secret, the tactical difficulties
would be at a minimum.

At the end of a week I found my Mr. Lee and made him a
counter proposal. I would accept his conditions provided that
I was permitted to select and take with me three key men, to
whom he was to guarantee five hundred dollars a month and
expenses. He agreed immediately. In a few days I found myself a lieutenant commander in the Chinese Navy. I had in
mind getting hold of three men I could depend upon—a chief
torpedo man, a chief machinist's mate and a chief electrician's
mate. With this solid support I felt that the thing might be
made to work.

There was Chuck Young, who had been paid off at the end
of sixteen years of service and who was now the engineer of a
ferryboat in San Francisco Bay, still operating a Diesel engine. I knew he could be lured. Jimmy Mann, my old chief
torpedo man from the boats in Panama, was at loose ends in
Seattle. I got off letters to them by air mail immediately.
That still left an electrician's mate. Jones was my choice, but
he had a wife and kids, and this was definitely a bachelor's
business. Wives have been known to talk, and the danger was
not inconsiderable. I could take him out, but could I bring
him back? So I decided to make a go without the chief electrician's mate. If I had decided otherwise, the adventure
might have ended differently.

I went down to the navy yard and reported to the com-
mandant that I intended to take a leisurely trip around the

world, and made arrangements with the paymaster to hold
my retired pay on the books until I returned. There was no
trouble about getting permission to leave the country. It all
seemed too easy. When Young and Mann arrived, we flew
away one bright morning for Hong Kong on the Clipper, and
evidently no one was the wiser.

Amoy was our destination. We were met on the dock by a
bright-looking young man in a light blue gown and a black
silk Chinese cap. His English was excellent. His military
manners were punctilious. He was my new second in command—a gentleman, somewhat of a scholar, a graduate of the
University of Hawaii, and an honor R.O.T.C. student of that
institution. My third officer was a product of the same university. I never had any complaint to make about my officer
personnel. They were industrious, efficient, courteous, and
later I was to find that they had guts. Both spoke excellent
English and both were fluent in Cantonese. This was fortunate, for without it the whole project might have soon bogged
down in language difficulties.

Even so, my discipline and internal organization were most
unsubmarinelike. Not to be able to talk directly to any member of the crew was a difficult situation for an old submarine
officer used to having an intimate knowledge of the charac-
teristics of each member of the crew and to treating them as
individuals. Then, my Chinese officers were army trained. It
was difficult for them to become used to the free-and-easy
discipline of a submarine; the most effective yet the most difficult discipline to maintain in a military organization.

To operate a complicated mechanism like a submarine, each
individual must be free to volunteer information, to discuss
when discussion is profitable, to exercise initiative and discre-
tion in carrying on his duties; yet in other situations he must
obey instantly, without question and without thought as to
his safety. The recognition of the subtle changes in the situation which determine where and when and in what circumstances these two widely different attitudes are demanded is

what makes a good submarine officer. If we could have worked together for a year or so, we might have acquired it. We hadn't the time. It was a subtle fault in our training. It proved to be a vital one.

The submarine herself was a pleasant surprise. You remember the hulks that line the embankment at Amoy—used to load and discharge cargo to the busy junks. She had been berthed inside of one of these, and over her superstructure had been built the replica of a Chinese junk. It had been well done. Her engines were run only at night, and there was nothing to indicate her presence to the casual observer. Nothing except the smell of human sweat and fuel oil and acid which characterizes a submarine the world over, and this soon lost its identity in the compound odors of shoreside Amoy.

I was astounded on seeing her. She was an S boat, no more nor less. You possibly recall the stories we used to hear about building Allied submarines in the United States just before we entered the war; how they had been built, disassembled and shipped by sections to Canada and thence to Allied ports. Well, here was one of them. They indicated that she had been Russian, probably been shipped to the White Sea and then overland to a Baltic port. Or perhaps she never had been assembled at all until long after the war. Anyway, there she was, an S boat of 1918 vintage, about eight hundred tons, four forward torpedo tubes and two main Diesel engines of about five hundred horsepower each, with a surface speed of about twelve knots, and probably about eight submerged. How she had got to this spot I never learned, but I figured she had lain in some back channel most of her life, until the present trouble started. Then, probably, she had been sold by the Russians to some enterprising Chinese.

Her hull seemed in serviceable condition—nothing to boast about, but fair enough—as well as I could determine without docking. Her valves and pump and air compressor were in working order. Her torpedo tubes could be fixed without too much trouble—nothing modern about them, but they would do. She had ten torpedoes aboard, and Mann reported that he could make them run straight and hot. Her deck gun was gone, but that would have been only a nuisance for the operation I intended. Her engines were old and cumbersome, but with a little patching they could be made to run from where we were to where we wanted to go. Not without breakdowns, perhaps, but she would "mote." Her motors were in fairly good condition. It was her storage battery that worried me most. Life in a back channel is not the best in the world for a storage battery. This one was old, about at the end of its useful life. There were no facilities for repairs, and we would have to make out as best we could.

I spent a month in training and preparation. Not long, but every day was fraught with danger that some inkling of our presence would leak out and bring the Japanese bombers on our heads. We worked all night and all day. Every night we charged the batteries with the engine and discharged them on her screw. The engine-room crew and the electricians got plenty of exercise, and Young reported that they would do. He groused and complained about little things, so I knew from of old he was having no big difficulties.

Young was in charge of everything aft of the engine-room bulkhead, and he reported directly to me. Neither of my young Chinese knew an air compressor from a thrust bearing, which was just as well. Mann took charge of the torpedo room. He picked out a couple of bright-looking assistants and took every torpedo apart and put it back together again right. We had one amusing difficulty. We couldn't get grain alcohol for torpedo fuel. In the end we distilled case after case of Holland gin with a still that Mann rigged up. We wouldn't have got anywhere without Young and Mann.

All day long I worked the crew at diving stations. We could not dive, of course. It was impossible to leave the dock until we were ready to go. But we could and did go through all the motions. Not much training for the bow and stern plane man, nor for the diving officer, but it had to do, and at the end of the month I think they had some idea about what they were up against. Wong turned out to be pretty well grounded in mathematics, so I made him my fire-control assistant. Loo became the navigator and diving officer. He caught on to the navigation quickly enough, having had some experience as a surveyor, and diving officers are born, not made.

Wong and I had a problem on our hands in that we had no tactical data, either on the submarine or the torpedoes, and no chance of getting any. There were no fire-control instruments, although the periscope was an excellent one and the gyrocompass worked all right. So we computed our own fire-control tables and made a couple of simple omnimeters for the fire-control calculations. I worked the poor fellow continuously and I drilled him on innumerable torpedo problems, until he could do them in his sleep. And so, one evening just after dark in early May, we went to sea.

We steamed out into the outer harbor, dismantled the junk superstructure and, as dark and alone and friendless as any wartime submarine, headed north through the Formosa Strait. Afraid of being sighted from the air, we submerged before sunrise and came up only after sunset. Progress was slow, because at night we could run only on one engine and charge batteries on the other. The batteries continued to be my worry. How I wished I had a good electrician's mate to watch them for me. They would stand the strain of an all-day dive, but there wasn't much left at the end of the day. The cells were ragged, and, after the manner of old batteries, you could never tell which cell would fail next.

I had had a number of heavy cables made up with special fittings on short notice, and I devised a system of jumping one out under a light load. We had to do it several times and the boys got rather proficient at it, and maybe too nonchalant. I explained to Wong and Loo what might happen if we ran with a reversed cell. You see, if one cell of a battery is so very much lower than the rest that it reaches the end of its capacity while the others are still going strong, the polarity of this cell reverses. The cell then charges in the reverse direction, and maybe all that happens is a loss of battery energy when you can least afford it.

But then again, if the battery becomes heavily loaded, the cell may gas—give off hydrogen at a heavy rate. I explained all this, and thought it made a deep impression. Maybe it didn't. I doubt now that even Young knew the whole danger. His training had been in the engine room. He knew what a battery explosion was, all right, but battery explosions came when charging the battery. Hydrogen, to him, as to every old-time submariner, was another way of spelling danger, but I doubt that he could visualize this slow building up of hydrogen concentration in the confined atmosphere of a submerged boat until, the explosive limit reached, we actually existed inside a bomb which any chance spark might explode.

It worried me though. I had one of my Chinese crew forever watch the voltage of the individual cells, with instructions to warn me whenever any one of them got too low. I used to let the crew smoke for ten minutes of every hour and watch their cigarettes for the telltale little blue flash that would indicate a hydrogen pocket. There was no need of making them stop smoking. If the hydrogen percentage got too high, the spark that would touch it off was sure to come from an open switch, the brush of a motor, or the blow of a steel hammer on iron. The gas is odorless, invisible and tasteless, and there was no instrument on board for its detection. I could only guess and be careful.

Well, it took us ten days to get up to the latitude of the Saddle Islands. A crew operating under wartime condition whips into shape in a surprisingly short time. At the end of ten days they behaved like veterans. It was a hard ten days, hard on everybody. But there was no whimpering. I knew that if they then could set foot on dry land, I would never see many of them again. I couldn't blame them. I've often felt the same way myself. Alone on the bridge at night, with every third wave coming over the rail and down the back of my unprotected neck, hanging on for dear life, just living from one minute to the next, I have often reflected that sub-marining is one hell of a way to make a living.

Just north of the Saddles, we took up station across the most probable route of the convoys coming down from Japan. One morning we were in the middle of one of those Saddle Island fogs, with a five-knot wind that blew the fog about in patches. One minute you couldn't see your own bow and the next the fog would lift and for an hour or more the day would be sunny. We didn't dare run on the surface, for fear the fog would clear like that and leave us exposed, but I came up every now and then, and when the fog was thick, lay on the surface awash to conserve my battery, diving at the first sign of clearing. We had 1917 sound gear that was worse than use-less. The periscope was the only thing we could depend upon.

At about five o'clock one of those patches of clear weather blew in, and down we went. When I came up to periscope depth later and ran up my periscope for a look-see, my heart nearly jumped out of my mouth. There, about five thousand yards ahead, lay a division of heavy ships and a whole bevy of light craft. Their sterns were toward me, and I thought at first that they had got safely past me, that I had missed the opportunity of the century by minutes. But I ducked under and ran toward them for ten minutes, and then looked again. We were closing on them. They were stopped and anchored, waiting for the fog to lift. So sure were they of their strangle-hold on China that the thought of a submarine never entered their minds. Their destroyers were out at about ten thousand yards, waiting for hostile planes, I suppose, and for mosquito boats that by some remote chance might find them way out there.

It was like shooting sitting ducks. I passed the word to get the tubes ready for firing. It seemed like a year, but it must have been less than a minute when Mann came back to the forward battery door and reported ready. I told him the firing order, told him to fire by hand if the electricity failed, but to get them off at all hazard. He rubbed his hand soberly on his jumper and nodded, but he looked up and grinned when I said, "Battleships." It was too easy. Poor Wong, with his tables and slide rules, didn't know what to make of it when he had so little to do. He plotted out my approach and called out the stop-watch time with the utter imperturbability of a Chinese, but I had never given him a problem as easy as this to do during his training, and I think he was worried that he wasn't doing enough.

I simply ran up parallel at fifteen hundred yards, making only one swift periscope exposure for check just as I threw the rudder over to come straight in. I held down her periscope then until the stop watch said I was in to eight hundred yards. My nerves were like violin strings. I seemed to be working like a slow-motion camera. Every motion took an hour, and it seemed ages before the simplest order could be carried out. "Time up!" "Up periscope!" I hope my voice sounded calm.

There she lay! A little left rudder. "Steady so! . . . Stand by! . . . Fire One!" You could feel the boat jar as she left the tube. I felt that I would have to ram my fist into my mouth to keep from ordering them all fired in the quickest succession. If I got them all off together, I was afraid they might run into one another before they reached the target. Something in the back of my mind began to count slowly.

"Fire Two!" I could see the wake of the first, straight and hot and true. The sub seemed to take an upward angle.

"Hold her down, lads! Don't let her broach now!" It might be the end of us, and it might spoil the whole show.

Good old Loo. He caught her in time. She was steady now at her depth.

"Fire Three!" There she goes. "One, two, three, four; one, two, three, four," the jigger in the back of my mind sang.

"Fire Four! . . . Take her down to a hundred feet! . . . Full speed ahead; hard over left rudder!"

We heard the full thud of the first torpedo explosion. We'd

hit her! We'd hit her! How do you like that, you so-and-so's? The jolt of the second hit!

Mann came back with a grin from ear to ear. He knew. He stopped to feel the shock of the third explosion and the fourth. Four clean hits! Four straight shots! Four tin fish in a battleship's guts. "Reload! Reload! Don't stand there, lad. Get those other torpedoes into the tubes. Let's try for another." Maybe four torpedoes wouldn't sink her. She was a big battleship. Matsui class, I think.

My God, would they never reload? It seemed hours. I wanted to look, I wanted to see, but every periscope exposure now might mean disaster before we could finish our job. We heard some distant explosions. Depth charges! A destroyer went over us like an express train over a bridge. There would be no more sitting ducks to shoot. We'd earn our game next time. But no more Japanese ships lying nonchalantly off the China Coast, biding their time, like a hawk watching a pigeon loft.

If we were sunk right now, the mortal wounds of that battleship back there would be only part of the damage we would have done. Endless days and nights of double watch, of zigzagging, collision at sea, attacks on net buoys, mine sweeps clearing the channels, and screens of many destroyers burning up their precious fuel every time a major ship had to poke her nose out to sea. The easy war was over for the Japs. Every floating stick was now a Chinese ally. They'd run themselves ragged with their own imaginations, if we disappeared from the earth this very minute.

"The tubes are ready to fire again, sir."

"Bring her up to periscope depth. . . . Easy now, don't broach."

You could hear the gyrocompass singing sweetly in her binnacle, the nervous slap of the chain on the stern planes as the plane man rod the bubble like a hawk to keep her keel level as we planed gently up and up. No one spoke but the diving officer, whispering in high-pitched Cantonese as he coached his plane man. The depth gauge said I could take a look now.

"Up periscope!" I walked her around to have a look at the whole horizon, so there would be no surprises. There lay the battleship, listed way over on her side. Her rail was under. I could see a propeller out of water. She was going to sink. They were trying to launch her boats. A couple of destroyers were standing by. The other two battleships had slipped their cables and were high-tailing it out of there. On the horizon a group of destroyers were depth-charging the daylights out of some poor fish-net float.

There wasn't any use wasting another torpedo on the big one. The fog was drifting in again; it would be dark in half an hour. There were plenty of destroyers, but with their shallow draft and agile maneuverability they were as hard to hit with a torpedo as a bee with a baseball bat. Besides, I wanted to save my torpedoes for big game. I let Wong and Loo have a look at the sinking ship. It seemed to improve their morale.

While Loo was taking a look around the horizon he cried, "Look, captain, another ship!"

Sure enough it was—a big cruiser, a ten-thousand tonner, with a destroyer on either side and a big bone in her teeth.

Here was going to be something. Her screen was well placed. It was going to be hard to get under them or behind them, and to fire from ahead would give an impossible angle, with an excellent chance that she could avoid a torpedo after she saw the wake. At the rate she was coming down the range, there wasn't much chance to maneuver. I couldn't close the range much, because there wasn't time. There wasn't time to plot her speed. I'd have to do the best I could on a quick estimate. I gave her thirty knots, a course two sixty, and decided on a ninety track, which would bring me, I figured, just in the wake of the near destroyer when I fired. I couldn't even make another periscope exposure, for fear of being seen by the screening destroyer. Everything depended upon that one glimpse and an estimate a little better than a guess. So "Down periscope! Full speed ahead!"

Wong figured out how long it would take for me to get to firing position. I watched the hands of the stop watch creep around. Now was the time! "Up periscope!" First I must locate the screen. It wasn't hard. She had missed running over us by yards. In clear water and with a bright light, she would have been able to see the shadow of our hull. Thank God for the Yangtze River mud that made the water like soup. We were in the white water of her wake. And Loo was having the devil's time holding her depth. On came the cruiser. "Stand by. . . . Fire One!" That was at her bow. "Hard left rudder!" Get her swinging, or I'll never be able to get four shots at her! No use timing these. "Fire Two!" I just felt the bump of the torpedo's leave-taking when I fired the third, and then the fourth, as her stern passed over my cross wires.

"All shots fired!"

"Take her down to a hundred feet!"

No explosions. Did I miss with all four? Then the dull thud of an explosion, and another, and a third so close that it sounded like one continuous shock. I guess the fourth missed. I never heard it.

"Get the last two torpedoes in the tubes, boys." Not much daylight left, but perhaps this fellow would take another fish to finish him off.

We were exhausted. We had been keyed up to a higher emotional pitch than humans are built to stand. My mind raced like a thing gone wild. Minutes dragged like hours. But somehow the torpedo-room crew managed to get those last torpedoes into the tubes. The destroyers were over us now, dropping depth charges frantically, at first so close that they broke the electric lights in their sockets, but then farther away as they lost the scent and went careening off on a wild-goose chase. We could hear nothing. Let's go up and take a look.

Cautiously we planed her up. Timidly I poked the periscope above the waves to have a look around. The fog was coming in again from the sea. I could just make out the

cruiser in the mist astern. She was way down by the stern.
I think she was done for. Doubtful if I could get in another
approach.

Then Young stepped up to my shoulder and said quietly,
"Captain, Cell Number Seventy-two has reversed."

Glibly I told him to jump it out. "Rip up the battery decks
and get those jumpers across. I'll hold her speed down as low
as possible while you do it. . . . Take her down to a hundred
feet."

She started down. There was no telling how long the cell
had been reversed, in the excitement. I guess the Chinese
boy didn't want to bother me with little details in the stress
of the attacks. We might be safe enough—it might be an incident—or we might be in a bad way. I took a look around
the horizon as she went down. Out of the mists to seaward
came a destroyer, trailing a cloud of smoke and pushing the
water away in her eagerness to get at us. She'd seen our periscope.

"Full speed! Damn the cell! Get her down! Get her down!"

The depth charge rocked us from stem to stern. Close, but
she was over. She'd have to turn to come back and attack,
and one spot looks just like another up there now in the fog.
She might lose us. The boys were working now in furious
haste to get at the cell. A little luck and we might be safely
out of it yet.

But we'd had a lifetime of luck in the last hour and we'd
played it out, ridden it to the bitter end. The depth gauges
showed her safely gaining depth. I could afford to slow her
down. I'd just given the order when it came. A sheet of blue
flame shot through the boat. It followed the hull plates and
flashed wherever moisture had collected. It made a blue halo
around the sweaty faces of the men. It danced around the
periscope. It danced in devilish glee across the manifolds. It
didn't seem hot; no one seemed burned by it. The pressure in
the boat dropped five inches in the flash of an eyelash. In a
way, we'd been lucky. Something had touched off the hydro-

gen before it was thick enough to be truly explosive. It just burned; there was still hope. If we could only come to the surface! But at the surface waited destruction.

I glanced at the depth gauge. We were coming up! Paralyzed with horror, the bow plane man had frozen to his controls with the plane on hard rise. Loo fought with him to take away the control. I tried to speak. I could feel the muscles in my throat form the words. My jaws moved, but I made no sound. I couldn't speak. The quartermaster screamed in silence. Loo shouted at the bow plane man without a sound. Our ears cracked with the diminished pressure.

At last Loo got the controls. I motioned for him to take her down. I jumped to the air manifold and bled air into the boat. I could speak. We were at periscope depth. The planes were on hard dive, but she was coming up. She broached. Her conning tower clear of the water. I jumped to the periscope. The destroyer had swung around. She opened fire with her bow gun. All her shots went over. "Take her down!" A shot. She was starting down. A terrific explosion right over my head. I was knocked clear of the periscope and sprawled on my back on the deck. She'd hit us in the conning tower. We were under. The water poured in from the conning tower. We dropped the lower hatch.

We did the things which would enable us to live for the next minute. I ordered all the watertight doors closed. The lower conning-tower hatch was closed, but the water continued to pour in through the voice tube. We fought desperately to close the valve in the voice tube. It was no use. We heard the roar of the propellers of the destroyer as she passed over our heads. Then there was a terrific explosion. All the lights went out. Then the motors stopped. The main circuit breaker had been knocked out by the jar of the depth charge. We switched on the emergency light. The main breaker was in again. We went ahead on the motors again, full speed.

The boat was getting heavy with the water coming in through the voice tube. The depth charges had possibly started a leak aft. We couldn't hold her up. Hard rise on bow and stern planes, and still she sank. A hundred feet . . . a hundred and fifty feet . . . going down faster. I made motions for Mann to take charge of the air manifold. Blow a little out of No. 2 main ballast. She was sinking more slowly now. Two hundred feet. Two hundred and twenty-five feet. She stops sinking. "Secure the air." She commences to rise. Now we try just as desperately to hold her down. I vent a little of the air out of the ballast tank. How long can this go on?

Do you appreciate our situation? A submarine submerges by virtue of suddenly flooding her main ballast tanks. These are normally kept full when submerged and empty on the surface. Any minor adjustment of weight is accomplished by pumping water into or out of smaller tanks. If we want to surface in a hurry, we admit compressed air on the top of her main ballast tanks and blow the water out through the Kingston valves in the bottom of the tanks. Now we are taking on water through the leaks so fast that the pumps can't handle the weight fast enough. We must use the compressed air. It gives quick action, but it's an expedient fraught with danger. The Kingston valves of the main ballast tank must be kept open. We decrease the weight of the boat by putting a bubble of air in the ballast tanks. If we go down, the bubble is compressed by the increasing sea pressure, and water comes in the Kingstons to fill the tank.

We get heavier. We go down faster. We have to blow more water out to stop her downward speed. She starts up. The sea pressure diminishes. The bubble expands; she gets lighter. Her speed upward increases. If it isn't stopped, she will break water on the surface. We must let some of the air out of the tank. Our equilibrium is unstable. Any tendency to rise or sink feeds on itself and multiplies its own effect. If we sink much below two hundred feet the pressure of the sea will be more than the strength of the hull can resist. The plates will buckle. We will rise no more. If we come up as close as fifteen feet from the surface, our hull will project above the surface and the destroyer will be on us like a cat on a mouse. We can't keep it up for long. Soon the water in the ballast tanks will all be blown out. We will no longer be able to compensate for the water leaking aboard.

But minutes are all we need. The fog is coming in, the sun is setting. A little darkness and a little fog, and we could come to the surface in comparative safety. Five minutes go by. I walk the tight rope between the surface and the crushing depth. "Blow a little out of main ballast . . . Secure the air." Mann is as steady as a rock at the air manifold. I watch the depth gauge in the feeble glow of the emergency light. The water is above the floor plates in the control room. It rises to the calves of my legs. No. 2 main ballast is empty. "Close Number 2 Kingston. . . . Blow a little out of Number One main ballast. . . . Secure the air." I'll have to surface and take chances with the destroyer. We haven't heard a depth charge in minutes now. "Blow all main ballast." The boat takes an upward angle. The water cascades back to the after end of the control room. We start upward for the last time.

Suddenly there is a furious pounding on the after battery watertight door. The door flies open and in streams a mob of screaming Chinese, crazy with fear. They run to the conning-tower hatch. They can't lift it for the weight of water and wreckage above. They beat on it with their fists. They fight and mill around the foot of the ladder. The salt water pours over the conning of the door and in on top of the battery. The decks are up, where they have been trying to place the battery jumpers. There is nothing between the salt water and the cell. It pours down on the battery.

I step to the door to look. Young lies across the cell tops, the cook's meat cleaver embedded in his skull to his eyes. He's dead. How long had he held off that milling mob from the door? I catch a whiff of the chlorine that is bound to come. Salt water in the acid of the battery, and a submarine becomes an automatic poison-gas plant to asphyxiate her own crew. My flashlight shows a thin trickle of greenish stuff seeping up from the battery covers. It won't be long now. I look at the depth gauge. We are on the surface.

The conning-tower hatch is closed forever. I tell Mann to open the forward battery door and go up on deck through the gun hatch. The gun hatch open, the crazy mob fights its way to the deck. I wait for the sound of the destroyer's gun. It doesn't come.

My control-room crew stood fast. They had had something to do and some understanding of what was being done. The idle engineers aft had had nothing to do but wait in the dark, feeling the violent angles the boat took, listening to the depth charges explode and to the swishing of the water in the control room. It was more than most men could stand. They didn't understand the danger of opening the door.

I told those who had stood fast to go on deck, and I followed them slowly up the ladder. It was rapidly growing dark, and the fog was so thick that a dozen destroyers could be within a hundred yards of you and never aware of your presence. The sea was calm. There was a long, low, lazy swell setting in and the boat rode with her stern toward it. Thirty men on a narrow deck a few feet from the water's edge; a boat full of poison gas below; the ocean alive with enemies from whom we could expect no mercy; no boats, a hundred miles from land—

Still, the conning tower was above water now, and that leak had been stopped. If we could get an engine started and patch up the broken steering gear in the conning tower, perhaps we could continue to work nearer to the land before daylight revealed our pitiful condition. Mann volunteered to have a try at inspecting the engine room. I couldn't ask him to do it. We both knew that his chances of ever breathing fresh air again were small. But it was our only hope. Wong insisted on going with him.

We tore up our shirts and made pads wet with sea water to tie over their mouths and noses. It's a fairly effective gas

mask for the very soluble chlorine, for a few minutes. I still
had my flashlight. We opened the engine-room hatch. It was
dangerous. The sea lapped within inches of the coaming, but
we had to do it. Loo and I sat above and guarded the hatch
while they dropped below.

I called to them every minute or so. It only took a few
minutes. The water washed closer to the hatch coaming. I
curled around the coaming to dam back the water with my
body, and called for them to come back up. The boat's stern
lifted to the next wave. They scrambled up the ladder and
fell coughing on the deck. The stern sank in the trough. The
water broke over and cascaded down the hatch. We slammed
and secured the hatch just in time.

I could guess what Mann had to report. The motor room
was half flooded. The watertight door might hold, but the
engine room wasn't in much better state. The water was up
to the floor plates. Every wave now washed over the engine-
room hatch. An hour or so was all she could last.

I called for volunteers to go below and get life preservers.
Loo talked to the crew. Three or four men stepped out. We
fixed them up with homemade masks, as before. They dropped
down the gun hatch. The gas wasn't so bad there. It was seeping forward, but slowly. The life preservers were passed up
the hatch, hand over hand. It was quickly done, but we
hadn't much time. In half an hour we had difficulty clinging
to the tilted deck, so I ordered the crew into the water. I
was determined she would make no Japanese souvenir. So
Wong and I worked aft and cracked the engine-room hatch
before we jumped clear. She lurched crazily once or twice,
then sank steady by the stern. We could just make out the
shadow of her bow as she went under, her bow planes sticking out like some impossible marine monster's ears. She was
a pig-iron wench of uncertain antecedents, but she had been
all mine and she met her end like a lady, with a long throaty
sigh for the pain our parting cost.

I could hear Mann cough for an hour or more as he tried

to get the chlorine out of his lungs, but we must have drifted widely apart. At daybreak I was still afloat. I can't remember any more. I regained consciousness aboard a Chinese fishing junk, lying in the bilges with the fish. And with the fish I was in due time delivered at Ningpo.

The rest was an anticlimax. I got hold of someone in authority only after difficulty. I wanted a boat to go out and see if they could rescue some of my crew, although chances were slim. Only one other survivor had been picked up by the same junk that fished me out, one of my enginemen. Of the rest I never succeeded in establishing the slightest trace. If any were picked up by the Japanese destroyers, judging by what happened at Nanking, I know what happened to them.

I wanted to organize a project to get another submarine. I'd earned a hundred thousand dollars, and I wanted to see the color of my money. I wanted a lot of things. In the end I was only too glad to get out of China with a whole skin. For the Chinese adopted the position that the whole story was preposterous. The Chinese engineman could testify only that there had been explosions uncomfortably close, and the boat had commenced to behave in a crazy fashion. The lights had gone out, and he had fought his way to the deck. Then the ship had sunk, and he was in the water. He knew that I had given her the *coup de grâce* by opening the engine-room hatch. In fact the Chinese authorities seemed at one time convinced that the simplest way out of their difficulty was to line me up before a firing squad for sinking a Chinese submarine. I think my engineman would have enjoyed that. He seemed to feel that he had a score to settle with me. I felt sorry for him. He had participated in one of the most telling blows that had yet been struck for the Chinese cause. And he was honestly ignorant of the whole affair.

I spent a week in a stinking Chinese jail. In the end they let me go. Just that! I got to Hong Kong by the grace of God. There I borrowed money for my trip back by plane.

I found two thousand-dollar payments had been credited to my account at the Bank of Hawaii, but by the time I had paid back the money I had borrowed in Hong Kong and re-outfitted myself, this was gone. Mr. Lee pretends to believe my story, but claims to be unable to do anything about my bonus. The Japanese, of course, will never admit the loss of two big ships. I'd sell out my claim for a hundred dollars in cash and charge the remainder to experience. But Young is definitely dead. The vision of that cleaver in his skull comes back to haunt my nights. And Mann is probably gone also. I blame myself for those two deaths. For my Chinese shipmates I have no regrets. It was their fight. I am ahead of the game in only one respect. In that one crowded hour I had my belly full of submarines. Do you know of anyone with an opening for an inexperienced real-estate salesman?

NORTH OF TERSCHELLING

THE SEAROVER was at Harwich when I reported aboard. I was glad to find her there. Since they had started evacuating the expeditionary force from Dunkirk, it had become difficult to predict the movements of naval vessels. The Searover was to be my first permanent billet, and I was anxious to make a good impression. Nevertheless, as I looked down on the submarine's decks from the depot ship, I had a peculiar sinking sensation. I had given up a comfortable post in the merchant marine and undergone several months of strenuous training to become navigator of such a packet. Moreover, I had been a bit puffed up about being permitted to do it. War doesn't make sense sometimes.

Lt. Comdr. Richard Gilbert was the Searover's commanding officer. I found him abroad, and the business of formally reporting for duty and logging in didn't take long. In fact,

my welcome aboard was so terse that I was taken aback. My
new captain was barely civil. The submarine skippers I had
known had little use for formalities and usually called their
officers by their first names. Captain Gilbert didn't stand on
ceremony either, but I can't say that he fell over backward
to be pleasant or agreeable.

"We will be under way just as soon as we finish fueling,"
he informed me. "If you had taken any longer getting down
here from London, I would have had to leave you on the
beach."

I thought this was a little unfair. Gilbert himself hadn't
known the night before that he would be at Harwich in the
morning, nor had I known that I would be assigned as navigator in the Searover. However, I had served with grumpy
captains before and I knew enough to hold my peace. I had
expected that the submarine wouldn't be long at dock. Every
element of naval power was needed at sea during those hours
of crisis.

"Get your gear stowed as quickly as you can," he continued. "If you are going to be any use as navigator on this
trip, I'll have to show you over the bridge and the control
room before we leave."

I commenced to wish that the Admiralty hadn't thought
so highly of the Searover's ex-first officer. He had just been
promoted to a vacant command, making way for my present
appointment. He must have been a paragon of good temper.
Despite all the other virtues one must possess, you still have
to refrain from striking your commanding officer to win promotion. That must have taken some doing by the end of a
long patrol, if this was a sample of Captain Gilbert's usual
mood.

We left Harwich in the early afternoon. As we passed
Felixstowe Point, I could see that a direct bomb hit had de-
molished the seaplane sheds at the air station. The air force
was valiantly contesting the control of the air over the narrow

seas, but there was no sure defense against night bombing raids. Every port at which refugees could be landed had suffered.

I had seen some of the refugees arriving at London from Dover, Ramsgate and Sheerness, through which the main tide of the evacuation flowed. It was a sight to sharpen a man's hardened resolution to the keen edge of desperation. Gilbert told me that a few had arrived at Harwich, but he also explained gruffly that the people of the Searover had seen very little of them.

"Too busy with our own affairs to borrow trouble from others," he exclaimed.

For the time being, there were no airplanes in sight. We were all glad of that. Until the Searover could reach deep water, into which she could dive, we had little defense against airplane attack.

As we rounded Sunk Light Vessel, we passed a destroyer headed in. Her decks were crowded with refugees. A light bomb hit had made a shambles of her forecastle. Behind her steamed a Hook of Holland packet, loaded to the gunwales with men.

"A few hundred more who will be glad to be in England tonight," I remarked to the captain as I watched them pass.

"They seem to have had a rough crossing," he replied, "but they ought to make it now. The air force must be holding its own over the strait, for a change."

It was about the first attempt I had heard him make at anything like general conversation. Perhaps I could draw him out of his crusty shell.

"Can you imagine what a raid in force would do, if they are coming across in scattered contingents like that?" I reflected.

"The battleships and cruisers can take care of any surface ships," the captain replied. "I doubt that the Jerries intend to risk their necks in a raid of any size. The tough part of our job is going to be to keep the submarines out of it."

After that the conversation died completely. We passed the lightship and headed northward, skirting the coastal mine fields. To the southward was where all the action was taking place. It was difficult to reconcile our northward course with that. I knew that a submarine would be of little use in the shallow waters off the Flanders coast, and the presence of our own submarines in the strait would only complicate matters for the surface ships. But somehow, to put the main fight astern of us seemed like desertion.

When we were safely on our new course, the captain turned the bridge over to a junior officer. I went below with him to the control room to study the operation charts. For the first time I commenced to get a complete picture of the task that lay before us.

"The Second Battle Squadron is at sea, cruising south of Brown Ridges," Captain Gilbert informed me. "They have a scouting line of light cruisers out, but they probably haven't much of an antisubmarine screen. Every destroyer the Admiralty can lay its hands on will be busy enough elsewhere. All our surface ships will stay south of this line from Smith's Knoll to the Texel, and the submarines must stay out of that area."

I could appreciate the necessity for that. The heavy ships would be very touchy about submarines. To venture into their area was to risk destruction by ships that were no less dangerous because they were nominally friendly.

"There is a neutral zone five miles wide from Smith's Knoll straight across to the southern end of Texel and then northward to Terschelling. North of it the submarine-patrol areas are laid out."

"Where is our area, captain?" I inquired.

"We have this area just north of Terschelling," he replied, pointing it out on the chart. "It looks as though they have given us the hottest spot they could find. Anything coming down from Helgoland Bight will naturally cut right through it."

I could see that I was going to have my work cut out for me. There was a mined area to the eastward and our own area was a narrow lane skirting the mine fields. Directly to the westward was the operating area of another submarine. Every submarine, I knew, had orders to attack any vessel coming into her operating zone. They would strike first and identify the victim afterward. Clearly, this was no time to go mooning around in the wrong part of the ocean.

"We will use the neutral zone going to our station," the captain continued. "If we get out of it into someone else's area, it will be our own hard luck."

He didn't have to add that there probably would be no lights to guide us and that we wouldn't be permitted to use our wireless.

"That's going to call for some close navigating," I commented.

"Whatever it calls for you will have to produce," he replied sourly. The captain was in no mood to take account of difficulties. The Searover had a job of work to do, and Gilbert intended to see that it was done, but I could see no reason why he chose to be so unpleasant about it.

At first I had thought his irascibility might be directed toward me personally, but he was snappish with everyone. What greatly surprised me was the good grace with which everyone on the Searover put up with his growls. Ordinarily, an ill-tempered skipper can be pretty sure of a sullen crew. The people of the Searover not only received their commanding officer's crusty remarks with equanimity, but quite often, I observed, they appeared secretly to enjoy his most cutting remarks. That this was actually the case, I was to find out later. Growly Gilbert had a wide reputation and his best bons mots were treasured and retold from ship to ship in the whole submarine force.

In the late-summer twilight we headed eastward down the center of the neutral zone. I took my departure on Smith's Knoll and set the course to allow for the currents we would encounter. Gilbert was anxious to get into his area before dawn and there was going to be but little rest for me until we were safely on station.

Luck was with me that night. I managed to pick up Terschelling just before the morning mists rolled in. The lightship was dark and silent, and actually sighting it was more a matter of luck than navigation, but it gave me a good fix when I needed it most.

I thought the feat might have called forth a little mild praise from the captain, but I had to content myself with the fact that even he could find nothing to criticize.

I stayed on the bridge, hoping I might be able to catch a couple of morning-star sights. It isn't well to trust too implictly in the position of lightships off the enemy coast during wartime. As dawn appeared, the weather commenced to get thicker, and by the time the sun rose we couldn't see more than a mile or two.

After I was certain there would be no star sights, I went below for breakfast and an hour or two of shut-eye after my all-night vigil. I had no sooner stretched out on my bunk than the diving alarm sounded. I bounded out of my bunk and into the control room, half expecting to find the Searover in the tense excitement of an attack.

The control room was about as peaceful a spot as I had found in a long time. The first flurry of opening the flood valves and vents and securing the main engines was over when I arrived. The diving officer was rubbing the sleep from his eyes and coaching the hydroplane men to take her down to the ordered depth. The captain was standing by the periscope.

"Take her down to sixty feet," he growled at the diving officer as he snapped the periscope handles into their securing position and lowered the periscope.

"Too thick to see a thing topside," he explained to me in a manner that was almost affable. "We have to maintain a listening patrol."

At sixty feet we slowed down until the ship was barely under control. The listener, tucked away in one corner of the control room, bent attentively over his instruments, constantly sweeping the full bearing circle, listening for the beat of propellers. The submarine settled down to an easy routine. Here at sixty feet we were much safer than we would be on the surface. There was no chance of being surprised and any vessel on the surface could steam right over us without doing us any harm. As long as the poor visibility continued, we would be able to hear farther than we could see. There was little likelihood that anything could get through our area undetected.

For the veteran crew of the Searover, submerged operation was no trick at all. For many of them it was a period of relaxation. The skipper decided that this was the best opportunity he was likely to have to get a little rest. He retired to his cabin, leaving the diving officer and me in control.

"Bring her up to periscope depth every hour or so, Orten," he told me, "and have a look around to see if the visibility improves."

I found that I had a hard time judging the visibility through the periscope. There were no marks to go by and the periscope itself cut out a portion of the precious light. It was nearly noon before I thought I detected any clearing. Then I called the skipper and asked him to have a look.

He agreed with me that the fog seemed to be a little thinner. I was commencing to be anxious about the ship's position. It was all right to correct for the known surface currents, but there was no way of knowing if their set and drift were the same here at sixty feet. After a prolonged submerged run at low speeds the accumulated error might be a serious matter. Besides, the captain didn't want to stay too long submerged. The battery had ample capacity for much longer underwater operation, but to discharge it too fully was to run the risk of being hampered by a low battery if we got an opportunity to make an attack.

Captain Gilbert decided to come up and continue our patrol on the surface, as we felt our way in toward the lightship to re-establish our position. I went up with him, hoping that we would get an opportunity to make a cast or two with the deep-sea lead. We went ahead on one engine, slowly, in the direction of Terschelling, and with the other engine we recharged the storage battery. I suppose the visibility was about two miles, but the fog was drifting in patches and it was never quite the same from one minute to the next.

The men were allowed to come up on the bridge in twos and threes for fifteen-minute periods, to get a little fresh air and a smoke. Gilbert and the coxswain stood on opposite sides of the bridge, constantly sweeping the water with their eyes. Their concentration was intense. Nothing that happened around them could cause them to lift their eyes from the water's surface. The men came up on the bridge for their brief peek at daylight and departed to be replaced by others. We steamed on like a ghost through the fog.

The helmsman still controlled the ship from below. The diving stations were fully manned and a listener was still at his post. After a while the captain had the forward ballast tank flooded. Trimmed down by the head, we felt our way in. If we found a sandbank in the fog, we would be able to blow tanks and back off before we were hard and fast aground.

The listener was not very efficient under these conditions. There were too many surface noises and the pounding of the engines drowned out all noise from astern. It wasn't a surprise then that we saw our enemy before we heard him.

The coxswain reported calmly, "Something dead astern, captain."

"Down the hatch, all of you," the captain ordered abruptly.

I stole a glance aft as I made my way to the hatch. There was a spot in the mist, I thought, more dense and solid than the rest, but that was all. My feet had hardly landed on the control-room deck before the diving alarm blared and I saw Gilbert slam the conning-tower hatch.

"Enemy submarine," he informed me, making for the periscope. "She swung around to the westward just before we dove, and I got a good look at her."

I was surprised at the change that had come over him. Under the tension of a submarine attack a man has a right to be short-tempered, but my irascible captain now seemed to radiate good nature.

"Right full rudder. Thirty feet," the captain ordered. "Going to close range if I can," he explained to me aside.

He ran up the periscope and peered intently through the eyepiece, fiddling with the focusing adjustment, trying to improve the vision.

"Can't see a thing," he muttered. "She either dove or the fog is thicker. . . . Take her down to sixty feet," he ordered the diving officer as he lowered the useless periscope. "Maybe we can pick her up on the hydrophones."

The ship slid downward to the ordered depth.

Suddenly the listener reported, "Torpedo!"

A second later we could all hear the whir of the torpedo's propeller right through the hull plating. It must have passed directly overhead. Gilbert's decision to go to sixty feet hadn't been a moment too soon.

"Well, that one didn't have our number," the captain announced jubilantly.

It was over too fast to be frightened about it, but as I reflected that sudden death had missed us all by a few feet I could hardly share the captain's elation. The next one might be another story.

Everyone had remained steady and unshaken at his appointed station, but I thought I detected, in the faces about me, those who shared my apprehension. Indeed, the captain's spirits seemed to act as a barometer for the crew. As his affability mounted, their nervous tension seemed to increase.

"Two knots," Gilbert ordered. "See if you can pick up the sound of his propellers."

Almost as soon as the screws slowed down, the listener reported, "Bearing one zero five, sir."

"Stop the starboard motor. Right ten degrees rudder."

He was going to bring the Searover around for a straight bow shot. With the uncertainty of range and of the speed and course of the target, an angled shot would be an almost certain waste of the torpedo. But to turn her took time.

We waited breathlessly for another shot from the enemy.

"Bearing eight zero."

"Get the tubes ready for firing. Depth setting forty feet."

"Bearing six zero, sir."

I suppose she was swinging fast enough, but to me the compass card seemed to be dragging slowly around.

"Bearing three zero, sir."

"Steady as you go."

The helmsman eased her rudder and steadied her on the course.

"Bearing two zero, sir."

She was crossing our bow from starboard to port, but at what depth, at what range and on what course and speed, we had no way of knowing.

"Stand by to fire!"

"Bearing one zero, sir."

It would be blind shooting. There weren't sufficient data to warrant the computation of a periscope angle.

"Fire One."

The listener could hear the noise of the torpedo's propellers as it sped away toward the target. It faded into the distance. Miss! It was too much to hope otherwise.

Then there followed more than an hour of waiting and listening. Occasionally the listener could hear the enemy's screws, but often the sound faded out entirely. Both ships were maneuvering to get into position for another shot. Both were absolutely blind, each feeling for the other and listening for his antagonist's movement, like blind men groping for each other in a dark room. One single successful shot meant victory for one and death to everyone on board the other.

The captain took the sound receiver from the listener's ears and tried himself to pick up the sound our very lives now depended upon. Occasionally he stopped the Searover dead in the water. That would serve both to throw the enemy's listeners off the track and to reduce the random noise level in his own receiver. Apparently the German was trying the same tactics.

Neither vessel could stay stopped very long. When the screws stopped, there was nothing to make the submarine keep her depth. As the way fell off the ship, she slowly sank toward the bottom or just as relentlessly rose toward the surface. The diving officer frantically tried to maintain the depth, but there was little he could do. To start a pump or to use the compressed air to transfer ballast would introduce another noise for the enemy to hear and to distract his own listener.

Neither vessel was able to track the sound of the other long enough to get into firing position. The motors on the hydroplanes and the rudder were cut out to reduce the noise on board the Searover. Then the helmsman and the hydroplane men were controlling the ship by brute force and, at slow speed, it took a large angle of plane and rudder to show effect. Enormous effort was required. The men dripped sweat and tired quickly. Every few minutes they had to be relieved.

The captain gave the earphones back to the regular listener. I could appreciate the struggle that must have cost him. Careful selection and constant training, I knew, had provided in the listener a man more adept with the sensitive apparatus than the captain was likely to be. Gilbert seemed to have complete confidence in his listener, but it must have been difficult to resign himself to the split-second loss of time it took the man to read his instrument and transmit the vital information.

It was becoming a battle of nerves, and Gilbert was the

man to win such a battle. Later I was to find that there were some who considered that the captain's cheerful nonchalance in dangerous situations was a superb act. I now quite disagree with that estimate of his character. Rather I think that his usual surliness and ill temper were a mask to propitiate the gods of chance. In the tightest situations he dropped it as no longer necessary and stood forth in his real character. For all his gruff words, there never was a more kindly and considerate man.

To some extent, however, the German had the better of the situation. The captain's primary fear was that his antagonist might give up the contest and slip away from him. At any cost, we must prevent that. The enemy had only the battle to worry him. If the German submarine could elude us, he could count it a victory. For the Searover, the worst thing that could happen would be to allow an enemy submarine to get by and gain the crowded seas that lay beyond. For us there could be no drawn battle. It was either win or lose.

There was a considerable interval while the listener reported no sound. I found the periods of silence the most nerve-racking of all. Suppose the listening apparatus had suddenly gone dead. Suppose the enemy had gained only a few thousand yards' distance, and even now was on the surface preparing to speed away and spread death and destruction to the cross-channel traffic. Thousands of men might die because of our failure.

Suddenly the sound of propellers was loud in the listener's ears, coming from almost dead astern. She was close aboard, coming up fast. We could all hear her through the hull, but before anybody could do anything effective about it, the hull rang to a mighty blow. It was like being inside of a bell. The ship heeled over to starboard and I staggered to hold my footing. We could head the wild thrash of her screws. The hulls clashed again and again. The two submarines, groping for each other blindly in the gloom of the sea depths, had collided.

Fortunately for the Searover, the blow had been a glancing one. We had chanced to come together on almost parallel courses.

"Stand by to fire!"

The screw beat was almost dead ahead now.

"Fire two."

The torpedo sped off in pursuit of the fleeing enemy. For a time we held our breath, waiting for the explosion we hoped to hear. Miss again.

"Nice work, John," Gilbert found time to say to the diving officer, who was struggling to regain depth control. "Have a look through the ship and see if we have any bad leaks, Dave," he told the chief engine-room artificer.

Abruptly, while the screw beat was loud in the listener's phones, the sound stopped altogether.

"All stop," the captain ordered.

I am sure he was the first to figure out what had happened. The German had had enough. He had stopped and settled on the ocean bottom. There he would make no sound and it would be impossible to find him. He would wait until the Searover grew weary of the search or until we drew far enough away to let him run for it.

Two could play at that game. As long as the enemy was here on the ocean floor he could do no damage. The Searover settled down on the sand of the ocean bottom to wait for the German to make the first move.

On the bottom, the Searover lay silent, like a dead log. The faint clicking of the gyrocompass was the only sound in the control room. Every man remained at his station, but for a long time no one moved. Back in the motor room there was a slight trickle of water along the shaft stuffing gland, but no one suggested that we start a pump. The pounding of a pump would reverberate through the still depths like a signal to disclose our location. Up in the torpedo room two tubes were empty. The captain refrained from reloading them because of the noise it might entail. All conversation was carried on in low tones, as though we feared that even the sound of our voices would be carried out into the water.

The Searover swung slowly until she was parallel to the tidal currents. We could feel her scraping and bumping along the bottom. The diving officer flooded a few tons of water into the variable ballast tanks to anchor her. Then we waited.

Time passed. The sun would be sinking in the west. The clock was all that told us the difference between night and day. The captain seemed absolutely imperturbable, but the nervous strain commenced to tell on me. As day faded into night I pondered the advisability of suggesting to the captain that we come up and set up a surface patrol. In the darkness it would be next to impossible for the enemy to see enough to conduct a periscope attack on the Searover. On the surface we might be able to spring a surprise on our adversary when he made a break for it. Could it be possible that the listener had failed us? A thousand possibilities went through my mind. Had I been in command, I know I would have succumbed to the temptation to do something.

The captain was made of sterner stuff. He must have read me like a book.

"How about a game of cribbage?" he suggested as calmly as though we had been seated in the wardroom after some quiet peacetime dinner.

I concealed my surprise as best I could and went in search of the cards. Squatted on the control-room deck, the cribbage board between us, we played game after game. The cook served sandwiches and cold food to the men, who remained at their stations. The listener stood attentively at his instruments. In all that dead expanse of sea he could pick up no single sound.

For the first few games we stood about equal. I confess that at no time was I able to give the game my undivided attention, and for a while the skipper wasn't able to do much better. Then his game seemed to improve, and I was no match for him. To watch him play, anyone would have thought there was nothing else on his mind at all, and that, I think, would have been the literal truth. Sometime during our cribbage match he had decided on exactly what he would do when the German made the first move. He had thought out all the details, weighed all the possibilities, and dismissed them from his mind. As we sat there playing cards he must have been quite sure that all of us had only a few more minutes to live.

"Home to deal," the captain announced, shuffling the cards with a flourish. You would have thought that the silly game was all that he considered important and that to beat me again would be a major triumph.

We played on for a while, the captain quite evidently enjoying the game. He groaned in mock anguish as it became evident that his hand would not count him out. If he was acting, it wasn't having the desired effect. Excepting only the captain, the nerves of every man in that control room were as tense as fiddlestrings. He was too keen an observer to try swank at a time like this. A submarine crew lives too close to its commanding officer to be fooled by dramatics. "Just three holes to go," he remarked as he shifted the pegs.

"But it's my first count, captain," I countered in a weak attempt to meet his enthusiasm. "Better resign now. You lost your opportunity when you didn't make it on that last hand. I have more than enough right here to put me out."

"I'll peg out on you," the captain replied, rubbing his hands before picking up his cards.

"Nine," I called, playing a card.

"And seven is sixteen," the captain retorted.

"I hear a pump bearing three three zero," the listener reported.

"Very well. . . . Your play, Orten."

The cards were rumpled and bent in my grasp. The suspicion that the captain had lost his reason under the strain crossed my mind.

"Eight for twenty-four," I responded to the captain's demand.

"She is turning over her propellers," the listener remarked.

"Blow Number Two main ballast," Gilbert ordered the diving officer.

"And seven is thirty-one for two, and I'll take those three points you failed to peg after you played the eight, Orten.

"Secure the air. All motors ahead. Open B Vent," the captain ordered in quick succession as the boat lifted.

"Cribbage is a game you have to give some attention to, Orten, my lad," the captain told me, rising from the deck. "Left rudder," he ordered as he took his stand directly behind the listener. "Secure the torpedo tubes."

The torpedo officer was as amazed at that order as I was. He seemed to hesitate for a brief instant before he hastened forward to obey. Soon there might be an opportunity to make an attack. There was a moment when I thought the captain was going to funk it and abandon the contest. Never again will I do him such an injustice.

"Three five zero, sir."

"Steady as you go. Secure all watertight doors. Stand by to ram!"

"Stand by to ram!" the diving officer repeated with a shout.

There wasn't sufficient time for the crew of the Searover to realize the desperate nature of the captain's action. If he succeeded in ramming submerged, there was little chance that anyone in either submarine would survive. Captain Gilbert was determined that this one enemy would not get through, if he had to keep the Searover there to guard her through all eternity. There was no time to weigh the cost, no time to compute the possibility of rescuing his submarine after she had suffered certain damage.

All that was behind him. He had made his decision. He knew how infinitely small were his chances of survival. There were four torpedoes in the tubes forward. If the shock of collision set off the half ton of high explosive, it would blow us all to kingdom come. But the enemy would go with us. It was on the slight chance of preventing the detonation of the torpedoes that he had secured the tubes. The heavy outer doors of the tubes would be some protection to the war heads. Their pistols hadn't been armed by a run through the water, but no one, better than Gilbert, knew how small was the margin of safety.

"Forty feet." He would still have to guess at the depth, but he banked all his chances on the probability that the German would rise rapidly to periscope depth and pause there before surfacing.

The enemy seemed to be crossing very slowly from port to starboard. He was close enough so we could all hear his screws.

"All motors, full speed ahead."

As the captain hurled his ship and crew through the water as a missile, he was afraid only that he would overrun or underrun his enemy and that she would receive only slight damage. Where the Searover struck would be largely a matter of chance, yet upon that depended who would receive the most damage from the collision.

"Tell the motor room to give me everything they've got without blowing the fuses."

I saw the captain grasp a stanchion and brace his feet for the shock. For a breathless instant I thought we had missed. Time seemed to stand still.

Then all hell broke loose. There was the sound of a mighty crash up forward. The Searover was trying to stand on her nose. Men were thrown to the deck in hopeless confusion. All the loose gear came down like a house of cards. The lights went out. The gyrocompass sheared its foundation bolts and came writhing down the deck like a live thing, crushing and grinding the helpless men on the deck. The captain somehow managed to keep his feet.

"Keep the motors full speed ahead!" he shouted above the din. At that moment, if he had known, there was no way to stop them. The electrician was scrambling in the darkness on the floor plates where he had been thrown by the shock of the collision.

The other submarine was hanging on our bows like a dead weight. The Searover was pointed down at an angle of thirty degrees. The captain was taking no chances of his enemy escaping him. He was going to carry the German to the bottom and there grind him into pieces against the sand like some gruesome sea monster with its prey.

Almost immediately the screws broke the surface. We could feel the whole ship vibrate and tremble as the propellers, pitched high out of the water, impotently fanned the air. It was as though the Searover shivered and shook with fear of the fate that was overtaking her.

"All motors stop!"

The electrician would be doing his best to stop those wild vibrations before that order reached him. In the darkness, and with the steep angle on the ship, he must have had a terrific struggle with the controllers. Then the shuddering of the Searover ceased as the motors stopped.

Our momentum and the weight of the enemy were still carrying us downward. There was another shock, not so violent as the first, but it scrambled men and wreckage together again in tumultuous chaos. We had hit the bottom, the enemy still locked across our bows.

Someone succeeded in turning on an emergency light. In its feeble gleam men were trying to regain their stations, scrambling over the wreckage of gear that had been the control room. Water spurted from half a dozen leaking rivets. One of the depth gauges had been carried away. A small but solid and powerful stream of water spouted from the broken fittings clear across the control room. It hit the interior-communication switchboard. Short circuits danced across its face like lightning flashes. The banshee wail of the short-circuited diving alarm added to the confusion.

The Searover was stopped, her bow a hundred and twenty

feet deep, buried in the hull of her enemy, her stern high in the air above the surface of the sea. Slowly I came to the realization that I was still alive. The torpedoes hadn't detonated. The Searover had taken the shock of the impact on her sturdy bows. The hull seemed to be still intact.

The crew was trying desperately to regain control and restore some kind of order. Men pulled themselves erect on the sharply inclined deck. A few more of the emergency lights were turned on. The scream of the diving alarm was stilled. In the sudden cessation of noise we could hear the screws of our adversary frantically struggling to get free. We could even hear them trying to blow their tanks, but soon sounds of life in the stricken ship ceased. We had won.

"Blow forward main ballast!"

With his purpose now accomplished, the captain was trying to extricate his ship and crew from the predicament into which he had plunged them. The engine-room artificer, who had the air manifold, was trying to make a broken leg sustain him as he crawled and wriggled toward his station. I reached it first. In the semidarkness my uncertain fingers found the valves. The hiss of air told me that the lines were still intact and that air was going through the valve.

For a long time she hung there at that sickening angle. There wasn't time to find out how much damage the Searover had sustained. We must get her to the surface if we could. I wanted desperately to live, to get the ship to the surface and breathe fresh air again.

Suddenly she lurched free of the dead weight on her bow.

"Blow all main ballast!"

Willing and more experienced hands were now helping me at the air manifold. She was coming up. She was on a nearly even keel.

"Secure the air!"

I saw the captain struggle up the ladder to the conning tower, climbing over the wreckage that was strewn everywhere. A puff of air swept past me, and I knew the hatch was open. No water came down. We were on the surface.

"Get the coxswain up here to wipe the oil off the bridge rail," the captain snarled down the hatch, "and tell Mr. Orten he can get a bearing on a light if he can get up here right away."

When I reached the bridge I found that the fog had lifted. Dead ahead of us was Terschelling, lit up like a Christmas tree, probably for our late antagonist. The smell of fuel oil was everywhere, but the sea breeze was sweet in my lungs. To starboard, the sea bubbled and frothed white. Down there, twenty fathoms deep, was one German submarine that would never harass the cross-channel traffic.

ENEMY SIGHTED

THE INDIAN OCEAN simmered like a witch's cauldron. Out of the brassy sky the sun poured down its intolerable heat. It sucked up the water out of the sea. It sucked up the moisture out of the bones of men. The submarine Petard rolled lazily in the greasy swell. The sea sighed and sloshed in the superstructure. The submarine rolled and waited, waited and rolled.

A mile to the southward the light cruiser Perseus also rolled and waited. The two ships forged slowly ahead at a scant five knots. For two and a half months the cruiser and the submarine had waited. At fortnightly intervals the Petard pulled up close to the Perseus and a boat came over with fresh provisions. Sometimes the fuel hoses were rigged between the two and the submarine drank Diesel fuel greedily from the cruiser. The rest was sheer monotony.

The sun was hours past the meridian, but it still beat down upon the water, reflecting back a blinding glare. On board the submarine, Lieutenant Commander Howe, the commanding officer, and Lieutenant Jordan, his navigating officer, surveyed the blue sea through the protective lenses of colored glasses. The open bridge afforded no protection from the sun. The burning rays bounced off the glassy surface of the sea and reflected on the green undersurface of their sun helmets and burned to a still deeper brown their already tanned and weathered faces. Despite the film of grease with which they protected them, their lips were cracked and sore with sunburn.

"Captain," said Lieutenant Jordan, "if I had realized, a month ago, that we would still be here, wallowing up and down in the Indian Ocean, in this heat, I think I would have been ready to jump over the side."

Mr. Jordan had a little habit of sucking air through his teeth. Each time he did it the captain winced and tried his best to look unconcerned.

"It has been a tough go, all right," the captain replied. " 'They also serve who only stand and wait,' I suppose, but it seems rather futile sometimes, doesn't it?"

The skipper leaned with his bare arm against the hot bridge rail. The burned blond hairs on his forearms stood out in bold relief against the tanned skin. Every now and then he carefully selected one of the sun-whitened hairs and pulled it out by the roots with a little jerk. Each time he made one of these little sacrifices to his boredom, the navigator, with conscious effort, lifted his eyes and looked away with studied indifference. The quartermaster kept his eyes glued to the compass. The ship had little more than steerageway and she responded slowly to the rudder. The radio electrician had given the quartermaster an amateurish haircut only that morning. The whitish crescent at the back of his neck was now slowly burning to an angry red.

"How much longer do you think they will keep us out here?" Jordan asked.

"Your information is as good as mine," the captain replied. "Another two and a half months perhaps. What's the odds? If you were on a ship operating in the north now, you might have a little difficulty considering such duty as this as a hardship."

"It can't be any worse than this," Jordan protested. "Too damn hot to stay below, and the sun burning you to a crisp, topside. Everything there is to be done on board we have done over and over again for a thousand times. Climbing the ladder up to the bridge is about the only exercise I've had in so long now I can't remember."

"If you were making port with three inches of ice on your decks, you would probably pray for a little of this heat," the captain argued. "You probably could stand a little boredom, too, after a patrol dodging mine fields and nets."

"I don't believe I would be able to hold out for another two months and still keep sane," Jordan remarked.

"The best plan is forget about time past and time to come," the captain suggested. "Take each day as it comes and don't let the next one bother you until it arrives. Anyway, no one requires us to keep sane as long as we are Johnny on the spot when something breaks loose."

For all his good advice, life on board the submarine was as irksome for the captain as it was for anybody else. In the close confines of the submarine everyone was constantly under the observation of his shipmates. Little mannerisms that ordinarily passed unnoticed developed into annoying habits. Each individual had acquired new idiosyncrasies, and these in turn became just as intolerable to his shipmates. Long ago, everything interesting that anyone had to say had been said. Long ago, the custom of a nightly wardroom bridge game had died from lack of interest. Everything readable had been read. The sun beating down on the thick steel hull made the bunks below too hot to lie on.

Each morning the two ships separated until the Petard was just visible from the Perseus. The cruiser then trained out her guns and went through a listless gun drill, using the submarine as a point of aim. When that was finished, the Petard submerged and made a practice approach on the cruiser as she steamed by at high speed. Neither exercise any longer held any element of novelty or surprise.

"My guess is that Intelligence has gone off half cocked again and that nothing will break loose," Jordan sighed. "I could stand it if I felt that there was anything more to this than just sloggin' up and down again."

"Don't you worry about that," the captain countered. "Not with Red Blair up there in the Perseus. Lightning always strikes somewhere close to that old sundowner."

On board the Perseus conditions were a little better. Among the five hundred and fifty men in her crew there was some chance of a change of personal contacts. Her decks afforded a limited opportunity to get about. The routine enforced upon her people was more varied. Once during the past month she had made the run into Colombo to refuel and reprovision. Even so, monotony colored their lives, and tempers were short. No one on board the cruiser had a shorter temper than Captain "Red" Blair, her commanding officer.

As the sun sank lower he paced up and down the bridge. He was a big man with the carroty red hair that had given him the nickname he had carried since his midshipman days. He was cursed with that light complexion with which the sun raises so much havoc, and despite the protection of the bridge awning his face had now been burned a beet red. It gave him the appearance of nursing a continuously suppressed rage.

On the port bridge wing the officer of the deck braced himself against the slow roll of the ship. Occasionally he lifted his binoculars to his eyes and swept the horizon. The quartermaster steadfastly regarded the compass and now and then gave the wheel a little flip this way or that to keep the lubber's line glued to the compass mark. The engine-annunciator men stood at easy attention. Two signalmen lounged against the flag bag. Above them the empty signal halyards slatted idly as the ship rolled. The officer of the deck glanced anxiously aloft to assure himself that the lookouts were attentive. In a few minutes now his relief would come clattering up the ladder. It had been a peaceful watch, but a moment's inattention on anyone's part would bring down about his ears the scornful wrath of the captain. He had no wish to test the extent of the Old Man's vocabulary in the closing minutes of the watch.

The navigator stepped out of the chart house, sextant in hand, to take his afternoon sun sights.

"At least we can be thankful for fine weather," he said pleasantly to Captain Blair.

"I'm damned if I can see anything pleasant about this

heat," the captain retorted. "I'd be thankful for a stiff breeze and a little cold rain."

The navigator grinned and continued on his way to the starboard wing of the bridge. If the Old Man was in that mood it would be best to leave him alone.

Captain Blair continued his walk up and down the bridge. It began to look as though everyone's calculations had gone astray. Perhaps that was the best thing that could happen, he reflected bitterly, but it was annoying to spend two or three months on a wild-goose chase. The Intelligence Officer's sources of information were obscure but they were generally quite reliable. They had been unusually sure that the Admiral Schroder was going to round the Cape and come into the Indian Ocean. But that had been a long time ago and the pocket battleship had not appeared. Something may have gone wrong.

He wasn't too sure he was pleased with the arrangement to meet her if she did appear. Depended too much on chance and luck. The possibility of getting the submarine into a position from which she could attack played too big a part in the projected operations. There was a good chance of disaster if things didn't work out that way. He had better have the captain of the submarine over to lunch to talk over the situation again if the weather continued fair. Cocky young squirt, but a lot depended on his skill and on the ability of the two ships to work together.

It was time to send up the plane for her evening observation flight. He went out on the bridge wing to watch the operation. The catapult officer was busy with his last-minute preparations. Long practice had made everyone efficient at his task. There was no longer any novelty even in a novel operation. There was not enough breeze stirring to make the cruiser change course to catapult the plane.

The pilot climbed up into the cockpit, exchanging places with the mechanic who had been warming up the engine. He fiddled for a moment with his controls and adjusted his goggles. The roar of the engine deepened in tone, shattering the silence of the vast ocean. The pilot waved his hand in signal and braced himself for the shock. The catapult officer flung down his upraised arm. In a deafening crescendo of sound the plane shot across the deck on the catapult tracks. The pilot's head was thrown back against the headrest in the shock of acceleration. By the time the plane had reached the end of the catapult it had gained flying speed. It shot off into the void over the water, dipped slightly toward the surface of the sea and commenced climbing to gain altitude. Soon it was a speck hovering between the empty sky and the empty sea beneath.

The sun was setting when the plane came back. It settled on the water like a huge graceful bird. The cruiser stopped to pick it up. Noisily it taxied to a position underneath the crane. With deft hands the pilot and his mechanic hooked on the slings. The pilot looked up to the bridge and shook his head in negation. The sea was as empty as it had been since the beginning of time.

The cruiser settled down to her nightly routine. Thanks to the plane's observations there was little chance of being surprised during darkness. Nevertheless, half the battery was manned; the men resting at the guns throughout the long night. In the full moonlight the cruiser stood out almost as clear as she had in the light of day. Excepting for the dim blue screened wake light for the submarine to steer by, no glimmer of light relieved the length of her shadow. Astern of her, the bulk of the submarine, huddled close to the water, could be discerned only as a dark blot on the surface of the sea. By two o'clock in the morning, when the moon set, the night would seem all the blacker in contrast to the brilliance of the illumination of the early hours of the night.

Sunrise found the crew of the cruiser at battle stations. That instant when the sun's ball tipped the eastern horizon was the critical moment of every day. One moment the sea was dark. The best eyes in the world could not pierce the

veil more than half a mile. Almost in the next instant the
horizon was twelve miles away. Anywhere in between, the
rapidly broadening circle might disclose a powerful enemy.
The surprise would be mutual, but it would be the Perseus
that would pay the toll. Her enemy's vitals lay behind thick
armor. The Perseus' hope of success lay in swift speed that
gave her the option of refusing action or accepting it only on
her own terms. With the visibility rapidly increasing she
might be caught at such close range that she could be
pounded to pieces before her seventy-five thousand horses
could pull her out of danger.

From the fire-control tower, Lieutenant Commander Fields,
the gunnery officer, observed his seventy-first consecutive
tropical sunrise. He carefully swept the distant horizon with
his binoculars. The plane had taken off fifteen minutes before.
It was out of sight. There was nothing to be seen. Low oily
swells traversed the lifeless expanse of ocean, unruffled by the
slightest breeze. Even the submarine had disappeared. Each
dawn she submerged to escape being caught in the widening
radius of visibility. It had been that way for months. Each
morning, an hour before dawn, five hundred and fifty men
had gone sleepy-eyed to their battle stations to await the
sunrise. Each morning the sun rose as it always had before.

Five hundred yards off the port quarter a disturbed patch
of water appeared. Through it the black hull of the Petard
shot to the surface. The white water cascaded off her decks.
An officer appeared on her bridge. The submarine was getting right along with her morning routine.

Lieutenant Commander Fields gripped the edge of the wind
screen and peered over the side. The peaceful decks of the
cruiser lay stretched out below him, her graceful outline projected against the flat surface of the sea. At each antiaircraft
gun a little knot of men stood ready. The covers had been
thrown back from the ready ammunition boxes and in them
he could see the gleaming brass fuse caps of the projectiles,
nested like eggs in a crate. The sight setters fumbled with

their telephones and every now and then glanced aloft, waiting impatiently for the word that would release them. The
main battery turrets betrayed no signs of the life that teemed
within them but every gun, every station was manned and
ready for action.

"Secure from general quarters," the talker on the captain's
circuit repeated to the gunnery officer.

"Secure," the gunnery officer ordered over the fire-control
telephone, as he commenced unbuckling the straps from
around his neck.

The group of men about the antiaircraft guns broke up.
Out of the turrets men climbed, suddenly clamorous and in
holiday spirits, like schoolboys at the dismissed bell. Another
moment of tension had passed. For the great majority of the
men in the Perseus, the grim realities had been dulled by
countless uneventful repetitions of the same dawn routine.
For Captain Blair and his gunnery officer this moment always
brought a sense of profound relief.

When Fields made his way down from the fire-control
tower he found Captain Blair taking his morning exercise on
the bridge. From the port wing of the bridge it was seventeen paces before the starboard pelorus barred his way. Wheel
and seventeen paces back. The signal quartermasters crowded
in the extreme corner of the port bridge wing to keep out of
the way. The officer of the deck threaded in and out of his
shuttlelike path, timing his coming and going to the harmoni-
ous motion of the captain. The early morning traffic to and
from the bridge was controlled by Captain Blair's motions as
the steam flow to a cylinder is controlled by a valve.

When the gunnery officer appeared, the captain paused.

"Good morning, captain," Fields greeted him.

Blair returned the greeting pleasantly enough. "How did
everything go this morning, Fields?" he asked apparently
more in a heavy-handed attempt at pleasant conversation
than for any information.

"Smoothly enough," Fields replied. "They ought to. We've

certainly had enough practice at it," he added, smiling wryly. "As a matter of fact I think the men are getting stale. The loading time in the turrets has been falling off a little lately."

Instantly he knew he had said too much. The captain's sunburned face became even redder.

"Damn it, Fields," he snorted, "I won't have it. Volume of fire and a little excess speed are the only elements of superiority I have over the Schroder. I expect you and the chief engineer to deliver them to the limit of the capabilities of the ship."

Fields thought the outburst was uncalled for. He knew, and so did the captain, that the Perseus was the best gunnery cruiser in the fleet. There had been no conscious slackening off. It was impossible to hold men to the peak of perfection for such a long period of time. His mouth set in a grim line. He did not reply. The captain resumed his pacing across the bridge.

Fields went down to the wardroom for breakfast. After breakfast he kicked off his shoes and stretched out on his bunk. It would be a couple of hours before the morning drill at general quarters. He could get a little rest. He had a night watch coming up and it would be too hot to sleep in the afternoon.

Above him on deck he could hear the wash deck hoses running and the pounding of the squilgees on the decks. In a few hours enemy shells might be ripping up those decks. It made no difference. Brass must shine and decks must be spotlessly white, as the outward badge of a smart ship.

He must have fallen asleep immediately, for he didn't feel the ship stop to recover the plane from the morning observation flight. When he opened his eyes he saw the pilot, still in his flying clothes, passing the door of his room.

"What do you see up there, Pete?" he called out to him.

"Nothing," was the disgruntled answer. "Just ocean. There is plenty of that around."

"Yes," Fields yawned, as he felt for his shoes. "There is a

lot of salt water in this vicinity and I think I've seen most of it."

From far aft in the interior of the ship came the measured Bong! Bong! Bong! of the general alarm as it commenced its clamor. There was a slight tremor through the ship. She seemed to have come alive and Fields knew she had increased speed. Over the loud-speaker system came the boatswain's mate's hoarse tones: "All hands to general quarters!"

Reaching for his cap Fields glanced at his wrist watch. Nine-thirty. General quarters. No rest for the weary. His feet found their way up many ladders to the fire-control tower, almost without volition. All his life, it seemed, had been spent running up and down ladders to the demands of brazen gongs and raucous bugles.

Remembering his conversation with the captain that morning, he decided he would hold the gun's crew in Turret Four after he had released the others, and himself witness a loading drill. It was quite true that morning general quarters had become a rather perfunctory affair. When they went to battle stations at dawn, there was always the possibility, however remote, that they would see action before they secured. There was little prospect of it later in the morning. It was pure drill. The Petard made an indifferent point of aim. All casualty drills had been repeated until they were sick of them, and loading drill had become pure labor.

As soon as he had given the word to secure, Fields hurried to Turret Four. Every extra minute that he held the men at the guns intruded on the time the first lieutenant would have them at their cleaning stations, and that didn't help matters either in the wardroom or the crew's quarters.

The Perseus was cutting through the water at high speed now. The water boiled in her wake. Every few minutes she made a wide change of course. The cruiser was making a high-speed zigzag run for the Petard to make a practice approach. The quarter-deck, as Fields reached it, seemed to be squatting low in the water.

Stooping low he crawled through the trap in the turret overhang and paused for an instant in the turret officer's booth, glancing about at the myriad of dials and controls and valves for the sprinkling system and the magazine flood controls. Everything seemed to be in order. He squeezed into the control chamber.

The turret officer was already there. There was hardly room for the two of them to crowd against the turret bulkhead. Nearly all the available space was taken by the gun breeches and the loading mechanism. Each man of the turret crew stood at his appointed place. From it he would be unable to move while the turret was firing. These seemingly inert and massive breeches would come charging back in recoil into that tiny space with the brutal, irresistible force of tons of metal in motion, each time the guns fired. Every man must keep clear of them or risk almost certain injury.

Through it all the turret would be sluing and turning as it trained on the target. It would be difficult enough for a man to keep on his feet, but the guns must be served. Accurately, safely and with the greatest attainable speed and precision, powder must follow shell into the waiting maw of the gun breech after every salvo.

Each powder bag that a man clasped in his arms bore the seeds of destruction for them all. If an enemy hit or an accident should set it off before the plug was safely closed on it, the whole turret chamber would be converted into an inferno that would incinerate everyone in it. If, then, there had been any carelessness in powder handling or if the protective measures were no less than perfect, the fire might spread to the magazine below and the whole ship would be instantly destroyed.

Fields pulled a stop watch from his breast pocket and nodded to the turret officer to proceed. "Load," he ordered.

The drill shells rolled onto the trays. The hydraulic rammers met them and hurried them along the loading trays into the yawning breeches. The rotating bands bit into the rifling with a hollow thud. As the rammers whipped back and the loading trays were pulled clear, the powder bags followed the shells into the guns. The plugs thumped home. On the right and left guns, the gun captains snapped on their ready lights almost together. Fields looked at his stop watch and nodded in satisfaction.

"You may unload and secure," he said as he retreated into the turret officer's booth. The turret officer followed him. "I know my loading time hasn't been so good lately," he admitted, "but I think it's mostly because the men are stale. I doubt that we would gain anything by any more drill."

"You certainly couldn't improve much on that performance," Fields admitted as he dropped through the trap on to the quarter-deck below.

The morning was nearly over. The Perseus sent a semaphore message over to the submarine asking Lieutenant Commander Howe to come aboard for lunch with Captain Blair. Acceptance was of course a foregone conclusion. Shortly before noon, both ships hove to. The cruiser's motor lifeboat danced over the heaving swells, looking tiny and frail on the great expanse of water. Lieutenant Commander Howe, slightly uncomfortable in a starched white uniform after the informal garb of the submarine, climbed the sea ladder and came aboard the cruiser. Both vessels got under way again at their crawling five-knot speed.

In the captain's cabin the two officers sat down to a luncheon that Howe knew was only an excuse for the conversation to follow. The young officer had a profound respect for the fighting reputation of Red Blair, but he felt under no obligation to endorse all the opinions of his superior. Blair, he knew, had but little respect for the capability of the submarine. Long years of experience had taught the older officer to bank his faith on the hitting power of his guns.

"I trust that everything on board the Petard is satisfactory?" Blair inquired.

"Yes, sir," Howe replied. "She is fit and ready. The crew is a little restive under the close confinement of submarine life and the heat is just endurable, but we bear up under it."

"Humph!" Blair snorted. "Two or three months at sea and these modern seamen consider they have cause for complaint. When Hughes and Suffern fought in these very waters men thought nothing of two years aboard ship."

Howe thought that there was little that could be compared between life on a ship of the line and the conditions on board his submarine.

"I'm not prepared to concede that Hughes' men were superior to mine or any better able to endure hardship," he answered.

"Perhaps, perhaps," Blair yielded. "I'll admit you have a lot to contend with. I presume that a few more weeks will see the end of it. If the Schroder doesn't arrive by then, everybody will be ready to admit that she isn't going to come at all."

"Then you feel it has all been a wild-goose chase?"

"Perhaps not. The enemy may have intended to send the Admiral Schroder into the Indian Ocean and had something turn up to change their plans. She could do a lot of damage here all right, but I imagine they would find the fuel problem almost insurmountable."

"It's strange we have heard nothing of her for so long. You would imagine that somewhere she would be sighted if she is at sea."

"Not so strange as it may seem," Blair replied. "The very threat of her coming is holding a lot of shipping in port and has forced the rest into convoys. If she picks up a stray tramp or two as prize, I imagine she would take adequate measures to see that they had no opportunity to use their radios. But two and a half months is a long time for her to operate without at least a rumor as to her whereabouts," he continued. "She must be getting short of fuel unless she has slipped back to port through the blockade."

Fuel, he reflected, might yet prove to be the key to the present situation. The pocket battleship might be lucky enough to pick up a Diesel-engined prize and acquire a little fuel in that fashion, but surely she would have to make more reliable arrangements for an extended cruise. Her cruising radius on her big Diesel engines was phenomenal, but she couldn't run on forever and the Indian Ocean was a long way from her base.

"If the Commander in Chief had been certain that the Admiral Schroder was coming here," Blair mused, "I think he would have sent a force more nearly adequate to handle the situation."

Howe was aware of what Blair was thinking. It nettled him a bit to think the cruiser captain placed such a low value on the potentiality of the submarine.

"The Petard will be prepared to hold up her end if we ever meet," he said somewhat testily.

"That is, if you can get within range, you mean," Blair countered. "Once you are forced down, you aren't much more effective than a mine field. With that slow submerged speed of yours, you will have to depend upon the enemy to come your way. What will you do if he doesn't care to play your game?"

That there was a lot of truth in the captain's contention, Howe had to admit to himself. Eight knots was the best he could make, once he was submerged. If the enemy had any warning of his presence it would be an easy matter for him to avoid the submarine. With the Schroder steaming at twenty-six knots, he would have to make contact within a narrow angle on her bow or he would never be able to get within torpedo range. Even then, if the enemy maneuvered radically in her brush with the Perseus he might not be able to close her. There was a lot of sound tactics in Blair's remarks, but it didn't make him feel any happier.

"I thought we were to depend upon Perseus to draw the Schroder into the submarine's reach," he suggested archly.

"That's the plan of action we've agreed upon," Blair replied. "I hope it works. Perseus advances and exchanges a few salvos at long range with the pocket battleship, then simulates being badly hit and retires behind a smoke screen. Petard advances to attack as the enemy advances to polish us off. It sounds fine on paper. Some desk strategist's ideas of war. Did it ever occur to you that Schroder may have other ideas?"

It had occurred to him, of course. The Admiral Schroder would be in the Indian Ocean for the purpose of commerce destruction. If she played a cool and calculating game, she would stand off the Perseus at long range and go on about her business. She could do infinitely more damage at commerce destruction than she could by coming to grips with a light cruiser. She would be bound to receive some damage in any hard-fought action despite her superiority of gun power and armor, and repairs would be impossible anywhere short of her home yards.

There couldn't be much doubt as to what would be the eventual outcome of any stand-up fight between the two ships; but even if the Perseus was sunk the pocket battleship might have to return and leave the Indian Ocean commerce to go on about its peaceful business. Just the same, Howe knew that the plan of action had originated in the submarine flotilla, and all his latent loyalties were aroused by the bitter reference to desk strategists. Personally, he was of the opinion that no enemy commander could resist the temptation to sink a light cruiser.

"In case she doesn't come within range of Petard," Howe ventured, "I suppose Perseus would have to use her superior speed to withdraw and we could try making a better contact later."

"I hate being decoy duck for a submarine," Blair growled, "and I dislike the prospect of withdrawing from any action once it is joined. I would feel personally responsible for all the damage she might do until she was run to earth."

Howe could appreciate the fighting instincts of the captain. He could bet that Perseus would play no passive decoy part, sound strategy or no sound strategy. Then, too, the Perseus was terribly vulnerable. One lucky hit and all her speed superiority would go glimmering and the rest might well be disaster.

It was time Howe returned to the Petard. Both ships stopped again, rolling lazily in the long swell. Captain Blair accompanied him to the top of the sea ladder.

"I would rather we had a heavy cruiser with us," he confided to Howe. "Then perhaps we could fight it out on any reasonable terms."

Howe was willing to concede the point. But that was just the trouble. There weren't enough cruisers to go around to protect all the possible hot spots in adequate force. He shook hands with Captain Blair in parting. Neither knew how soon their theories were to be put to the test nor how much chance was to color the situation.

Evening came. The Petard's officers were crowded together in the little wardroom for a cheerless meal, like many others that had preceded it. It was characteristic of their boredom that no one expressed any curiosity about the captain's recent visit to the cruiser and that Howe felt no urge to discuss tactics with his officers. The war news they had heard on the afternoon short-wave broadcast schedule had not been very cheering. The dinner proceeded in silence.

A messenger from the radio room appeared at the wardroom door and handed in the carbon copy of a message that had just been received. The communication officer excused himself and retired to his room to struggle over the message with code book and cipher. Around the wardroom table interest picked up a bit.

"What's in the wind now, I wonder," said the engineer officer, breaking a long silence.

"Probably some routine report," the captain replied dejectedly. "Anyway, we won't have to answer. There are some advantages to a radio silence."

The conversation died back into silence. In a few minutes the communication officer was back. His face betrayed his suppressed excitement as he handed the decoded message to the captain. Howe read it through rapidly. He struggled to get free of the wardroom table as he handed the message to the navigator.

"Here, Jordan," he ordered, "plot in our position on the chart and let me know course and distance to Suvadiva as soon as possible." The captain was already on his way to the bridge.

The engineer read over the navigator's shoulder: "Tanker Momus left Batavia noon of the twelfth with cargo of Diesel oil. Reliable information she intends to fuel the Admiral Schroder at rendezvous in vicinity of Suvadiva Atoll."

"That reads like it will call for a little more speed," said the engineer, picking up his cap from the sideboard. As he passed through the control room he could hear the jingle of the engine telegraph above the subdued clatter of the engines. At last they were going places.

By the time the skipper reached the bridge, the cruiser had already swung to a northeast course. Evidently she also had intercepted the message and Captain Blair had lost no time in acting on it. Howe rang up full speed. The submarine rapidly accelerated to her best sustained surface speed of fifteen knots. He threw the rudder over and followed in the cruiser's wake. In the bright moonlight the Perseus was so clearly outlined that the faint gleam of her blue wake light was hardly necessary for him to maintain position. The increased speed stirred up the semblance of a breeze. Life on board the submarine took up a quicker tempo with the swifter beat of the engines.

There was a faint flicker of light from the port bridge wing of the Perseus. The signalman of the Petard carefully aimed his blinker tube and answered.

"Course zero two five, speed fifteen." Blair would waste no time at unnecessary night signaling. What might have to be explained could be done with less chance of detection by semaphore after daybreak.

The navigator called up to the bridge through the control room voice tube to tell the captain that the positions were plotted if he cared to have a look at them. The captain dropped down the ladder and blinked for an instant until his eyes became accustomed to the light.

"Here is Suvadiva," Jordan explained, pointing to a tiny dot south and a little east of the tip of the Indian Peninsula. "I've run up my evening star sights and here we were when we changed course just now. At fifteen knots we can make it about two o'clock in the afternoon day after tomorrow. I've plotted the tanker's run from Batavia and if she makes ten knots and sails great circle, she can reach Suvadiva eight hours ahead of us, or about dawn Tuesday morning."

"Humph!" Howe snorted. "It's a wonder they can't be more timely with their information. What have they been doing for the past week—sitting on this message to see if it will hatch?"

He was aware that to acquire this information at all had called for a nice piece of intelligence work somewhere. The difficulties of getting it out of a country that was then neutral might well account for a week or ten days' delay. It was still timely enough to act upon but there was no denying that if it had come in a day or two sooner their problem would have been greatly simplified.

They kept on during the night at fifteen knots. Howe could well imagine Captain Blair's state of mind. Perseus was tied to the slower submarine. At the submarine's best speed they might arrive at Suvadiva too late to be fully effective. Two-thirds of the cruiser's seventy-five thousand horsepower lay idle beneath her deck. It is always irksome for a fast ship to be held back by a slower consort. Now that the matter of a few hours might mean all the difference between success and failure, Howe knew that Captain Blair would be using his justly famous vocabulary in invective against the Petard. With five hundred yards of water between the ships he could afford to grin at the thought.

He didn't envy Captain Blair the decision he would have to make. It was well within the range of possibility that the Schroder would be waiting at Suvadiva for the tanker. If the weather was calm enough for fueling at sea without the protection of the atoll, the enemy might run down to meet the Momus. With good luck he could complete his fueling in eight hours and then he would be free for another two or three months' operation. All of the Indian Ocean lay before him. There was no reason why he shouldn't venture into the Pacific. The prospects for the officer who was responsible for letting this ship get away were far from pleasant.

On the other hand, if the Perseus left the submarine behind and then came to grief under the guns of the pocket battleship, it would make a holiday for the armchair tacticians for years to come. Dividing his forces in the face of a powerful enemy! It wasn't done. He was damned if he did and damned if he didn't. The only possible vindication of whatever decision he made would be success. Critics could always find sound reason for any decision that led up to a successful operation. And of course there was the small matter of the lives of five hundred and fifty men to consider and the possible destruction of a beautiful ship.

Howe never had any serious doubts as to which way the decision would fall. Not with Captain Blair in the driver's seat. There wasn't much chance of the Admiral Schroder being allowed to calmly complete her fueling while the Perseus hung back to retain the support of the submarine. Blair would fight with any force he could bring to bear.

A few minutes before dawn the Petard submerged. She stayed on the surface until it was already commencing to get gray in the east; but despite the urgent need of haste Howe was unwilling to risk the chance of continuing on the surface during sunrise. The best chance he had of getting into action depended upon the complete surprise that would be effected by the presence of a submarine in these waters. If the enemy suspected a submarine trap, he would be just that much more wary. The Schroder would be coming up from the southwest. Their courses might be almost parallel. There was no use being sighted by a scouting plane. Captain Blair's temper would not be improved by the additional delay, but it couldn't be helped.

He was up again as soon as there was clear daylight. He could depend on the Perseus to maintain a good lookout for planes and let him know if one was sighted. From the viewpoint of the submarine, there were a good many advantages to operation with a cruiser.

The Perseus was several thousand yards ahead by the time he surfaced. It seemed as though Blair was trying to urge them on to greater effort than their laboring engines could make. Howe lived in constant fear of an engine casualty. To steam for two or three days at top power put a terrific strain on his engines. He had every confidence in his engineer, but the slightest mishap would cause him to slow down for two or three hours. He dreaded the withering scorn of Captain Blair in that event.

When the cruiser stopped to pick up the plane after the morning reconnaissance flight, the submarine was able to regain her position. But the Perseus lost no time. Very soon she was ahead again, demonstrating her impatience at the slow speed of her consort. They labored on during the long day, the Petard doggedly making her best speed.

The plane was catapulted for her evening flight. A signalman appeared on the bridge wing of the Perseus. Captain Blair was notoriously chary of his signals. There had been no flag-fluttering discussion of the situation so far. Howe knew before the signals came over that Blair had reached his decision.

"After recovery of the plane, Perseus will increase speed to twenty-five knots. Petard continue to rendezvous Suvadiva at best speed."

He had been right in his estimate of Captain Blair. The Perseus would close in on the tanker and risk the chance of running smack into the Schroder.

After the Perseus had left the submarine behind, Blair felt as though a load had been lifted from his mind. He fully realized the danger of his position, but his decision had been made. The Perseus was a handy ship. He had every confidence that the cruiser would give a good account of herself under any conditions. He turned in and spent the most restful night he had had in weeks.

An hour before dawn the crew of the cruiser sprang to life to the insistent clamor of the general alarm. Whatever was waiting for him at Suvadiva, Blair was going to be fully prepared to meet it. Before the first faint gray showed in the east, the plane was in the air. The sun breaking over the horizon found every man at his battle station. There was steam up to the throttle for her full thirty-two knots.

To the northward Blair could make out the low island of the atoll. For the rest there was nothing.

"Secure from general quarters," he told the navigator, who had relieved the officer of the deck. "We seem to be the first arrival at this party."

The guns' crews straggled out of the turrets to stand around the deck in little knots of men who gazed off into the vacant sea. The possibility that they would be surprised at dawn was past.

"Have breakfast served as soon as you possibly can," Captain Blair ordered. "You may dispense with the morning routine. I want the men to get all the rest they can. We have a long day ahead of us."

"Plane returning on the starboard bow!" the foretop lookout reported.

The cruiser's plane closed rapidly. She flashed across the bow, banked and turned, and winged away again to the eastward. It was the agreed-upon signal that something had been sighted that demanded investigation. The pilot was forbidden the use of his radio, except in case of emergency, for fear of prematurely disclosing the presence of the cruiser.

The Perseus swung round gracefully to the new course, leaving a wake of boiling white water astern and heeling slightly to the rudder. The general alarm called the men back to their battle stations. Blair rang for full speed. A big white roller appeared on either bow. She seemed glad to feel her full power again, after the long months of lolling through the warm water under bare steerageway. The plane streaked away ahead of her.

In a few minutes the foretop lookout reported, "Sail ho! Dead ahead!"

It wasn't long afterward that Captain Blair knew he had caught the Momus, caught her unguarded and alone. At the rate the cruiser was gliding through the water, the upper works of the tanker heaved rapidly above the horizon. Soon they could make out her decks from the bridge of the Perseus. The tanker stood on serenely. Probably she still thought she was making her anticipated contact with the Schroder.

Suddenly the Momus became aware that something was wrong. She commenced a lumbering turn away from the approaching cruiser. Her attempt at flight was almost ridiculous, like a waddling duck fleeing from a fox.

"Drop a shell alongside of her," Captain Blair ordered the gunnery officer.

Turret One swung out a few degrees to port. The guns raised their ugly muzzles in unison. The left one barked once. The haze of smokeless powder gases drifted over the bridge. The thin whistle of the retreating shell filled the air. The sound died away long before the shell arrived at its destination. A splash arose abeam of the tanker.

"The tanker is using her radio," the communication officer reported. "We are trying to jam his signals, but we can't tell how effectively we are doing it."

"Make signal by flag hoist in International Code to cease using radio," Captain Blair ordered his signal officer.

The signal flags stood out stiffly in the thirty-knot breeze of the cruiser's own making.

"Tell the gunnery officer to give him another round," Captain Blair directed his telephone talker, "and tell him to put this one close enough to put the fear of God in him. If he can't understand signals, he will at least be able to understand that language."

The right gun of Turret One fired once. The shell splash appeared on the starboard side of the tanker and very close aboard. Tons of water from that splash must have drenched the decks of the Momus.

"The tanker appears to have stopped signaling," the communication officer reported.

Captain Blair turned to Commander Lang, his executive officer. "Get your prize crew together. Lieutenant Commander Johnson will go as prize master. Send him up here to me for instructions. Get two boats ready for lowering."

In a few minutes Lieutenant Commander Johnson appeared on the bridge. Forewarned by the ship's organization bill that he would be prize master, he had had his bag packed as soon as the tanker had been sighted. The prize crew was already assembling on deck. The bugle called the boats away. The Perseus was losing no time about the operation.

"You sent for me, sir," Johnson addressed the captain.

"I did, sir," Blair replied. "You will take over that ship as prize. But not until you have conducted a regular visit and search. I'll have nothing irregular about this business. You will go in the first boat with a boarding party. Remember that the boarding party may not be armed when boarding but may have arms in the boat. Examine the papers and cargo if necessary. The prize crew will be in the second boat."

Johnson smiled at this strict compliance with the regulations by a commander who had evidently determined to make the tanker prize.

"I understand, sir. I am to examine her for evidence of un-neutral behavior."

"If she has Diesel fuel aboard, she's a prize. I don't give a damn how her manifest reads. And I want you to lose no time shilly-shallying about it. Your prize crew will be right behind you. Call them alongside and take her over as soon as your visit and search is completed. I want those boats back in half an hour."

"Aye, aye, sir," Johnson acknowledged. "What are my orders after I take her over?"

"You will follow Perseus back to Suvadiva. From there you will set a course to Colombo. Perseus will then steam south to rejoin Petard. I anticipate no difficulty, but keep your eye peeled for the Admiral Schroder."

"What are your instructions in case I should be overtaken by the enemy?" Johnson asked. He knew it was a delicate question, but now that the subject had been brought up, he felt it worth while to be protected by definite orders.

"You will sink the tanker, sir," Blair ordered. "And be damned sure you do a thorough job of it."

"Aye, aye, sir," acknowledged Johnson, smiling at the captain's forthrightness.

"Very well, then. Your boat is waiting. Carry out your orders."

While this conversation was taking place, the Perseus had approached to within a few hundred yards of the waiting tanker and had stopped. The first boat now cleared the side and the boat with the armed and organized prize crew followed her.

It wasn't long after Johnson had been observed climbing up over the tanker's side that a signalman appeared on her bridge. The semaphore flags flicked their message across the narrow stretch of sea separating the two ships:

"Momus Maru out of Batavia for Yokohama with cargo of Diesel oil. Have made her prize in accordance with instructions."

The prize crew was already clambering aboard the Momus. Soon the boats were returning. In less than an hour after the Perseus had stopped, the two ships were under way again, retracing their way to Suvadiva. The tanker wallowed along in the wake of the cruiser.

The Perseus was again tied to a slow-moving consort, and it was nearly two hours before she could get rid of her. It was nine-thirty before the Momus Maru set her course for Colombo and Perseus was free to turn southward to rejoin the Petard.

For Captain Blair it was two more hours of anxious uncertainty. The Admiral Schroder was almost certainly somewhere in the vicinity. The Momus Maru had had ample opportunity to bleat out all her troubles over the radio. The enemy would know that he would have to fight for his fuel. He would believe that he had the preponderance of force on his side and he would be eager for battle. Until she rejoined the Petard, Perseus could at the best put up an ineffectual running fight, with very little chance of inflicting any great damage on the pocket battleship.

The tanker worried him. The chances were that the Schroder was still to the southward, but there was a likely possibility that the enemy might be lucky enough to make first contact with the prize. His directions to Johnson had been clear enough. It was difficult to imagine a situation in which the tanker could be taken in broad daylight, without an opportunity to use her radio. Perseus could always overtake the prize in an hour or two. The enemy wouldn't have an opportunity to fuel even if Johnson failed to carry out his implicit directions.

He smiled grimly to himself at Johnson's request for instructions. There was no question but what the junior officer was right. He was asking for the reasonable protection of positive orders to cover a situation that was only too likely to occur. Well, he had his orders. They should be positive enough. The responsibility rested squarely on his, Blair's, broad shoulders. It belonged there. It was too late in life for him to begin to hedge with indefinite instructions.

Nevertheless, he could envy the freedom with which the junior officer might now act. Johnson had known as well as Blair what should be his proper action if the Schroder overtook him. Now he could do what he knew the situation would require and still walk into court with clean hands.

If the Momus Maru was sunk, there would be a court all right; with a good deal of hullabaloo, and justice the last thing to be considered. He was familiar enough with the Declaration of London and all that grave nonsense contained therein about the rights of neutral shipping. Strange how, when serious and apparently sensible diplomats got together, they utterly neglected to regard their ukases from the view of the officer at sea who would eventually be bound by them. It was a lucky thing for him that the tanker had made that abortive attempt at flight. And for her to clear for Yokohama and be overtaken at Suvadiva was sheer stupidity. He would have no difficulty vindicating his action in taking her prize, no matter what the outcome.

To sink her now, that was another matter. He would be a fool to hesitate if it became necessary. But what still passed for international law, if anybody was willing to concede that that phrase had any meaning left, took a very serious view of the destruction of a neutral prize. If the Momus had to be sunk, there would be a great hue and cry. The easy way for the diplomats to get out of it would be one of those long dignified notes of apology to the imperial government. He could almost dictate the closing paragraph: "The officer responsible for this unwarranted action has been relieved of his command."

Well, there was no help for it. He had to get on with the war. He would have to accept the responsibilities of his command as he accepted the authority. Naval officers had been faced with that since navies began.

The lookout reported the submarine in sight. Captain Blair could hardly suppress a little sigh of relief. Let the enemy come on. He was as ready for him as he ever would be. His capture of the tanker had actually improved his tactical situation. The enemy would be looking for a fight. It would be easier to predict his maneuvers. The submarine had a better chance of closing to torpedo range. Here would be one of those novel situations where both sides believed they had the preponderance of force. Both antagonists would be eager to join action. If he played his cards right, the submarine would be an ace up his sleeve, to spring as a surprise at the right moment and turn the tide of battle his way.

The Perseus swung to a northerly course again, the Petard following in her wake. The tanker was a good forty miles ahead. Captain Blair would feel better when he had her in sight. Then there would be no chance of a slip-up. At the submarine's best speed they were closing in on the prize a good five miles every hour. The enemy could appear any time he chose. Blair smiled to himself, thinking how confident the Admiral Schroder would be, standing on, secure in the belief that he had only a weak light cruiser to batter to pieces with his heavy guns. He probably felt sure, too, that his appearance would spring a big surprise on his antagonist. Well, there would be more surprises than one in the action that was to follow.

On the Petard, Howe had spent a restless night. It wasn't very comforting to be left behind when action was imminent, even though the reasons were overpowering. He spent a sleepless night, urging his engineer officer to demand still greater effort from his laboring engines. In the engine room the watch was doubled. Every gauge, every instrument, was constantly watched for the first indication of trouble. Ordinarily, he felt a lift of exhilaration from machinery running at full power with the smoothness of perfection, but now he felt only impatience at the inability of the ship to attain greater speed.

At dawn he made the briefest submergence he dared. After the submarine surfaced, he had the torpedoes withdrawn from the tubes one at a time to have their final adjustments rechecked. Somehow he felt that today was the day they would make their run. Feeling a compelling desire to see them himself, he left the bridge for the torpedo room. As the men returned each torpedo to its tube they patted its bright steel afterbody. They, too, felt that they were seeing their charges of many months for the last time.

While he was in the torpedo room the communication officer reported that a strange vessel's signals could be heard coming in through strong interference. He could only guess that it would be the tanker attempting to signal to the Schroder. It didn't do much to relieve his anxiety.

When the Perseus appeared over the horizon he had had to dive until he could be certain of her identity. It wouldn't do to come charging down on the surface on the wrong ship. The Perseus came up over the horizon rapidly. When he could recognize the familiar upper works through the periscope, he surfaced and ran down to meet her, feeling as though he was welcoming an old friend returning from some long journey.

The Perseus wheeled about to a northerly course and slowed down to his speed. Howe adjusted the submarine's course to conform and followed in the cruiser's wake. Blair sent him over a short signal: "Tanker Momus Maru has been made prize. This force will continue at fifteen knots on course three five zero to cover retirement prize on Colombo."

Captain Blair had made a daring division of forces almost in the face of the enemy, accomplished his objective and recombined his forces without mishap.

The two vessels continued onward, certain now that contact would come at any minute. On the light cruiser the men lounged about the decks in apparent enjoyment of the release from ordinary routine. Both airplane engines were kept warmed up by turning them over under power every half hour, but otherwise there was nothing to remind them that anything out of the ordinary was expected.

It was nearly three o'clock before the expected happened. "Sail ho!" the foretop lookout reported.

"Where away?" the officer of the deck inquired.

"Broad on the port quarter, sir! I can't make her out, but there seems to be an airplane flying above her."

It was the Admiral Schroder. No other ship in these waters would be operating with aircraft. For the last time in the Perseus the general alarm sounded and the men hurried to their battle stations.

"Make the signal, 'Enemy sighted, bearing two one five,'" Captain Blair ordered. "All engines full speed ahead."

The Perseus shot ahead almost directly away from the enemy, leaving the Petard rapidly behind. The submarine commenced turning in the direction the signal had indicated. From her low bridge nothing could be seen as yet. She would have to run down much closer before the pocket battleship came within her horizon.

"Catapult the plane!" Captain Blair ordered. It was for this that he was running away, much as it griped his fighting soul. He wanted to get both his planes off before the guns opened up and the blast of gunfire ripped the fabric from their wings. He was depending on the planes to help him lay a smoke screen behind which he could dodge in case of necessity and under whose cover he might be able to approach to decisive range. Both planes had had their bombs removed and replaced by smoke tanks. Peterson, the senior pilot, had strenuously protested that decision, but Blair had a very clear idea in his mind as to how the action might develop. The certain assistance of the smoke was better than the speculation of damage a few light bombs might do to his agile and well-armored antagonist.

The plane took off with a roar. While they were hoisting the second one to the catapult, the Perseus made her turn toward the enemy. Blair would take his chances of getting the second plane off while he was closing the range. Shortly after he made the turn he passed the Petard, on the surface and still making top speed.

"Tell the engine room to commence making smoke," Blair ordered. He would need that smoke later on, and under its cover the Petard would close to attack while still making fifteen knots on the surface. The second plane got off, and also as she did so the gunnery officer reported the first enemy salvo. Twenty-seven thousand yards. The Perseus had a long way to go before she could return the fire. He could hear the six eleven-inch shells rumbling and roaring as they came. Splashes arose close aboard. Close aboard and on both sides of the ship. Straddle! Straddle at twenty-seven thousand yards! He knew then that he was going to have a hard battle. This ship could shoot.

He put the rudder over and changed course to port. It would throw off the enemy's fire control, for they would have a hard time discerning minor changes of course at that range. Sure enough, the second salvo landed three hundred yards to starboard. He turned toward its point of fall. Chasing salvos. He was depending upon the enemy's thoroughness in correcting the fall of shot to save the cruiser from being hit. It was an old dodge, too old to keep an alert enemy guessing very long.

Abruptly he was aware that a new element must enter his calculations. High up in the cloudless sky and well over to port, out of reach of the cruiser's antiaircraft guns, the enemy plane was rapidly gaining spotting position. Now he must pay the penalty for that initial run away. That and his careful preparation had given him two planes in the air to the enemy's one, but it had also given the enemy an opportunity to advance his one plane.

Something must be done about it immediately. The plane would report his maneuvers and her spotting would greatly improve the accuracy of the enemy's shooting at long range. Far worse than that was the danger of discovery of the

Petard. The submarine was coming down under cover of the cruiser's funnel smoke. It couldn't be depended upon absolutely to conceal her.

"Open fire on enemy aircraft, bearing two nine zero," he ordered his gunnery officer. The plane was far out of reach of the antiaircraft battery, he knew, but it would do the men good to hear the sound of their own guns. It was trying to be under fire and not able to return it. The battery opened enthusiastically.

The third salvo fell. A miss to port. The range was closing nearly two thousand yards every minute. If his luck would only hold out for a few minutes longer, Blair thought, he might be able to give them something to think about.

"Order the planes to drive off enemy spotting aircraft," he directed.

That was an order he was reluctant to give. The planes had been maintaining a position in readiness to lay down a screen at his direction. He might need that screen, need it badly.

The white bursts from the antiaircraft guns were all far short of their target.

"Cease firing," Blair ordered. No use wasting ammunition.

The fourth salvo came over while the antiaircraft battery was firing. It was another straddle. The ricocheting shorts burst after impact with the water and sprayed the side of the Perseus with shell fragments. There were holes in the stack and one of the boats was shattered. As he looked aft he could see that there had been a casualty among the crew of the antiaircraft battery.

If Blair's initial maneuver had given the enemy time to advance his plane, it must also have seriously misled him. At twenty-five thouand yards the Admiral Schroder could have made a target practice out of the engagement, for the Perseus could not reach him at that range. The light cruiser had the superior speed, but closing the range would have been a slow process if the enemy had fought a retiring action. No doubt she thought she had the element of surprise on her side. Perhaps she expected the overmatched Perseus to retreat as soon as the first few salvos established her identity. At any rate, she kept boring in and the range was down to twenty-two thousand yards.

Blair saw that his planes had received his orders over their short-wave radio. They were advancing together on the enemy plane. He hadn't seen them drop their smoke tanks. He hoped that they had not. The extra weight would handicap them in their climb to the enemy and in a dogfight later, if it came to that. With two planes to one, they would stand a good chance of bluffing the enemy plane into retiring to the protection of his own antiaircraft guns. He hoped his own pilots would be content with that. He needed only a few minutes. Just a few minutes, and how badly he would want that smoke screen when he wanted it.

In the next few minutes Blair was too busy to follow what was happening in the air. But Peterson, the senior pilot, had a good idea of what was expected of him. He held on to his smoke tanks and advanced as though he intended to fight it out right there, but it was with relief that he saw the enemy bank and turn and wing its way back toward the Schroder. He followed, not pushing the chase too hard, and when the first puffs of antiaircraft fire appeared, he retired. He could wait. The enemy plane would come back. After he had finished his smoke mission, Peterson could afford to risk his plane.

In the fire-control tower directly above the bridge, Fields was beside himself with anxiety lest an unlucky hit should wipe out half of his battery before he could return the fire. Twenty-one thousand yards. They had been under fire for nearly four minutes. He had to clench his teeth to keep from shouting the order to commence firing.

"We will open fire to port," the talker on the captain's circuit informed him.

Until then, except for the zigzags to dodge the enemy's shells, they had been heading almost directly at the enemy.

The after turrets, unable to bear on the target, were still trained amidships.

"Turrets Three and Four," Fields ordered, "train out to port and follow the pointer in train and elevation."

He could see the bow swing away from the enemy until they were on such a course that his after turrets would bear.

"Commence firing," came the order.

"Commence firing," Fields repeated over the fire-control telephone.

The response was instantaneous. A hundred and fifty men in those turrets had been tensely awaiting that order. Almost before the words were spoken the first salvo was off. The whole ship trembled to the shock of eight six-inch shells simultaneously leaving the guns. Almost before the concussion had ceased, the second salvo left the ship. And then the third not far behind it.

"Check fire."

The plotting room long ago had had instructions for those opening salvos. Far down below in the interior of the ship, men had been busy over instruments and plotting board, working out the rate of change of range and deflection, assembling the data from various observers and instruments and sending it out to the guns. Those first three salvos were sent out spaced to fall five hundred yards apart in range. Then they would wait until the shells fell and correct the range by spotting

While they waited the Schroder scored her first hit. Fields distinctly heard the hit and felt the shock of impact.

"Hit in the forecastle abreast the anchor engine," he heard the damage control lookout report.

His own salvos were falling. Short! Short again! Straddle!

"Up five double oh," the spotter called.

"Resume fire."

All eight turret guns responded in unison. Fields could feel the air leaving his lungs with explosive force. He had been holding his breath, waiting to give that order.

Eight seconds. Another full salvo, all off together, as though the Perseus was firing at an inanimate target. Fields felt better. He hadn't been able to bear the thought of all that training, all that preparation, being wiped out on any part of his battery by one lucky enemy shell before he had had a chance to return the fire.

There would be five or six salvos in the air before the first one fell. He felt a glow of pride replace his nervousness as his battery continued to pump out shells at a prodigious rate.

Smoke appeared at the forward hatch. The repair party advanced in the lee of the turrets to fight the fire the hit had caused. The Perseus would be lucky if a forward hit didn't clip a knot or two off her speed.

"Down two double oh, left one," Fields heard the spotter call out. They were on the target. The spotter, in his passion for perfection, was making minor corrections to get the mean point of impact at the center of the target.

Below on the bridge Blair was intently watching the fall of shot. It was too far away to judge their effect but the sea around the Schroder was alive with splashes. They must be getting hits. Between fifty and sixty shells were falling around his antagonist every minute. At that range the six-inch shells could not penetrate her armor but they could disrupt her fire control and cut her superstructure to pieces.

The Schroder's fire control hadn't suffered yet. With the decreasing range, her rate of fire had increased. She was getting off two salvos nearly every minute. The Perseus seemed to have a charmed life. Great geysers of water rose out of the sea on either hand. Tons of water from the splashes were falling on deck. Shells that hit the water burst after impact and their splinters were the worst that the Perseus had to contend with. Shell fragments penetrated the thin sides of her superstructure. At the antiaircraft guns the inactive men were being bowled over like tenpins. Blair noted with approval that the battery officer was ordering the men to lie down on deck. Almost at his elbow a signal quartermaster was hit by a fragment. That there was worse to come, he knew.

Glancing aft, Blair could see the thick black pall of the funnel smoke lying close to the water. For the first time in months he was thankful that there was no breeze. The smoke would lie. Back on the quarter-deck, men were throwing over what must be the last of the smoke floats. Their white fumes streaked the black pall of funnel smoke.

It seemed as though they had been under fire for hours. Six minutes had passed since the Schroder's first salvo. There was the shock of a direct hit, followed by the burst of the shell. It must have been on Turret One. It was silent now. The guns still trained out toward the target, but they were mute and motionless.

At eighteen thousand yards, Captain Blair couldn't see that he had made much impression on the enemy. She still fired regularly. He had only six guns now with which to reply, but those six guns were still firing with clocklike regularity.

Then the Perseus took another hit. The bridge itself tottered benoath the captain's feet. The mast wavered and for a brief instant he thought it was going to fall. There was a volcanic roar—almost under the bridge, it seemed. The air was filled with white-hot steam. The bridge personnel threw themselves on the deck to escape it.

Lying flat on the deck the captain yelled to Conn, "Right full rudder."

As soon as he could breathe he got to his feet. He could feel the ship slowing down. The Perseus would have to get into the smoke screen, or the end would come in a few minutes. The forward boiler room had taken a direct hit. It would be some time before he knew the full extent of the damage, but he couldn't doubt that it was extreme. He eased the rudder and the light cruiser limped toward the smoke screen and temporary security.

The after turrets got off a couple of salvos, ragged and uncertain, as they tried to keep on the target with the Perseus swinging under full rudder. They were entering the screen when she took another eleven-inch shell, in the vicinity of the torpedo tubes. It burst just under the deck.

Just before the Perseus reached the cloud of black smoke, Captain Blair saw his two planes race across the range, close in toward the cruiser. The smoke trailed out behind them. At a crucial moment his planes hadn't failed. He hadn't seen them return from the chase. There had been no orders. Peterson's practiced eye had instantly recognized the emergency. From out of the sky the lacy white curtain dropped toward the sea. They were mercifully hidden from their enemy. All firing ceased.

Captain Blair took the telephone away from his talker to speak directly with the damage control officer in central station.

"What is the extent of our damage?" he asked.

"Turret One is out of commission," the damage control officer replied. "She took a direct hit on the face plate. Everybody in the turret chamber was killed and the turret jammed in train. The handling rooms were not damaged. We have a few tons of water aboard up forward from the first hit and a little port list. I'm taking it off by shifting fuel oil. I haven't had complete reports from the last two hits, but the forward boiler room seems out of commission." He seemed relieved that the damage was no more extensive. He had drilled at casualties worse than this.

The engineer officer's voice came over the telephone. He had evidently been waiting to report.

"We took a hit in the forward boiler room," he reported. "Both boilers there are damaged beyond repair and everybody in the boiler room was killed either by the shell or the steam. The after boiler room is all right, but the man on the port bulkhead stop valve was killed before he could get it fully closed. We have steam right now on only one boiler but in ten minutes I'll have steam up in the other one and we can still make twenty knots."

It could be worse, Captain Blair reflected as he asked the

gunnery officer to report. Twenty knots was only six less than the Schroder could make when she was built. The engineer officer was conservative. He would probably make her do considerably more than twenty when the time came.

"I've still got six good guns," the gunnery officer reported. "I've just ordered the handling room crew of Turret One to transfer ammunition to the other turrets."

Blair remembered that Fields had always feared getting into a long-range engagement and shooting himself out of ammunition. At the rate at which he had been laying down his salvos, it wouldn't take the Perseus very long to empty her magazines. He reflected wryly that it was only a day or two ago that he had rebuked Fields for letting the loading time of the turrets fall off.

"Nice shooting this afternoon, Fields," he interjected. "You might need Turret One's ammunition yet at the rate you have been getting them off."

Fields was almost speechless at the captain's rare words of praise. "Both port antiaircraft guns were dismounted by that last hit," he continued, "but the starboard ones are still intact. The port torpedo tubes were destroyed. The gunnery department is ready to continue the action," he concluded.

He had hardly finished before he was aware that the Schroder was ready and willing to continue also. He heard the dull boom of the Schroder's guns. The salvo landed over and a little way to port. The smoke seemed as thick as ever, but suddenly there was a little rift. He caught a glimpse of the enemy's plane. Their topmasts must occasionally show to the plane and she was directing the fire.

"Captain!" Fields reported. "The enemy's plane is spotting through the smoke screen."

"Very well," the captain replied. That enemy plane was persistent. It must have returned to its station immediately after having been driven off.

"Order the planes to attack the enemy aircraft," he directed the radio room.

High aloft, the Perseus' two planes got the word over the radiotelephone immediately. Both of them were out of the smoke. Peterson commenced flying in a wide circle, waiting for his wing man to join up in the echelon formation they had agreed upon for the attack. They had spent a great deal of time during the long months the Perseus was at sea, talking over just what they would do to meet certain situations.

The second plane was alert. She was in position before Peterson had completed the first circle. Peterson dropped his smoke tank. It went tumbling end over end into the sea. No need being loaded down with useless impedimenta. Their smoke mission was ended. He had pleaded for an attack mission. Now he had got it. It was up to him to make good. There was a sinking feeling in the pit of his stomach nonetheless.

They were speeding toward the enemy plane now and gaining altitude rapidly to get above their antagonist. He was far out beyond the edge of the screen, wheeling and circling, intent on his efforts to get a glimpse of the Perseus. So intent he was that at first he didn't notice their approach.

Suddenly the enemy pilot became aware of his danger. He nosed his plane down, turned sharply to the left and streaked into the smoke screen. It was an unexpected maneuver and the Perseus' planes were still too far away to interfere. The smoke that hid the Perseus served equally well to conceal her enemy.

But Peterson, from his previous contact with him, thought he could predict what his antagonist was going to do. He would retreat again to the protection of the Schroder's anti-aircraft guns. Peterson refused to be drawn into the murk of the smoke where anything might happen. He wheeled his formation and stood out beyond the edge of the screen.

Sure enough, the enemy plane came out of the smoke like a hare breaking cover, flying very close to the water to prevent an attack from below. Peterson let go a few bursts from his machine gun to warm it up. It wouldn't be long now. He raised his arm in signal. He could see that his wing man had already eased out of formation and was flying abreast of him, ready for the next phase of the attack.

"Here we go," he shouted.

He nosed his plane down. Both planes came down at a sharp angle, one on either side of the tail of the retreating enemy. With the speed of their descent they were overtaking him rapidly. Peterson was aware of the observer in the after cockpit of the enemy plane pointing a gun in his general direction. With an attacking plane on either side, he couldn't keep both of them under fire. One of them should surely get him.

At about a hundred and fifty yards he opened up. He could see the smoke of his tracers in the air. The stream of bullets hit the water at first, then the stabilizer, and creeping up, sewed a seam of machine gun bullets along the fuselage.

It was over in an instant. At this altitude there was no spectacular flaming wreck. The enemy plane nosed over sharply and immediately met the water in one mighty splash. She was gone. And not a moment too soon. Above him, Peterson could see the white shrapnel burst of the antiaircraft guns from the Schroder as he wheeled to retire.

For the Perseus, the immediate menace was removed, but her security was temporary and very precarious. It would only be a matter of a little while before the smoke would commence to drift and dissipate. She was stopped in the densest part of the screen, the preparations to make her ready going ahead with feverish haste.

The planes had no sooner been ordered to attack than the Petard came steaming through the fog of smoke. She was close aboard. On the bridge of the Perseus they could hear the clatter of her engines. From the few scattered men on the deck of the cruiser a ragged cheer arose. There was a lone officer on the bridge of the submarine. He waved his cap in reply, then turned and climbed down the hatch. Captain Blair could distinctly hear the woof and hiss of the Petard's vents as her tanks flooded. Under the water and into the smoke the Petard disappeared. All their hopes of eventual victory were with her now.

Howe had been the officer to wave his cap at the cheering men on the decks of the battered cruiser. He had been poised for instant submergence since the Perseus had signaled that the enemy had been sighted. Below all hands were at their battle stations and he alone with his quartermaster kept the bridge. It was of the utmost importance that he keep his fifteen knots surface speed as long as possible, and he was grateful for the smoke that enabled him to do so. When the Perseus loomed up through the murk, he ordered the quartermaster below. It was time to dive. He didn't dare hold on any longer.

A glance had told him of the beating the cruiser had taken. The forward turret was trained out away from the others. The midships was a shambles, and, worst of all, she was stopped. He felt the gripping necessity of haste—haste and a sure approach, or the Perseus wouldn't survive much longer.

As Howe slid down the hatch, he sounded the diving alarm. "Take her down. Fifty feet," he ordered.

In the hushed silence he watched his diving officer take her down and level her off at fifty feet. In the close confines of the control room, with the watertight doors closed between them and the rest of the ship, surrounded by men who had shared his every waking moment for months, Howe felt a glow of confidence. They were ready—ready for anything that might happen—and these men, he knew, would follow him without question wherever he might lead.

"Two knots. Up periscope." Still in the smoke screen. Howe could see nothing. "Down periscope. Eight knots."

He waited for what seemed an eternity. They must be out of the smoke now. "Two knots." The periscope slid silently upward. They were clear.

Howe could see the top and the bridge of the Schroder. "Ten thousand yards. Bearing three five zero, angle on the bow fifteen port. Down periscope. Eight knots."

"You are twenty-six hundred yards from the track, captain," Jordan, the fire-control assistant, announced. "If she is making top speed, you have just eleven minutes to get in with a straight bow shot and a ninety track."

"Come left to course one two zero," Howe ordered.

"I'll run on this course for two minutes," he told Jordan. "Then I'll swing down to meet her." He saw Jordan snap his stop watch.

"I'm going to fire angle shots with the bow tubes," Howe informed his assistant. "Parallel and opposite courses. We will reserve the stern tubes for the unexpected."

Howe was going to lose no time dallying. Eleven minutes would seem like eleven years to the Perseus, and anything might happen in that time. He was going to cut all the time he could off the approach. The Schroder apparently thought she had everything her own way. She was steaming on, oblivious of everything except the necessity of finishing off a badly damaged light cruiser. Any moment the smoke screen might lift enough to bring the Perseus under murderous fire.

"Two minutes, captain."

It was like a drill. Howe was aware of nerves tense to the breaking point. The indivisible responsibility for the effectiveness of his ship, for the success of the whole action, for the final outcome of events of momentous importance pressed down upon his mind. Those about him seemed oblivious of any excitement.

"Two knots. Up periscope. Range sixty-five hundred, angle on the bow ten port, bearing seven nine. Down periscope."

"Come right to course two one two, eight knots," he ordered. "All tubes ready for firing. Bow tubes ninety degrees left angle. Give him twenty-five knots."

He could be oblivious of excitement, too, if so much didn't depend upon his success. It was a setup. The target was coming down on a straight course at a steady speed with no screen. She probably didn't suspect a submarine within thousands of miles. It only remained to get off his torpedoes before being sighted. That was going to be the hard part. The sea was smooth and oily. Sharp eyes would detect the least ruffle on its surface.

"Looks like you've got her, captain," Jordan said calmly. "You will be just a thousand yards from her track when you complete the turn. Four minutes to go."

Four minutes. The ship slowly turned around the compass. She had yet to complete the turn. God, how slow she swung. He would depend upon the listener to track her and keep him informed of her progress. No more periscope exposures until they were ready to fire. If she changed course in the meantime, there would have to be some lightning calculations when he looked again.

"All tubes ready for firing, sir," announced the chief torpedo man. Howe glanced at the array of ready lights. Forward and aft in the torpedo rooms the torpedo men would be standing by the tubes, their eyes on the gauges, waiting for the telltale thud of the torpedo leaving the tube. The Petard was at last steady on the firing course.

"Bearing three four zero," the listener reported. "Bearing three three five."

It was the waiting that was hardest, waiting and not knowing what was going on on the surface. Suppose the Schroder had suddenly decided to change course away from him. At the speed she was making, he would have lost all chances of getting in by the time he looked.

The hand of the stop watch crawled around the dial with slow deliberation. Two minutes to go.

"Bearing three two five, sir. She is coming down rapidly." One minute to go.

"Two knots." He waited as long as he dared for the speed to fall off the ship. There could be no feather on a day like this. "Up periscope." Crouching low to the eyepiece, he followed the periscope as it rose, stopping it as soon as he could see. *There she is. She seems close. They must be inside a thousand yards.*

Howe set his periscope to the firing bearing. The Schroder still had a little way to go to the cross wires. "Stand by!"

He saw the flash of a gun. The Schroder commenced a turn toward him. He had been sighted. A gleam of the sun on a glass, a tiny feather in that smooth sea—it made no difference what it was. The damage had been done.

"Fire One." He would fire a wide spread as rapidly as he could.

"Fire Two. Right five degrees rudder." The Schroder was turning rapidly. He couldn't hope for four hits now.

"Fire Three."

She could avoid some of them, but at least one of that wide spread would get her.

"Fire Four. . . . Right fifteen degrees rudder. Eight knots. Stand by the after tubes."

They felt the dull jar of a mighty explosion. The Schroder had been hit. Howe saw a huge column of water arise well aft.

It was mere guesswork now. The Schroder herself wouldn't know what she was doing, hit like that while swinging to full rudder.

"Give her fifteen knots. Make her course two seven zero," Howe called out.

"What's the setup on a straight stern shot? Ease the rudder, steady as you go."

Things weren't quite so calm about him now. The diving officer was having trouble keeping the depth after the rapid discharge of torpedoes forward had spoiled his trim. The fire-control assistant was peering over his table of instruments to complete the data the captain demanded. The quartermaster was steadying on the new course.

Three or four guns were blazing away merrily at him. The splashes arose all around the periscope. At eight knots his periscope would be displaying a big white plume. To hell with the gun fire. He could only lose one of his periscopes. No ship was going to get away from him with only one hit after an approach like that.

"Periscope angle one nine eight, sir," the fire-control assistant answered.

Here she comes. The fire-control data wasn't likely to be within miles of being right, but the Schroder had closed the range by her maneuvers. He wouldn't miss with both.

"Fire Five." She was still firing. Those raindrops must be machine-gun bullets. "Fire Six."

He saw one of the torpedoes rise straight up out of the sea, stand for an instant on its tail, and then drop back. Defective torpedo. Everything happened all at once.

The jar of an explosion shook the boat. *That's two, anyway,* Howe thought. He didn't see it. Suddenly the periscope went black. Some one of the many missiles that had been falling around it had hit the periscope. He swung the emergency eyepiece cover in place.

"Down periscope, eight knots. All tubes reload." Two hits were not enough. She would have a lot of fight left in her. Give her time and they would be able to take the list off her. Damage to her screws and her rudder might be serious. She would be slowed down a lot and there would be something on her mind now besides the destruction of the Perseus. But the battle wasn't over.

"Come right to course zero one zero."

If she had been slowed down sufficiently there would be an opportunity to get in another attack. The Petard was in a bad position to attack again. It would take minutes to rectify it and reload the tubes. Before those minutes were over, the situation had changed again. Captain Blair was now ready to take charge again, and what he did must have been as great a surprise to the Admiral Schroder as it was to Howe.

While the Petard was making her approach, the Perseus was lying to, but her crew had not been idle. The wounded were carried below and the surgeon and his assistant made them as comfortable as possible. The dead, too, had to be taken out of sight. It made an appalling total. The turret magazines were replenished from the unexpended ammunition in Turret One. The damage control officer worked the list off the ship.

Their more serious damage would require a dockyard for repairs. Steam was being raised in the after boiler room. The repair party cleared away some of the loose wreckage on deck. Crews for the undamaged antiaircraft guns were reorganized from the men of that battery who remained alive and un- wounded. The minutes passed.

The engineer reported, "We are ready to make twenty knots, captain."

"Sound the general alarm," the captain ordered. "Tell the gunnery officer to stand by. We are going in again."

The navigator glanced at him in astonishment. Like nearly everyone else in the Perseus, he had expected the cruiser to retire as soon as she could make reasonably good speed. Re- tire and thank their lucky stars if they didn't have to fight again. In all the months they had served with him they had failed to gauge the temper of their captain.

"All engines full speed ahead."

The Perseus commenced moving through the smoke. Cap- tain Blair conned her around until she was again headed for the enemy. The Schroder, too, was in for another surprise. The Perseus was a battered ship, but she was far from beaten yet.

In the fire-control tower, Fields stood tense and ready. His guns were still loaded and primed. They might make contact now at short range when the Perseus cleared the smoke screen. The first few salvos might decide the battle. He would have to get in the first blow. He strained his eyes to penetrate the smoke that was flying past him.

Suddenly they shot out of the screen and an unexpected sight met his eyes. He had expected to engage almost bow to bow again, but the Schroder had been trying to cut around the flank of the smoke screen when the Petard got her. She was far over on the port bow. No longer did she look like a ship with victory in her grasp.

The captain put the rudder hard over and the Perseus changed course sharply to port, leaving the enemy on the starboard bow at as sharp an angle as he could and still get the after turrets to bear. In the seconds it took the ship to swing and for the turrets to train on their target, Blair had an opportunity to size up the situation.

The Admiral Schroder was headed to the westward, putting the Perseus on her starboard bow. Her speed was not more than ten knots and it is probable that she was having difficulty making that, for she was listed to port and well down by the stern. That list was to prove very important to the Perseus.

The Petard, he then realized, had completed a successful attack. The Admiral Schroder was a badly damaged ship, but that she was still a fighting ship he was shortly to find out. High overhead the Perseus' planes circled above her. The enemy plane was gone.

"Commence firing," Fields ordered. It was his turn to get in the first salvo, and at that range his guns would hardly miss. The sea around the target was a forest of splashes. He could see the hot red glow of hits on her armor. The air above her was filled with the smoke and debris of shells bursting in the superstructure.

She was vainly trying to make smoke, throwing smoke floats over the side with abandon. She wouldn't have time to make an effective screen. At this range the battle would be over in a few minutes.

"Four thousand yards," Fields heard the range-finder operator intone. Four thousand yards and his six-inch shells could penetrate the Schroder's armor. He heard the staccato bark of the antiaircraft guns, jubilant now that they had a target within range.

The forward turret of the pocket battleship returned the fire of the cruiser. Shortly afterwards the after turret got off a salvo. Those on the Perseus could plainly see the movement of the guns. Her turrets were firing independently. Pointer fire. The shells they had rained on her in the early phase of the action had had their effect. Her fire-control system was disrupted. Her turrets were firing under local control. One of her five-point-nines opened up. The others must have been out of action.

The Schroder's eleven-inch shells rumbled far overhead and struck the sea a full two thousand yards beyond the cruiser. Then Captain Blair realized how fortunate he had been in making his second contact. With the Schroder's list, at this close range, she couldn't depress her turret guns sufficiently to hit the Perseus. For a full two minutes the cruiser was under the effective fire of only one five-point-nine. In those two minutes the Perseus was pumping out salvos, eight every minute, forty-eight shells a minute, and many of them were hits.

For the first few rounds that one five-point-nine was wild. Then the Perseus took a hit aft. It must have been the next shot that went through the barbette of Turret Three. Turret Three was silent. The battle belonged to Turrets Two and Four, but they were still firing on director and making very good practice.

The enemy was slowly turning toward the oncoming Perseus. She was trying to get around to such a bearing that her list wouldn't make her fire over. But she was maneuvering clumsily. There must have been something wrong with her rudder or her steering control. Her after turret was silent. If the Perseus was suffering casualties, the enemy was also taking a beating and her armor was no longer sure protection.

The forward turret fired. One shell clipped through the top of the cruiser's smokestack. The Schroder's bows were pointed straight at the cruiser. She could depress her guns to get on her target now.

The two remaining turrets of the Perseus were steadily pouring out shells. The range was down to three thousand yards—point-blank range for both contestants. From the tops, machine guns opened up with a wild clatter. From high out of the blue the planes came down, one after the other, in a wild dive, their engines moaning and racing. Over the decks of the Schroder they swooped, spraying her exposed personnel with machine-gun bullets. The five-point-nine was silent after their dive.

An eleven-inch shell made a direct hit on the Perseus, almost underneath the catapult. With its tremendous energy, it went right through the ship and out the port side, bursting more than a hundred yards away and showering the disengaged side with shell fragments.

Turret Four got off a late salvo. It was wild and high and to the left.

"Turret Four! Get on the target," Fields shouted into the transmitter.

"Turret Four, aye, aye!" came back the answer promptly, but faintly and far away. Fields was yet to realize that he was very deaf from the blasts of the guns.

He had his eyes on Turret Four for the next salvo. He was looking right at it when it happened. There was a blinding flash on the face of the turret. Almost instantly a great sheet of flame leaped skyward. He held his breath and waited for the explosion that would send them all to the bottom. It didn't come. But Turret Four would answer no longer. Even as he chided them, all of the men in that turret chamber had been incinerated, roasted alive by powder charges that the hit had set afire. Fields could remember his prayerful thanksgiving that somehow the fire had been prevented from reaching the magazine.

It was the last distinct remembrance he had for some time. He was only dimly aware of the next terrific explosion, and then he was down on the deck of the fire-control tower. There were jagged splinter holes in the wind screen as he tried to shake the fog from his mind. His spotter lay beside him. The director operator was slumped over his smashed instrument. The others were uninjured, but they seemed to have no comprehension of what had happened.

Fields pulled himself painfully erect. His legs seemed to wilt under him. "Turret Two! Local control!" he yelled into the transmitter. No answer. He snatched another telephone from a dazed talker. "Main fire control out of action! Turret Two shift to local control!" No answer.

Not until then did he realize that Turret Two was firing. Firing steadily and rapidly under local control. He glanced at the enemy. Turret Two was getting hits. His leg refused to hold him up any longer. It crumpled under him and he sat down again on the deck. He looked at it in amazement and saw that it was mangled horribly.

Down on the bridge, Captain Blair had seen his main battery wiped out turret by turret, until only one was firing. Still he kept boring in. Well he knew that it's your own casualties you know most about. You never hear about the enemy's until after it's too late.

He glanced aft just in time to see a torpedo salvo leave the tubes. All through the ship, men cut off from one another by shell fire and casualties, their normal means of communication gone, were taking independent action to fight the ship to the last bitter end. That was where training told. It wasn't until afterwards that he learned that the torpedo officer, finding that he could no longer communicate with anyone, had left his instruments and charts and made his way to the tubes. There was only one unwounded man in the torpedo crew but with his assistance he had trained out the tubes, estimated the firing angle and himself had fired the salvo. Under the circumstances, it wasn't surprising that the torpedoes had missed but it was that kind of spirit that won the battle.

When the ricocheting short burst high in the air right over the ship, it had decimated the bridge crew. Miraculously, Captain Blair escaped. There was a slight pause in the firing from Turret Two. When it was resumed, Blair knew from the motion of her guns that she was firing pointer fire. Main fire control out of action.

He watched the Schroder. He saw two shells together strike her only remaining effective turret. The next salvo seemed to land in the same place. There was a blinding flash. A mighty roar came over the short stretch of water. Before his eyes the pocket battleship disintegrated. A great pillar of smoke and fire arose three hundred feet in the air. There were huge pieces of wreckage turning over and over in it.

Then he could see the stern of the ship standing straight up in the air, the propellers still turning over slowly. She was gone.

There had been no cheers. It was too awesome a sight for cheers. She had been a gallant ship and she had been well fought. She was gone with all of her crew of valiant men. After the turmoil of the action, the silence was oppressive.

"Torpedoes!" someone shouted from the wrecked bridge wing. "Torpedoes on the starboard bow!"

The captain stood impassive. He made no move to save his ship. No cry could rouse him. He was stone deaf. Both his eardrums had been ruptured by the gun-fire. Too late his own eyes saw the menacing white torpedo track.

"Right full rudder!" he shouted; even as she commenced her turn the Perseus was hit. Suddenly the whole forecastle seemed to heave bodily upward. A great column of water geysered high into the air. The ship lurched sickeningly under the mighty shock.

After all the punishment she had taken, the gallant Perseus was to receive her death blow after the action was over. For the first time that day Captain Blair felt sick at heart. It was the irony of fate that in the Schroder, at the very instant of her destruction, someone now dead had released the torpedo which was to avenge her.

"Secure from general quarters," Captain Blair ordered. "Get the men out of the turrets and handling rooms." It was just thirty-four minutes since the Schroder had fired her first salvo.

Blair was still not ready to give up his ship. Men rushed

forward with shores and planking to bolster up the collision bulkhead that kept the Perseus afloat. All that men could do to save her they did. The forecastle kept sinking lower in the water.

The first lieutenant came on the bridge to report in person. It was necessary to communicate with the captain by pad and pencil.

"The bulkhead was weakened by the first shell hit. There are a number of holes in it from splinters. The water is gaining on us. We have not more than three hours." It was a losing battle against the sea.

The Petard came through the pall of smoke still hanging over the sea where the Admiral Schroder went down. There was very little wreckage left afloat to mark the spot.

Howe found only two dazed survivors of that terrible explosion to rescue from the water. Then he maneuvered the submarine solicitously near the stricken cruiser, acutely aware that he was unable to offer her any assistance. When the end came, the Petard would be too small to take aboard all the survivors.

In the circumstances, it was a heartening sight to the weary men on the cruiser to see the ugly bow of the Momus Maru come poking around the edge of the thinning smoke screen. Johnson had had his orders to go to Colombo. When he heard the gunfire he had chosen to disobey them. A tanker wouldn't be much good in a naval action he knew, but there might be some service to perform. All his instincts were to close on the point of contact. Colombo could wait. It was a fortunate decision.

As the sun sank lower in the west there was nothing to do but abandon the sinking ship. She was doomed. To delay until after dark would only mean unnecessary loss of life; lives that, Captain Blair now realized, were bound more closely to him by the experiences of that hard-fought action.

"Send a signal to the Momus to send boats," he directed. "All hands stand by to abandon ship."

Fields was among the first to go, among the other wounded. When he arrived aboard the Momus they took him directly below. He made no protest. He had no wish to watch the Perseus make that final plunge to the bottom of the sea, freighted with the bodies of so many of his shipmates. It was most fitting, he knew, that they should man her through the long, peaceful years to eternity. But they had been close to him and he loved the ship too well to watch her go.

When Captain Blair sent his signal to send boats, Howe broke out his little wherry and stood by close aboard the sinking ship. Most of the survivors, he knew, would be transferred to the Momus, where there would be facilities for their care, but he wanted to be prepared for any emergency.

The last of the boats shoved off. The Perseus was sinking very rapidly, going down by the head. The forecastle was nearly awash. Quite unexpectedly a figure appeared on her bridge. It was Captain Blair. Howe shouted for his boat to go alongside the cruiser and take him off.

Very deliberately Captain Blair walked down the ladder from his bridge for the last time. Somewhere, somehow, sometime he had found the opportunity to dress for the occasion. He was meticulously attired in the full dress uniform of a captain, the gold lace of his epaulets gleaming in the setting sun, his cocked hat set at a jaunty angle, his sword dangling from his side.

As though there was nothing more urgent on his mind than a formal call on some visiting admiral, he made his way to a point abreast the waiting boat, buttoning his white gloves as he came. His last salute to the side was unceremonious. It was only a short drop into the boat now. Somehow the captain managed the scramble into the tossing little boat without the slightest loss of dignity.

Howe, watching the little tableau, decided he must rise to the occasion. "Four side boys," he ordered, as he scrambled off the bridge.

There was a moment of confusion. Side boys hadn't been

seen on board that submarine since King Neptune had been welcomed aboard in ancient farcical ceremony. But out of the group of men collected topside four side boys were pushed forward and took their traditional places at the sea ladder as the boat approached. They lacked only the boatswain's pipe.

Never had a captain been welcomed by a more motley group of side boys. A seaman had borrowed a hat two sizes too big for him and it dropped about his ears. A Stillson wrench protruded from the hip pocket of an engineer. In a sweaty undershirt and greasy trousers, Howe waited at the head of the lane they formed to greet the red-headed old fighter.

Never had more heartfelt honors been rendered to a captain. As Howe watched the shivers precede one another up the naked spine of a torpedo man, he realized that his men were just as proud as he was that Captain Blair was one of them in a service to which they had all devoted their lives.

"With your permission, sir," said Captain Blair as he stepped over the side of the Petard, saluting the colors.

A thousand times afterward Howe thought of something fitting to reply. Now he could only mutter, "Aye, aye, sir," inanely.

Together, the two commanding officers climbed to the bridge. Together they watched the end of a gallant ship. She had been abandoned none too soon. In the fading twilight she suddenly lurched forward, standing almost straight up on her bows. With a muffled roar the boilers broke loose from their foundations and crashed through the forward bulkhead. She went down with a rush. For a brief instant her colors alone were visible, fluttering from the staff. She was gone.

Captain Blair stood at rigid salute to his colors. In the gathering darkness Howe was sure that he was the only one to observe that there was moisture in the old man's eyes as he watched her go. Howe brushed the salt spray from his own eyes. Strange where it came from on such a calm evening.

BATTLE STATIONS!

WE HAD had a hard week. With stadimeter and pelorus, the fleet submarine Otter picked her way through the ordered array of the fleet, looking for the exact hole into which she must drop her anchor.

"On the bearing, captain," the navigator said, looking up from the pelorus.

"All back," the skipper responded.

There was a swirl of white water as the screws bit in astern.

"Let go the starboard anchor!" The cable rattled out around the wildcat as the anchor dropped into its appointed place on the ocean bottom ten fathoms below.

The skipper, Lieutenant Commander Hunt, swung his leg over the bridge rail and turned to the waiting quartermaster on the bridge.

"Secure the bridge and main motors. Tell the electrician he can shut down the gyro."

Wearily, he climbed down to the deck below. Lieut. Joe Swift, the navigator, tenderly stowed the stadimeter in its little wooden box and followed. It was a relief just to get off the bridge.

The deck force heaved the heavy awning up from below and commenced spreading it over the forward deck space. The captain sought the sheltered side of the conning tower and squatted on his heels in the scant shade it afforded, tilting his cap over his eyes against the glare of the bright sun on the blue water. In a single movement he whipped off his black necktie and opened his shirt at the throat. The navigator joined him in silence. The charging engines coughed and sputtered, and then settled down to the long, wearisome task of charging the batteries.

After the main motors had been secured, I saw the charge

135

well started and gave my charging orders to the electrician's mate on watch. Wearily I checked again the figures on the Monthly Summary of Performances and scrawled "Hamilton Wade" in the space marked "Engineering Officer." Fussing over a mass of paper work was too much to ask after that week's operation. I had to get topside.

The sun still shone and there was still some air in the world untainted by the smell of fuel oil. It had been three days since I had seen the sun. We had been diving at sunrise and staying down until dark, guarding the channel against the entrance of these very ships with which we now consorted. My ears were tired from the clatter of machinery, and the sight of even the bare brown hills of the Seven Islands was a relief from the gauges and meters that had been too long before my eyes. Every year, it seemed, the fleet maneuvers were tougher than the year before.

The awning had been spread before I got topside. The mess boy had hustled some folding chairs up from the wardroom and the captain was leaning back in one of these in sheer enjoyment of inactivity. The crew was straggling up to get the air. While the charge was going on, it would be too hot below for relaxation. In a few minutes, below-decks would be left to the engine crew and the electricians of the charging watch. The chief torpedo man, Simpson, asked the captain's permission to use the motor launch for a fishing trip, and then mustered a crew to break out the boat and get it into the water. The submarine was settling down to a normal week end in port with the fleet. There was no incentive to go ashore. A hot bath on the tender, a little relaxation, and Monday morning we would be at it again.

I squatted on the deck alongside the skipper.

"How about fresh water, captain?" I asked. "If we can go alongside the tender before we sail for home next week, I can open up the shower bath and I'll secure the evaporators on the charging engines."

"Don't depend on it, Hamilton," he replied. "If a breeze

springs up from the south, we couldn't lie alongside the tender in this anchorage. I know the evaps make the engine room hot, but there is no help for it. I'll send a boat over to the tender later, so the crew can go over for baths. I think I will go over myself to see the movies after dinner, if I can muster courage to shift into white uniform."

"Do you think we'll really sail for home next week, captain?" the navigator asked. "After all, Old Whiskers has kept us here two weeks after our scheduled departure."

"Can't tell, Joe," the captain answered. "The international situation still looks touchy, judging by the radio press. Wish I could see a real newspaper. . . . What do you think, John?" he asked my assistant engineer, as he ambled back from the forward hatch. "Is your father going to take us back home next week?"

"I wouldn't know, captain," Barston replied. "I am, unfortunately, not one of my old man's confidants. If I had any influence, we would be bounding over the deep blue sea for home right now."

"Looks bad to me," spoke up Jackson, the young communications officer. "We passed Destroyer Division Ten going out as we came in this morning. If the Commander in Chief is putting out security patrols, he is still afraid that something might break. My bet is that we stay right here until the whole thing blows over. After all, that invasion is a direct violation of all the peace treaties, and if the powers-that-be decide to do something about it, the old boy would want the fleet concentrated in just about this spot."

"You don't know my old man," Barston said. "He has always held that the first sign of trouble from that direction would be a determined submarine attack on the fleet. In this exposed anchorage he would have security patrols out at the first whisper or even just for a week end's exercise."

"What do you think about it, captain?" I asked. "Do you think there is any real danger of war coming out of this mess?"

"No, I don't, Hamilton," he replied. "After all, this fighting is thousands of miles from our coast line. I don't blame the admiral for keeping his finger on his number. He can't afford to take any chances, but I think it will blow over in a week or so."

"I hope you're right, skipper," Barston said. "I think I'll go over to the flagship and bum a meal off my father and see if I can pick up any dope. We can't sail for home too soon for me."

"Oh, that baby of yours will keep, John," Jackson kidded. "You know the old saying about a naval officer being necessary at the laying of the keel, but quite useless at the launching of a new Navy Junior."

"Yes, I know that one," Barston retorted, "and when I was a bachelor I thought it quite funny too. Anyway, this one has been launched two whole weeks now, and I think it's about time he stood a skipper's inspection."

The petty officer of the watch approached and reported, "Motorboat from the tender standing this way, captain."

Across the bright blue water the motorboat bore down upon us, her spotless gray hull and gleaming brass reflecting the glare of the sun, piling up the water ahead of her in a rolling, white-crested wave. She shot across our bow, made a wide and handsome sweep and came alongside our starboard sea ladder. The division engineer made a leap for our low deck, vaulted the rail and shouted, "Haul out!" to the coxswain. The boat pulled out a little way and waited with her engine idling. The skipper's face broke into a broad grin.

"Why, hello, Frank," he greeted. "I was just thinking that I'd come over to the tender after dinner tonight and we could have a game of chess when the movies were over."

The division engineer's face was grave. "No chess tonight, I'm afraid, Fred," he replied. "The Oryx is getting under way to come alongside the tender now. You will follow her after she shoves off. You are to fuel to capacity and take on stores

for extended operations. Send your exercise heads over to the
tender and take reserve war heads for all your torpedoes. The
division sails at midnight under sealed orders."

The smile froze on the skipper's face. "What's the dope,
Frank?" he asked.

"I don't know, Fred," was the reply. "You are to be completely ready at midnight for any eventuality. The Division
Commander will see you in his cabin when you get alongside,
and he will give you your sealed orders then. Other than that,
I know no more than you do."

He waved his boat alongside. The skipper walked over to
the side with him. They stood a moment in conversation. He
leaped into his waiting boat and stood down toward the
Ocelot to deliver his disturbing message there. In silence we
watched the wake of the speeding boat stretch out behind her.

Two hours later we were alongside the tender, gulping in
fuel oil through the heavy hoses. The fresh-water tanks were
filled to overflowing. The deck force wrestled frozen beef into
our refrigerator space. The brightly painted exercise heads
went aboard the tender. Gingerly, the shining steel war
heads, with their heavy loads of T.N.T., were lowered into the
torpedo room. Target-practice shells went to the tender and
our magazines were refilled with live ammunition. With a
heavy heart I went about the business of sounding the tender's cargo-fuel tanks to check my receipt of oil. Everyone
kept busy with the ominous preparations, in order to avoid
discussions which no one had the stomach for.

The division engineer hailed me from the tender's rail.
"Send up those two patched cylinder heads you are carrying
for spares, Wade," he directed. "Draw two new ones from
stores. You had better draw a couple of new spray valves, too,
and make sure you have a full allowance of spares."

"How about my allotment?" I asked. "With this lub oil
I've drawn today, I won't have a nickel left."

"I'll take care of the allotment," he answered. "Take what

you need and sign a chit for it to the storeroom keeper. Tell him to bring the chits to me. This is no time for your Scotch instincts to show!"

In two hours our preparations were complete. The skipper came down from the division commander's cabin, buttoning a couple of envelopes into his shirt pocket. He climbed to the bridge in silence. We slid out away from the side of the tender, and the Ocelot took our place. Commander Dryden, our division commander, stood by the tender's rail and watched us go. When all the preparations were complete, he would shift over to the Ocelot to sail with us at midnight. The engines chugged away on the interminable job of pumping amperes into the battery.

Midnight rolled around too soon. In darkness we weighed anchor.

From the dark deck the boatswain's mate reported: "Anchor's up and secure, sir."

From the bridge came the skipper's muffled, "Very well."

We didn't know it then, but that was the last time we were to hear that familiar exchange on the good ship Otter.

Without a light showing, the five submarines threaded their way through the anchored fleet. A destroyer, with all her lights aglow, led the way, and the five shadowy hulls of the submarines followed her in silence. Out past the outermost ships of the fleet we steamed, out beyond the darkened security patrol. The destroyer swung from her course. We plodded on.

As we slid past her bright lights, she hailed from her bridge, "Good night and good luck!"

"Good night!" the skipper answered through the megaphone. Then he leaned over the bridge rail above me, looked down and ordered, "Rig for diving!"

I slid down the torpedo-room hatch, and a seaman closed it after me. Only under the most tragic circumstances would I ever see it opened again. The well-trained crew was busy preparing the torpedo room for submergence. I went back to the control room and took my place at the diving controls. The lights on the control board winked from red to green as the ship was rigged.

My electrical officer stepped in from the forward engine room and reported, "All rigged forward, sir!"

The assistant engineer came from aft and reported all rigged aft.

Through the voice tube I reported to the bridge, "Ship rigged for diving. Main ballast flood valves closed. Main induction open."

In reply came the reassuring voice of the captain, "Very well. Ventilate the hull and battery outboard. Station the submerged cruising section. We will continue on the surface, prepared for a dive the minute anything is sighted."

A few minutes later the captain climbed down from the conning tower. He selected one of the envelopes from his shirt pocket and opened it under the lights of the diving station. Silently he passed it on to me to read. My eyes glanced over the familiar form.

"Form scouting line, ten-mile interval, course three one zero. Dive when necessary to escape observation from ship or plane. Maintain continuous listening watch on six hundred kilocycles, but observe radio silence except for contact reports or other vital information. Keep all torpedoes in full wartime readiness."

Except for that ominous sentence about the torpedoes, it was familiar enough. We had been through it all many times before on maneuvers. We were still not at war, thank God!

The captain called the torpedo officer and told him to fit all torpedoes with war heads and to load all the tubes. Then he returned to the conning tower to lay out the course, write his night orders and give the necessary directions to the officer of the deck. I excused the torpedo men from the diving station for their work on the torpedoes, and disposed the remaining men to cover their stations in their absence. We settled down to a familiar routine.

At four o'clock the torpedo officer came back to relieve me at the diving station. He had been working all night on the torpedoes. The tubes were loaded. I walked back to the maneuvering room to see how things were going in the machinery spaces. Our lives dropped into their customary pattern without confusion.

Four hours on watch for everybody except the captain. Four hours off to check the machinery operation, supervise the communications, navigate the ship, check the torpedoes daily and get what rest we could in the time remaining. The navigator and the communications officer took the bridge watch. The torpedo officer and I relieved each other at the diving station. My assistant engineer and the electrical officer stood watch in the maneuvering room in general supervision of the engines and the electrical plant, with the additional duty of coding and decoding all messages. The captain would relieve the navigator to work out his sights. It was a hard grind, but we knew from experience that we could live through it for days on end. Fortunately, the veteran crew could carry on indefinitely with little checking from the officers, whose watches chained them to their cruising stations.

At breakfast the next morning, the captain, Jackson, Barston and I sat down to a cheerless meal. The others kept the watch until we could relieve them. None of us had had more than a few hours' sleep the night before. Inevitably, the conversation turned to the situation in which we found ourselves.

"Do you think it's war, captain?" Jackson asked.

"Not yet, at any rate," he replied. "The situation must be tight indeed for the Commander in Chief to want a distant patrol shoved way out toward the enemy, but, as yet, we have no order for hostilities. I hope to God they never come. Perhaps in a few days we will be recalled."

I wriggled out of my seat behind the wardroom table. It was time to go on watch.

"Captain," I said, "I hope you are right."

On the second day out, we had to dive to escape being sighted by a tramp steamer. We went down to periscope depth the minute her masts appeared above the horizon. There we stayed, forging very slowly ahead to conserve the batteries. On our right, the Ocelot, invisible from our low bridge, might also be able to see the masts of the merchantman and be forced to dive. To the left, the Orcus would also have to dive, but the Orion and the Oryx, on the extreme left flank, would continue on the surface.

As the steamer neared the beam, I turned over the diving station to the torpedo officer and climbed into the conning tower to have a look at her. She passed not more than a thousand yards away, plugging along at nine knots, wallowing comfortably in the low swell, all unmindful of the eyes that were watching her every move. She seemed a symbol of peace and comfort. Three times seventy men had taken six thousand tons of submarines fifty feet below the surface of the sea to allow her to pass in peace. Unaware of the disturbance she had caused, she went purposefully on about her proper business. In three days she would be safe in port, the deck winches clattering over her cargo holds. There was no such peace in store for us.

We were down more than two hours. When we surfaced again, we had to charge ahead at sixteen knots to regain our position in the line. I went up on the bridge after the dive, for a smoke and a breath of fresh air. The sea was serene and empty. Astern, the wake stretched away to the horizon, as though the ocean was too indolent to erase the mark that we drew across her peaceful surface. In the immense expanse of blue, the low squat hull of the submarine shrank into insignificance.

Four days, five days we steamed on, listening for the message that would recall us. The flying fish skittered from under our bows, flashed for a brief instant in the sun and sank again into the endless sea. Man is a strange creature, to reach across the vastness of the ocean wastes to seek out his fellow man and destroy him.

One day we saw a mother whale lying on the surface, suckling her young. Lazily she finned over, first on one side, then on the other, to give her feeding infant a breath of air as it nursed. When we drew too near, she took fright and sounded, her great black tail standing straight up in the air as she dove straight down. We, too, were hunted things and could find safety only deep down beneath the surface.

The captain leaned against the bridge rail and sucked his pipe.

"I suppose if war does come," he reflected, "we have one good chance of a quick victory."

"What chance is that?" I asked.

"Well," the captain replied, "the enemy is pretty cocky. He probably would take a chance at the southern Islands at the very beginning of the war, in order to make a big splash in his home country. If the Commander in Chief could lure them away from support of their own bases and then fall on them with his full force, perhaps, and only perhaps, he could annihilate their whole force in one grand and glorious battle. If he won, there would be nothing left for them but to sue for peace, and victory might come before the economic pressure of war changed things too much back home."

Two more days on the course and we would be in sight of the enemy coast. Early one morning about three o'clock, a message came in from the division commander. I knew that it must be important, to cause the Ocelot to break radio silence. I sent it back to the maneuvering room for decoding. The skipper was in his bunk. I called him on the ship's telephone and told him that I had a message from the division commander and that it was being decoded. The decoded message and the skipper arrived in the control room simultaneously from opposite directions. I read the message over his shoulder:

"Hostilities commenced at midnight. Carry out instructions contained in Envelope B."

The captain handed me the message sheet. "In defense of peace, we go to war," he sighed. He fumbled in his shirt pocket and produced the second envelope of sealed instructions. When he had read them through, he passed them over to me to read. They were short and concise. Some of the paragraphs stand out in my mind:

"The mission of this division is observation. Attack only when assured of inflicting major damage on enemy capital ships. Observe and report all enemy movements. . . .

"This division will maintain patrol off the port of Sofala. Submerge during daylight, charge batteries and rectify position during darkness. Broadcast results of all observations while on the surface at night. The enemy main body is believed to be concentrated at Sofala, and it is further believed that he will soon make a southward sweep from that port in full force. . . .

"This division will report departure of the enemy main body, their course and disposition. After departure of main body, each ship will act independently to trail the enemy. Endeavor to obtain position ahead of enemy each dawn, in order that screen may be penetrated and main body observed during daylight by submerged operations. . . .

"Division commander in Ocelot. Guard six hundred kilocycles, maintain radio silence, except to transmit information of vital importance."

It would be a difficult mission to complete. We might wait in vain off the enemy port until our fuel and provisions were nearly exhausted. We would then have to return with nothing accomplished. While we were waiting we could count on the enemy's surface and air patrols making life very interesting to us. Neither in daylight nor in darkness would we ever have a minute of security, not an instant during which we could relax our vigilance without the probability that disaster would descend upon us in one of a dozen different forms. If it had been tough going before, we still had been able to adjust our lives to the hard routine. Now we knew that this had been only a prelude, just light training to harden us to what lay before.

If the enemy left port while we were on patrol, the task before us mounted to Herculean proportions. Each night we must play a gigantic game of blindman's bluff in an endeavor to gain a position ahead. If we succeeded in that, there would follow a contest in skill and luck in which we would strive to outwit the enemy defense and penetrate into the very heart of his formation. Countless observers in surface ships and in planes aloft would be constantly watching for the slightest betrayal of our presence. Listeners would be straining their ears to catch the noise of our propellers.

We could count on an enemy fleet speed of about twelve knots because of his necessity to conserve fuel on a long cruise. Our own maximum speed of eighteen knots gave us a scant margin. During a part of each daylight period we must trail on the surface. If the enemy maintained an active airplane patrol on his wake, it might be impossible to obtain a position at dusk from which we could dash by his formation during darkness. No submarine division had ever attempted a more difficult mission.

It was easy to see what the Commander in Chief had in mind. He hoped to use his submarine scouts to guide him to a contact between the two main battle fleets in the very first days of the war. If he could get his battleships into a position from which they might strike, then information of the enemy's movements would be of much greater importance than any damage our torpedoes might assess against him. If our admiral could successfully bring the two fleets together under conditions advantageous to himself, then he might be able to win a decisive victory and virtually end the war before the economic pressure was fairly felt at home.

The second morning we arrived at our station. War had meant no difference in our routine. It had removed some ambiguities from the situation. Before the open declaration we might have found ourselves in a difficult position if we encountered enemy vessels. Now, at least, we knew what to do.

Each of us had a front ten miles broad to patrol. An hour before dawn we dove. Back and forth we patrolled at the slowest speed we could make and still control the ship. The battery must be conserved for the long submergence and still have enough reserve power left over to close the enemy if he came out.

It was monotonous work. The needles of the depth gauges hung as though painted in place. Around and around the periscope an officer continuously walked, scrutinizing the surface of the sea and the sky above. The hours dragged by. It was monotonous, but still each minute was fraught with danger. Every time the periscope showed a feather, there was the possibility that it would be sighted by a patrolling plane. A moment's inattention at the diving station might result in exposing our naked and defenseless hull above the surface or might start us down to dangerous depths. Eternal vigilance was the price exacted for safety.

The air grew foul. Exertion became exhausting. We must conserve our oxygen and chemicals for an emergency. As the carbon-dioxide percentage went up and the oxygen in the air decreased, we were overcome by a dangerous listlessness intensified by the monotony of our work. Lassitude was our chief danger. Even though we knew the danger that surrounded us, it was difficult to maintain the constant attention necessary to keep us constantly on our toes.

The second day at our station we observed an enemy cruiser making port. The Ocelot followed her to the harbor entrance, carefully submerged and at a safe distance, following exactly in her wake to avoid the probability of a mine field. Behind the low headlands she could see a sea of masts. That night she relayed her information to us. The quarry was there. Like cats at a mouse hole, we watched the harbor entrance.

The nights were no less wearing than the days. We lay on the surface and charged batteries; five black hulls intently forever watching for the shadowy shapes of enemy patrols; poised for a crash dive to the safe depths of the ocean at the first alarm. Safety depended on seeing the enemy before he saw us. The strain on the bridge watch was almost unbearable. Each morning we prayed for the dawn that would see us safely below the surface. Each evening we prayed for the darkness that would permit us to come up and breathe fresh air again.

On the fourth night there was a sudden flare of searchlights on the southern horizon. Then there came the flash and the rumble of distant gunfire. One of our ships had been caught on the surface. We had no way of knowing how she fared, but at two o'clock in the morning, when we all reported our positions to the division commander, the Orion remained silent. There was still a possibility that she was being kept down by surface patrols and was unable to use her radio. We could only hope for the best.

On the afternoon of the sixth day, the enemy destroyers and cruisers commenced coming out in force. They swarmed over the surface of the sea. Planes came out and seemed to fill the sky. If we remained at periscope depth, there was grave danger that the planes would be able to make out the shadow of our hulls in the clear, sunlit water. We had to sound below periscope depth and trust to the listening gear.

Down we went to a hundred feet. Attention shifted now from the periscope to the listener. With the stethoscope stuffed in his ears, he twisted his sound gear from side to side. Perspiration dripped, unnoticed, from his face. The captain intently watched his expression as he paused now and then to listen more attentively on this bearing or that one as a new sound caught his straining ears.

"Destroyer on bearing zero three five, captain," he reported. "Seems to be standing this way. There is another one over on the port bow."

The ocean swarmed with destroyers, their depth charges ready to let go at the first sign of our presence. Intently we listened for the slow beat of the screws of the heavy ships.

About an hour before dark they came. We must take the risk of a periscope exposure. We planed up. The captain was there at the periscope. At sixty feet he checked her rise and eased her up ever so gently to fifty-five. Cautiously he poked only a foot of her periscope above the surface. With the dignified pace of pomp and power, the big ships came out. They cleared the harbor entrance and set up their zigzagging courses. We paralleled their base course and watched. They were surrounded by a myriad of screening destroyers. Not much chance of a successful attack. Our mission was observation. We let them go by.

An hour after sunset we surfaced and broadcast the information that the enemy was at sea. With our main engines on the screws and our charging engines on the batteries, we set off in pursuit. On our own darkened bridge all eyes scanned the black water for enemy ships. Suddenly, from the inky void on our starboard beam, a dim light winked out a strange recognition signal.

"Down! Get her down!" The diving alarm blared. The engines hissed to a stop. The bridge personnel tumbled down the conning-tower hatch. In the sudden silence I could hear it thump shut. But it was too late. A searchlight beam swept the surface of the sea. The conning-tower eye ports glowed as it found its target.

In maddening deliberation she took her own appointed time in leaving the surface. Thirty seconds. The decks were awash. We could hear the boom of gunfire close aboard. The bow planes were under now. They found a bite in the water, pulling her under. The depth-gauge needles wavered and hung. Forty seconds. An explosion aft. The sound of rending steel. We had been hit. Fifty seconds. The conning-tower eye ports were under. Sixty seconds, seventy seconds. She was under; going down fast now. Seventy, eighty feet. I made no attempt to check her. I wanted plenty of water over her.

The destroyer passed directly overhead. Her drumming screws made a noise like a train going over a trestle. Wham! The first depth charge. It felt as if it were right on top of us. The whole boat was shaken. Light bulbs broke in their sockets; men were thrown off their feet by the force of the explosion.

"Water in the main engine room!" How badly was she damaged? I had to know.

"Take a look aft, John," I ordered Barston.

"Aye, aye, sir!" came his ready answer. He beckoned to a machinist's mate to follow, opened the engine-room door and stepped through and dogged the door down after him. I never saw him again.

The boat was getting heavy. I couldn't hold her up. It must be a sizable leak. We sank to one hundred and fifty feet, both bow and stern planes on hard rise now. She took a big upward angle, but she continued to sink.

"Blow safety!" I ordered. The high-pressure air whistled through the blow valve. I stepped to the conning-tower hatch and reported to the captain: "Bad leak in the engine room, captain. Can't hold her up with hard rise on everything. I'm blowing safety."

The depth-gauge needles hung and then started back. She was coming up. Coming up sluggishly, as though she were tired and wounded. But I'd caught her and checked that sickening dive. With a thud like a quarry blast, another depth charge let go.

"Get her down!" the captain called from the conning tower. "Flood safety."

She went down like a rock.

"I can't hold her, captain," I reported.

"Put her on the bottom, Ham," he ordered.

"All motors stop!"

A hundred and thirty, a hundred and forty feet. Like a dead thing, she sank toward the bottom. The extra weight of water flooding in aft gave her a fearful angle down by the stern. It became difficult to stand. We had to clutch at anything we could reach to keep from sliding and falling into the after end of the compartment. Everything loose came clattering and sliding along the floor plates. She seemed intent on standing on her tail.

"Blow the after group," I ordered.

The angle eased a little, but she continued down.

The lights went out. The water had flooded the after battery. I sent the electrician forward to disconnect the forward battery before short circuits in the flooded compartments sapped the battery energy and heated the cables and connections to the burning point. In the dry compartments they shifted what load they could to the forward battery.

Down she went. More slowly, now that the after group was dry. A hundred and sixty, a hundred and seventy. A light shock, a shudder. She was on the bottom. The angle came off her as her bow settled on the ocean floor. She lay still and dead. A hundred and seventy-five feet of salt water rolled over her. We heard more depth charges, but they were farther away now. In the boat there was silence. In the feeble glow of the emergency lights, my men stood motionless at their stations. The azimuth motor of the compass ticked like the beating of a heart.

The captain came down from the conning tower. Together we peered through the small round deadlight into the engine room. Solid black water met our eyes. The engine room at least was flooded. We called the maneuvering room and the after torpedo room on the ship's telephone. No answer. We

tapped signals on the bulkhead. No answer. Half of the crew
was back there in eternal silence. A half hour went by. The
sound of the propellers receded and died out.

"Blow main ballast," the captain ordered.

The air whined into the tanks. We could hear the air from
her flood valves bubble along the side after all the water had
gone. The depth gauges never even quivered.

For the next half hour we tried every known device, every
trick, every expedient we knew. It was useless. The Otter was
on the bottom in one hundred and seventy-five feet of water,
and there she would stay forever. We were trapped.

We were in desperate plight. As the last effort failed to
budge the Otter from the bottom, no one found it necessary
to be reminded how hopeless was our situation. We all knew.
There within sight of the enemy coast line, no rescue ships
would hurry to our aid. No rescue chamber would ever be
lowered to snatch us from the jaws of death. We would never
hear the reassuring tramp of heavy diver's shoes upon her
deck. We were left to our own devices. If we succeeded in
getting out of the boat with the aid of the submarine escape
lung, there would be no vessel on the surface to receive us.
We would only substitute one form of death for another. In
the silence we could hear the slow trickle of water from the
cable glands through the bulkhead to the flooded compartment.

The captain tried desperately to keep us busy at tasks that
would keep our minds from dwelling on our plight. The electricians were busy making emergency connections from the
forward battery to the lights and the sound-signaling oscillator. The deck force he set to work overhauling and assembling life preservers in the torpedo room. The pitiful remainder of my engineers commenced counting and examining
the submarine escape lungs and collecting all available oxygen
tanks in the torpedo room.

Eventually, even his ingenious mind gave out of ideas.
Intense activity would soon result in raising the carbon diox-

ide content of the air and cut down the length of time we could continue to live. Not that it mattered much. The situation was hopeless. Whether we died early or late could make but little difference.

The oscillator was wired up now to the forward battery by an emergency hookup. At intervals of a minute or so, the sound man sent out the Ocelot's call. The Ocelot had been to the northward of us. It was barely possible that she, too, had been kept down by the light surface craft and that she hadn't been able to start in pursuit of the enemy fleet until late. Her course might take her near us, within range of the sound of our oscillator. I wasn't sure what good it would do if the Ocelot became aware of our predicament, but the captain evidently had no intention of attempting an escape before he got in contact with her. The weird and ghostly notes of the oscillator sounded along her hull at evenly spaced intervals of time. It was something to do.

After the electricians had finished reconnecting the battery, we were able to afford a couple of lights in each compartment. It seemed more cheerful that way. In the control room there was the steady trickle of water from the leaks through the stuffing boxes where the cables and fittings pierced the bulkhead to the flooded engine room. It wasn't a cheerful sound. The control room wasn't a popular place. The men distributed themselves through the remaining compartments, lay on the bunks, sat on the deck, moved about as little as possible, stared into space and waited.

I was more fortunate in that I had a task that kept me occupied. With the aspirator and a little box of chemicals, I went from compartment to compartment, sampling the air and testing for carbon dioxide. In order for us to live, the carbon-dioxide percentage must be kept below 6 per cent. If we were to attempt an escape with the lung, I would have to keep the concentration below 1 per cent, for the increased pressure would intensify its effects. As the concentration crept up, I broke out the sealed can of soda lime and spread the absorbent powder on mattress covers throughout the compartments. The torpedo room called for special consideration, for it was from there we might attempt an escape. I spread a good supply of soda lime on the top of the upper bunks, high above where the water would reach when we flooded the compartment.

There were thirty-seven of us left. The engine-room bulkhead had divided us into almost exactly equal parts. A half of us still lived, without much hope of life, here in the forward end of the ship. A half of our number were dead back aft— drowned at the engine controls; dead in the after torpedo room; caught in the intricate maze of cables and piping in the maneuvering room. We didn't speak of them as dead.

With the greatest care, we refrained from discussing them at all. The electrical officer was gone. The torpedo officer had happened to be in the after torpedo room. Barston I had sent to his death with an order slung nonchalantly over my shoulder. He had gone with a cheerful "Aye, aye, sir."

When we thought of them at all, we considered them lucky. They had it over with. We still had to face it. Only the habit of carrying on kept us alive. The carefully installed habit of never giving up while the slightest capacity for resistance remained was stronger than the instinct for life. None of us were free from disturbing thoughts as to how well we would meet the end. The fear of fear was a very real thing.

I know that for me life held no prospects worth the struggle. Considered apart from my responsibility to the crew and to the service, I would be willing to meet death more than half-way. One swift bullet from an automatic would be better than the lingering wait. Two weeks of constant, wearisome, nervous strain, with very little sleep, had beaten me down until I would willingly sell out for the prospects of eternal peace.

If I survived, I would someday have to look into the blue eyes of little Jane Barston and tell her that I had sent John to his death before he had ever even seen his son. I would have to face my admiral, not as an admiral but as John's father, and tell him how his only son had died. If he won a great battle, the world would heap honors on his head. They would be empty as ashes now for him and a gray-haired old lady as they faced the end of life forever alone.

Entombed in our prison of steel, we patiently waited. Waited for death to arrive and release us. Patiently waited for death to bring peace and relief. Into our bones crept the chill of the ocean, the numb, lifeless cold of the depths of the sea. Every breath that we breathed brought the end ever nearer—the end that we feared, yet would welcome at last. Life was a burden too great to be borne by us, a burden we would gladly relinquish for peace.

Time alone would soon rob us of initiative. In time, in spite of our chemicals, the carbon-dioxide percentage would creep up so high that it would be suicide to attempt to use the lung. Nothing would then remain but lingering death as the oxygen supply slowly decreased and the poisonous concentrations of carbon dioxide built up. All that our chemicals could do would but delay the inevitable end.

If we chose to attempt the ascent with the lung, the outcome could be hardly less certain. The ascent through one hundred and seventy-five feet of water was not lightly to be regarded. Only those in the best physical condition and so psychologically constituted that immersion brought no vestige of panic could ever hope to make it successfully. We had all had experience with the lung in drill ascents, and this gave us some confidence. But none of us had ever come up from such a depth, and before each drill ascent we had gone through a rigid physical examination to weed out those not in the pink of physical condition. The prospects were that many of us would not reach the surface alive. Yet we must all be bound by one decision. We must either all go or all stay. For those who successfully reached the surface, far from any possible aid, there would be nothing much left to do but quietly drown.

The oscillator plaintively whined the call of the Ocelot. The hull shivered like a living thing as the hopeless notes went out into the water. The notes changed! The sound man was sending out a message! I slid off the wardroom transom and set out for the torpedo room. The captain was bent over the listening sound man. He looked up.

"We have contacted the Ocelot!" he announced.

The Ocelot was on the surface. It was midnight up there, and as black as the inside of your hat. In the sea around her might still lurk the light forces of the enemy. She would not dare to show even the gleam of a light. But it was ears she needed now, not eyes, to guide her toward us. With her listening gear she should have no trouble locating our oscillator. Neither would any enemy ship that might chance to hear us. But it was a chance we had to take.

Quickly the skipper informed the Ocelot of what he knew about the enemy—their course, their dispositions and the position where he had last observed them. It was military information of the most vital nature. We learned that our radio broadcast had got through. The Oryx and the Orcus were away in pursuit. The Ocelot had been coming down through our position to trail the enemy when she had picked up our message. In a tense message the skipper described our predicament.

The sound man spelled out a message from the division commander:

"Make escape with submarine lung. Ocelot will stand by on the surface to rescue survivors."

From a military viewpoint, perhaps, it was a wrong decision to make. The Ocelot still had a mission to perform. As she lay stopped on the surface she would be a fair target for any chance enemy. Each minute she remained, the quarry got farther away. He knew he should leave us to our fate.

Who can blame the division commander if he found himself unable to do so?

Quickly we all gathered in the torpedo room. The forward battery door was dogged down tight behind us. The skipper counted noses. We were all there. We kicked off our shoes and each man donned a lung, adjusting the straps until they fitted snugly in place on our chests. The captain gave us our instructions and lined us up in the order in which we would ascend.

"We will have to get rid of one of the torpedoes to clear the tube for flooding," the captain said. He turned to the sound man. "Tell the Ocelot to stand clear. We are going to fire a torpedo on course one eight five," he ordered. . . . "Get Number Two Tube ready for firing, Simpson," he ordered the chief torpedoman, "and you can take care of the flooding, too, when the time comes," he added. "We will flood through Number Two Tube Drain and Inboard Vent. Take a bonnet off the drain manifold."

Simpson opened the outer door of the torpedo tube and built up the pressure in the impulse tanks. Thank God we still had plenty of high-pressure air. By the time the preparations were complete, the sound man reported that the Ocelot was ready.

"Number Two Tube, fire!" the captain ordered. We could hear the torpedo rumble as it left the tube. It would probably bury itself in the mud of the ocean bottom before the control mechanism found time to function.

"Jackson, you will make the first escape," the captain directed. "You're husky and a good swimmer. After the pressure is equalized, I will want you to go to the top of the hatch with your lung and see that everything is clear. Then you are to come back to the compartment and Childs will stream the buoy. The Ocelot will have a boat in the water, but I doubt that they will be able to find the buoy in the darkness. When you get up, cling to the buoy and yell until they find you.

"All of you follow Jackson in the order I have lined you up. Don't wait for orders. County twenty after the man ahead of you disappears up the hatch, and follow. Don't charge your lung with oxygen until the man ahead gets ready to go. When the pressure comes on, open your mouth and swallow hard, if you feel it in your ears. Remember that we can't stop after we have once started flooding. You will have to stand it. . . . Unlock the hatch, Childs," the captain ordered the chief electrician's mate.

Childs climbed up the ladder and disappeared into the hatch trunk. We could hear him spin the operating wheel. Not a drop of water leaked by the hatch. The tremendous pressure of the water above kept it as firmly on its seat as though twenty tons of lead had been placed on the hatch cover. No power we had available would be able to budge it until we had built up a pressure within the compartment equal to the sea pressure. Then it would lift from its seat by the pull of heavy springs, and if it did not fly all the way open, Jackson would easily be able to open it wide when he made his inspection.

Childs returned to the torpedo room and hooked the loose coils of the ascent line over his arm, free for running.

"You can drop the hatch skirt now," the captain told him.

They unclamped the skirt and it lowered into place. It made a two-foot extension on the hatch trunk that already extended deep down into the compartment. Together, the trunk and skirt would form a water seal between the hatch and the compartment when flooding had progressed far enough. As the water flooded in from the bottom of the torpedo tube, the air would be compressed and trapped in the upper part of the compartment. Because of the seal, the air would not be able to escape when the hatch was opened. In the upper part of the compartment there would be a big bubble of air which we could breathe while each man awaited his turn at the ascent.

The pressure would build up as the flooding progressed,

until it finally reached sea pressure, nearly eighty pounds on every square inch. The water coming into the confined space would cause the pressure to rise. With high-pressure air available, we could bleed air into the compartment to increase the rate of pressure rise. That would both increase the size of the final air bubble available and dilute the carbon dioxide, against which we must guard now. When the pressures finally equalized, the hatch would open. But the air that we breathed must be under tremendous pressure, and it was there, we knew, that the danger lay.

We knew that we were bound to have some trouble. We couldn't expect to gather together thirty-seven men and not find a few with slight colds or sinus infections that would clog the Eustachian tubes. If that little tube between the ear and the throat was not open, the pressure couldn't equalize behind the eardrums. Then, too, the pressure had strange effects on certain individuals. They would become dizzy, perhaps hysterical and quite unaccountable for their behavior, as though they were in the last stages of intoxication. With the intense nervous strain we were already under, anything might happen. We all knew it. But it had to be all or nobody, and there was no hope of surviving in any other manner. We were ready.

"Open Number Two Tube Drain and Inboard Vent," the captain ordered.

The water shot into the boat in jets of tremendous force under the full head of a hundred and seventy-five feet. Instantly the pressure commenced to rise. The captain started bleeding high-pressure air into the compartment. The hiss of its escape added to the roar of the incoming water. I looked about me at the strained faces. Several men commenced swallowing hard and rubbing their ears. Relentlessly the pressure increased.

An engineman's nose began to bleed. He wiped his face with the back of his hand and looked with fascination at the blood. Suddenly he yelled with the excruciating pain in his ears. He moaned in torment. The eardrum ruptured. He sobbed in sudden relief. A tiny spot of blood appeared on his ear lobe. The pressure kept increasing. As the air was compressed the temperature increased. Despite the cold water that swirled about our legs, our faces were bathed in perspiration in air of boiler-room temperature.

In a corner a couple of men giggled like schoolgirls. Intoxicated by the increasing pressure, they broke into raucous song:

> *"Crash! Crash! Crash! the boats are diving;*
> *Flood ballast through the salvage line.*
> *Hoist away the brimming cup,*
> *We'll go down and ne'er come up ——"*

Their voices were high-pitched and nasal as their vocal cords strove to adjust themselves to the unaccustomed density of the air. I must have been a little drunk with the pressure myself, for I remember that I thought the ballad very touching and appropriate. I became sentimental at the thought of the times I had heard that old song in barrooms and at cocktail parties all over the world.

I was suddenly sobered by the look on the drawn white face of Doane, the radioman. The water was up to our thighs now. The air seemed unbearably hot. Still the water flooded in and the pressure relentlessly increased. The captain continued to bleed high-pressure air into the compartment as he noted the progress of the flooding and the condition of the men about him.

When the water was within a few inches of the hatch skirt, the hatch cover began to flutter open and shut. A solid stream of water came down the hatch trunk. It continued only a few seconds, but it seemed a long time. The sight of water pouring in on us from above in a huge stream was nerve-racking. It seemed that nothing on earth would be able to stop it before we were all drowned. The water level quickly reached the tip of the hatch skirt and the flooding stopped. In the center of the compartment we had to swim now. We hung on wherever we could and waited.

Suddenly Doane let out a wild yell and started half crawling, half swimming toward the hatch. I tried to reach him. Panic might spread like wildfire now and disaster would be upon us. I saw the captain find a footing on the ladder and brace himself as Doane came toward him. With his arms swinging wildly, Doane was not an easy target. The captain watched for an opening, came around with a wide haymaker swing and caught Doane right on the button. It was a quick and merciful knockout. I was close behind him to catch him as he fell back in the water.

"You take care of him, Ham," the captain said. His coolness had a sobering effect on all of us.

Jackson was already charging his lung with pure oxygen through the light red rubber tube. He passed the charging chuck to the next in line, put the mouthpiece between his teeth and adjusted the nose clip. The captain nodded to him to go ahead. Jackson inhaled deeply and exhaled again into the lung. Satisfied with its operation, he ducked under the hatch skirt and climbed the ladder.

We could hear him fumbling around. The hatch thumped as he pushed it all the way open. In a minute or so he was back in the compartment.

"It seems to be all clear, as far as I can feel," he reported to the captain.

Childs streamed the balsa-wood buoy up the hatch. The line ran out rapidly through his hands. The line slackened suddenly and he knew the buoy had reached the surface. Then he secured the slack of the line to a pad eye. Everything was ready. Jackson had recharged his lung with oxygen. He ducked under the hatch and was gone. Childs could feel the tug on the line as Jackson slid up it toward air and life.

"Next man!" the captain ordered. He shivered slightly with the chill of the water, although the hot air in the compartment seemed to burn the exposed skin of our faces.

The next man grabbed the buoy line and followed Jackson. At twenty-second intervals the others followed. The captain stood at the hatch and slapped each man on the back as his turn came. It seemed to take an eternity, but actually it could have been only ten or twelve minutes before the navigator, the captain, Doane and I were alone in the compartment.

I had done what I could for Doane. I splashed water in his face and slowly he regained consciousness. It was evident that his terror had not left him. With the help of one of the men, I bound his arms and legs with a heaving line. He made no outcry, but his eyes reflected the terror and hysteria that overwhelmed him.

The navigator charged his lung. Before he slipped the bit in his mouth, he turned and said: "Good-by, captain. . . . Good-by, Ham."

The captain wrung his hand in brief farewell. "Good-by, Joe," he said.

By his white, drawn face and labored breathing, both the captain and I felt sure that we would never see him again.

Together the captain and I pulled Doane to the hatch. The captain reached into the overhead and pulled down the little emergency medical kit from where he had stowed it in a niche by the hatch to keep it dry.

"Here, Ham," he said; "secure the bit in his mouth with adhesive tape."

I held Doane's face well above the water, wiped it dry with a bit of gauze and shoved the bit home between his teeth. Then I plastered over his mouth and nose with adhesive tape.

The captain had taken a short length of iron wire that he had found somewhere and was twisting it into a loop at his belt. It was a few seconds before I caught the significance of his action.

"Slip up to the top of the hatch, hold on and help me to get Doane through the hatch," he directed.

"No, no, captain," I protested. "It will be hard enough to make it alone! You can't possibly take Doane up with you!"

"Do as you're told, Hamilton," he commanded.

I knew that tone in his voice. How I wish now that I could have disobeyed his last order to me. But the habits of a lifetime can't be undone in a moment of stress.

"Aye, aye, sir!" I replied, adjusted my mask and slipped up the hatch.

I had difficulty holding myself down against the upward tug of the inflated lung. I found the hatch wheel and hung on. I didn't dare lose contact with the ascent line. To lose it would be to lose the chance at life.

It was only a second before my groping hand felt Doane's hair. I eased him through the hatch. My fingers found his belt and I hung on. The captain was right behind him. He felt for Doane's belt and guided by my arm, found it. I knew that he was twisting the loop of wire from his own belt through Doane's, working clumsily in the total darkness, handicapped by the necessity of holding on to the buoy line with one hand. I held Doane down as he worked. The captain's elbow nudged me sharply twice. I wrapped my legs around the line and slid upward.

Pulled upward by the buoyant effect of the inflated lung, I had to check my rate of ascent by holding myself down on the line in order not to come up too fast. I knew that I must take at least four minutes for the one hundred and seventy-five foot journey to the surface. I had to come up slowly to allow time for decompression. Above all, I must remember to breathe into the lung. I had to combat the normal tendency to hold my breath while under water. If I had done so, the pressure in my own lungs would soon have exceeded the sea pressure. The sea pressure constantly decreased as I slid upward. When I breathed into the lung, the little flutter valve at the bottom automatically kept the pressures inside and outside my body equalized.

If the pressure became greatly unbalanced, disaster would be the immediate result. The excess pressure would rupture the delicate membranes of my lungs. Bubbles of air would find their way into my blood stream and I would die, either immediately or soon after I reached the surface. Fortunately, I had been through several practice ascents before at drills in the escape tower. I did the right things with little conscious thought.

After what seemed a lifetime, I reached a knot on the line that told me I was fifty feet from the surface. I had an almost overwhelming desire to let go the line, make a dash for the surface and get it over with. But I held on and inhaled and exhaled into the lung slowly ten times. Before I left that stop, I was aware of the captain right behind me on the line. There were knots in the line at ten-foot intervals now. I paused at each one and made sure the captain was right behind me. I was sure he was coming along all right at twenty feet.

From the last stop I slid slowly upward. Suddenly I felt a hand under my arm, and a voice said, "O. K. now."

I looked up and saw the stars that I had thought I would never see again. I spit the bit from my mouth. I clamped the flutter valve shut with my nose clip to conserve the remaining gas in the lung and make it act as a life preserver. My hands found the gunwale of a small boat.

"The skipper is right behind me," I said. "He will need a lot of help because he is bringing Doane up with him. I'll stay in the water to help him."

The seconds passed. Nothing happened.

"He must have lost hold of the line," I told them in the boat. "He was right behind me at the twenty-foot mark."

I left the boat and commenced swimming around in the darkness to see if I could find anything on the surface. I think I must have got a little frantic. The officer in the boat called for me to come back. I told him to go to hell. I continued to splash around. It might have been ten minutes. Of course, we didn't dare show a light, but it is probably just as well that I didn't have one to show just then. My hand hit something in the darkness.

"Here he is!" I shouted. "Come help me! Help me!"

They sculled the boat over to me. Still bound together, we pulled the captain and Doane into the boat. In the crowded boat we couldn't do much, but in a minute we were alongside the Ocelot and I had him on deck and commenced artificial respiration.

"Take them down the gun-access hatch to the control room," the division commander's voice ordered from the darkened bridge.

Someone undogged the gun-access hatch and we quickly lowered them to the control-room floor. The hospital corpsman relieved me at the artificial respiration. Doane was undoubtedly dead. The blood oozed from his mouth and nose. His face was purple and his chest appeared crushed.

The captain was in better shape. He must have lost the line somewhere near the surface and, encumbered as he was by Doane's body, he had drowned before he reached the surface or before help could get to him. Frantically we worked over him. I felt the engines start up as the ship got under way again.

"Down, hold, release, rest! Down, hold, release, rest!" We kept it up as hope faded. It must have been an hour or more.

Commander Dryden stood over me. "It's no use, Hamilton," he said. "He's gone, I'm afraid."

I had known it for some time. I could feel his muscles stiffening.

"Yes, commander," I assented. "He's gone."

"You know we will have to bury them at sea, Wade," Commander Dryden told me. "Tonight! Now! Before dawn. It's tough, I know, but there is nothing else we can do."

"He would want it so, commander," I answered.

Someone brought me an iron weight. I lashed it to his feet. I took off his class ring. His wife would cherish that memento, if I ever got it back to her. We hoisted them back up the gun-access hatch to the deck. The splash that he made we couldn't hear above the slap of the seas on the gun sponson.

Slowly I climbed up to the bridge and down through the conning tower to the control room. I mustered my men from the Otter. It didn't take long. Of the seventy-four men who had been in the Otter two weeks ago, when we had left port, but twenty-two remained alive. Only twenty-one of the thirty-four enlisted men who had left the torpedo room were picked up on the surface, and I was the only officer to survive.

Jackson, I believe, had reached the surface. The boat that the Ocelot had lowered had been unable to locate the buoy of our ascent line in the darkness. Then they heard someone shouting in the water. It had been a few minutes before they could reach him. They found the buoy. Two men were swimming around in a dazed condition. Neither of them could remember calling out. They never found Jackson. Whether he had drowned before the boat could reach him or had died from air embolism, no one will ever know. I am certain that it was his shout that brought the boat to the buoy and saved the rest of us. He had left the torpedo room of the Otter determined to do just that, and his determination had carried him through. Death itself had not been able to prevent him from carrying out his orders. When the boat found the buoy, they simply held on to it and picked the survivors off the line as they reached the surface.

I reported to the division commander.

"Have the hospital corpsman examine your men, Wade," he directed. "Let them turn in for tonight and tomorrow. Then, if they are fit for duty, we will put them on watch with the Ocelot's crew. I want you to write out a complete report of everything that happened in the Otter while the memory is fresh in your mind. When you have finished and feel sufficiently rested, report to me. I'm going to make you a sort of one-man staff, and you will take care of all the code and decode work for me."

That morning two of my men from the Otter showed symptoms of mild attacks of the bends. One showed the characteristic rash across his belly and the other had severe pain in his knee. There wasn't much we could do for them. There was no practical way we could put them under pressure again. Fortunately, they both came around all right. I put the others on watch with the Ocelot's men.

In the evening I reported to the division commander and handed him my written report. Briefly, he reviewed our situation for my information.

He hadn't heard from the Orion in more than three days. No report had come in from her the fourth night on patrol after the Otter had seen the gunfire to the southward. He hadn't heard or seen a sign of her since. We could only assume that she was gone. She had probably been caught on the surface at night much as the Otter had been, and the Otter was gone. That left only the Ocelot, the Oryx and the Orcus to carry out our assigned mission.

The Ocelot had had a terrifying experience the day before the fleet came out. Apparently, planes had found her shadow in the water as they patrolled high overhead. Her first intimation of trouble had been bomb explosions that racked her from stem to stern. She had gone to a safe depth immediately —beyond the penetration of the searching eyes in the plane— but surface ships with depth bombs had hurried to the spot.

They had evidently followed her with sound apparatus, and she had had a narrow escape. At a hundred feet depth she had dodged this way and that at slow and silent speeds, making every effort to suppress each little sound incident to her operation. Relentlessly, they clung to her track. Depth bombs exploded near and far as they bombed the whole area of the ocean in her vicinity. Finally she had had to seek safety on the bottom in two hundred feet of water. For hours the destroyers searched the surface above her, as she lay silent

and helpless on the ocean floor. It had been a near thing, but
with approaching darkness the enemy had given up the pursuit. We were confronted by an alert enemy, now aware of
our presence, and we had a very difficult mission to perform.

Thanks to the Otter's timely radio signals, the Orcus and
the Oryx had been able to gain a favorable position ahead of
the enemy fleet on the course we had signaled. A couple of
hours before dawn, soon after the Ocelot had left the grave
of the Otter, the Oryx had sent in a terse message reporting
the midnight position of the enemy main body. They had
evidently changed course soon after darkness, but luck and
guts had circumvented that maneuver. The Oryx must have
penetrated into the very heart of the enemy formation during
darkness and lived to tell the tale.

We hurried on in pursuit as twilight turned into darkness.
At eight o'clock we received a message from the Orcus. She
had contacted the enemy main body that afternoon. From
her position ahead, she evidently had been able to dive under
the enemy's screen and observe his whole disposition. She had
been kept down nearly all day, and now she was far astern of
the enemy, only a few miles in advance of us.

The Ocelot and the Orcus were in a hopeless position to
catch up that night. But the Oryx had had a little better
luck. By dodging every enemy patrol and seizing every opportunity to run at full speed on the surface, she had been
able to maintain a position close to the rear of the enemy
fleet. The Ocelot and the Orcus couldn't do much but attempt
to gain a favorable position by dawn. Then, if we could hold
it during daylight in the face of enemy surface and air patrols,
we might be able to do something the next night.

That night the Oryx intended to repeat her feat of contact-
ing the enemy during darkness. But her luck must have
played out. Whether she was bombed from the air at twilight or ran into enemy surface patrols during darkness, we
never knew. She disappeared from the face of the earth without a message and without a trace.

By dawn the division commander realized that the Ocelot and the Orcus were alone now. They were both astern of the enemy. We couldn't hope for contact with the main body during daylight hours. By darkness he would have had more than twenty-four hours in which to evade us. If he had made a wide change of course, we might lose him. The division commander ordered the Orcus to search a lane forty miles to the eastward, while we continued on the last reported course of the enemy main body.

Dawn found us within a few miles of the enemy's most probable position. We had to dive during the uncertain dawn light, and each hour we stayed down meant that the enemy would gain at least ten miles that we must strain every rivet to catch up. A half hour after sunrise we were up again, charging ahead with every ounce of effort the engines could put into the screws.

That day was a nightmare. Four times we were forced under by airplane patrols. Four times we made it before we were sighted. Perfect visibility and a cloudless sky were on our side. After each dive we surfaced as soon as the patrol had disappeared. Each time we surfaced we knew the terrific danger of emerging with an airplane patrol almost directly overhead in the blind spot that our periscope couldn't cover. Death might descend upon us from the sky almost before we could get a man on the bridge to scan the danger angle. Our luck held. As the afternoon wore on, we still held our position fifteen or twenty miles astern of the enemy fleet.

No reports came in from the Orcus. We could only guess that the enemy was not to the eastward. He must be dead ahead or to the west. Our repeated plane contacts indicated that he was not far away from us.

We dove at sunset to avoid the risk of contacts in the uncertain twilight. We were up again in half an hour. Again we were in relentless pursuit.

In the darkness we steamed on. On to a prodigious game of blindman's buff. The enemy didn't dare use searchlights, for fear of prematurely disclosing his position. Stealth was the only game we could play, invisibility was our only armor. It was a battle of straining eyes against straining eyes, and in this the advantage was with us. Our low black hull was harder to see against the black surface of the sea than the gray bulk of the surface ships. Barring tricks of light or a sudden chance encounter close at hand, like that which had undone the Otter, we could observe without being observed. But in this game of I spy, we, as the hunter, were much more vulnerable than the hunted. If we were tagged, we were out of the game for good.

I kept the bridge with the division commander. Lieutenant Commander Jameson, the captain of the Ocelot, and the regular officer of the deck were with us. Two trusted and experienced enlisted men kept constant watch on our wake. Each officer kept a sector on the seascape under constant surveillance. The controls had been shifted below. Only the officers and the lookouts were on the bridge. Every diving station was manned and ready. A machinist's mate was at each throttle and each clutch. The electricians stood ready at the motor controls. The main-ballast flood valves were already open. We rode on the vents, poised for instant submergence.

By midnight we knew that we must be among them or that we had missed.

In a tense whisper, the officer of the deck reported, "Look, captain! There, on the port beam!"

It was impossible to keep from stealing a look. I turned my head from the sector I must guard at all costs. Very faintly, on the port beam, I could make out the dark bulk of a ship—either a destroyer or cruiser. Occasionally the white top of a wave showed at her bow. The captain moved over to the hatch.

"No, Jimmy," the division commander ordered. "We'll have to ride it out on the surface and hope she doesn't see us. I've got to find the main body, and if we dive now, it will be hopeless. Alter course twenty degrees to starboard and keep going."

In low tones, the captain gave the necessary orders through the voice tube to the steersman below. "Stand by," he added. "Everybody stand by for a quick dive."

On the altered course, we slowly left the destroyer astern. Her dark bulk melted into the black sea. There was no easing of the tension on the bridge. We leaned far out over the rail, as though the few inches we could project our bodies over the sea would increase the range of our vision. Wide-eyed, we stared into the darkness, conscious of each flick of an eyelash and annoyed that the necessity of breathing detracted from the concentration of our gaze at the black void of the night. The crests of waves took ominous shapes and our imaginations peopled the ocean with a host of enemies.

"There! Over there on the starboard bow!" I pointed.

It was a heavy ship, a battleship. Silent as a shadow, her high bulk loomed up from the sea, as dark and unfriendly as a rock rising up from the ocean. We were between the flank screen and the heavy ships. We altered course back to port and steamed on. Soon we could make out the bulk of another ship ahead of the first. Our course now paralleled them. Slowly we pulled by the long column, less than a mile away. Our low black hull, we knew, blended with the color of the sea, but to us it seemed that we must stand naked and visible to a myriad of eyes searching for us from the decks and the masts of the monsters as we passed them. Behind a hundred guns the gunners stood ready to blast us out of the water.

Six heavy ships we passed. We might have made a successful night torpedo attack, but if we did, we would certainly have to dive, and we couldn't prejudice our chances of getting our information into the air. It was two o'clock by the time the last of them had faded astern.

There were three other battleships at sea. We could only assume that they must be in column astern of the first ship we had sighted. The aircraft carriers were probably beyond our reach. Every hour now we put four or five good miles between us and their battle line. We needed that distance, so we could dive before dawn and let them run past us while we were submerged. We didn't dare open up on our radio, for fear a spark on a wet antenna might betray us.

Four o'clock. The division commander dictated a message to me. I went below and coded it while an enlisted man took my place as lookout. I came back to the bridge with the coded message in my pocket.

"Don't release it until I tell you to, Wade," the division commander ordered, "but stand by the radio room, and if we start to dive, get it on the air."

I turned to the hatch. "Dead ahead," I heard the captain whisper to the division commander.

I peered into the darkness. The phosphorescence of her wake had betrayed the cruiser ahead of us.

"Change course thirty degrees to starboard," the division commander ordered. "Eight minutes—keep on that course eight minutes and then come back to the old course parallel with them. We will have her just out of sight on our port beam. Probably the anti-destroyer screen. . . . Take that message to the radio room, Wade," he ordered. "Tell them to open up at the first diving signal. Then you can come back up here to me."

When I returned to the bridge, we were just coming around to a course paralleling the cruiser's. She was out of sight now, and ahead of us, because we had lost distance by our maneuver. Fifteen minutes later we sighted another cruiser to port. We slipped by between the two of them.

It was four-thirty. The sun would rise about six. By five-thirty the sky would be gray enough to outline us against the horizon. We would have to be down by then to avoid being sighted.

At five o'clock I went below to release the message. We broadcast the all-important information: "Two o'clock position enemy main body: Square ninety-seven. Battleships in company with destroyers and cruisers." Twice we sent it out, addressed to no one in particular, hoping it would be picked up by someone who could relay it to the admiral.

"Send it out again," I ordered, my eyes on my wrist watch, waiting for the diving signal.

The radioman reached for the key. He paused, adjusted the earphones and picked up a message blank instead. He looked up.

"Commander Cruise Force receipts for our message," he reported. "He has something to transmit to us."

I stepped into the control room and bent the voice-tube megaphone toward me. "Bridge! Bridge!" I called.

"Bridge, aye, aye," the officer of the deck whispered, as though to admonish me for my loud tones.

"Commander Cruise Force received our message. He is transmitting to us now."

The message came over immediately. The cruisers must realize our urgent need for haste. I reported its receipt to the bridge.

The bridge personnel came down the hatch. The engines sighed to a stop.

"Take her down," the captain ordered from the conning tower.

The skipper was afraid to use the diving signal, for fear its blare might be heard by an enemy too close aboard. The vents opened. Silent as death, we slid beneath the waves. An audible sigh of relief went through the ship.

I bent over the task of decoding. When I had finished, I brought the message to the division commander.

"Midnight position our main body: Square forty-three. Major engagement imminent. Make every effort to observe and report daylight position enemy main body."

"Run at a hundred feet depth," the captain ordered. "Four knots."

We continued on a course parallel to the cruisers. The enemy would be overhauling us at eight knots or more. In the boat, silence reigned. Only the low whine of the motors could be heard, and the occasional grind of the bowplane operating shaft. The division commander came down from the conning tower and went forward to stand by the listener at the sound gear. I went with him.

Immediately we could hear the screws of the enemy cruisers. They came up from astern, passed safely over us and were gone into the silence ahead. A half hour passed. On the surface, the sun would be just over the horizon, dispelling the morning mists, bringing relief to other eyes that had also strained all night peering into the darkness.

On the starboard beam we could hear the whine of high-speed propellers. We listened in vain for the slow, deliberate beat of the screws of the heavy ships.

"I'll have to have a look," the division commander said. He threaded his way back to the conning tower and I followed.

"Bring her up to fifty-five feet," the captain ordered to the control room. "And for God's sake keep her under control and don't broach her!" he added.

The depth-gauge needle slowly slid back around the dial. It pointed to fifty-five feet.

"Up periscope!" The captain walked the periscope around, examining the whole horizon. He paused near the starboard beam. "Cruiser bearing: Zero eight five," he said. "Range: Six thousand yards. Angle on the bow: One hundred and thirty port. She is making all of sixteen knots, maybe eighteen. There is a whole slew of cruisers beyond her on the same bearing. I don't see any heavy ships. . . . Wait! Dead astern! Bearing: One eight zero. I can just make out the fighting tops of big ships. Down periscope!"

"We've got to close quickly," Jameson," the division commander remarked.

The captain nodded. "What's the collision course, Pete?" he asked his navigator.

The navigator twisted the white dials on the iswas. "Two seven zero, captain," he replied.

"Come right to two seven zero! Eight knots! One hundred feet!"

The whine of the motors increased in pitch. We slid back to one hundred feet.

"How long can I run on the course before I am abeam of the heavy ships?" the captain asked.

The navigator consulted his instrument and tables. "Twenty-five minutes I make it, captain," he said.

"Make it twenty," the division commander interjected. "Have a look at ten minutes. They might change course on us."

The captain nodded and clicked the stop watch he wore on a lanyard around his neck.

"Pete," he said to his navigator, "I will want you to work out the speed of that ship. Figure she is on the same course as the cruiser we just saw. I'll give you a bearing on the second observation and my estimate of the range."

We could only stand and wait as the ship swam through the depths. We knew that her batteries could only keep her going for an hour at this speed. We had already used a good spot of that precious battery energy that morning. Now it was flowing out of her like heart blood through a severed artery.

The minutes wore on. The hand of the stop watch dragged its weary way around and around the dial. Ten minutes.

"Two knots!" the captain called out. "Fifty-five feet!"

We could feel the way drop off the boat. We planed upward.

"Up periscope!" He twisted the instrument around the horizon for a hurried look. "There they are!" he called. "Range: Eight thousand yards. Bearing: Zero nine three. Angle on the bow: Thirty port. They've got a tight anti-submarine screen, but I don't believe they've been zigzagging. Down periscope!"

"They are making eighteen knots," Peterson interjected. "Their course is two one zero. Periscope angle for a straight bow shot is zero one eight."

"The bearing is holding up nicely," Captain Jameson said. "At this speed I can get into a beautiful attack position. To hell with the screen! I can get under or through it."

"Afraid not, Jameson," Commander Dryden retorted. "You wouldn't have enough battery left to get out of here, and I've got to get this information to the admiral. Slow down to four knots. We'll get in close enough for detailed observation."

"Maybe you're right, commander," Jameson agreed. "But I'd like to sink a couple of torpedoes into those babies. So far, we've taken all the punishment. I'd like to dish out a little. They've stepped up their speed to eighteen knots. When they go by, we'll never be able to catch them again. It's our last chance."

"Primary mission is information, Jameson," the division commander added. "I appreciate your feelings. It's tough. Slow down and let them go by."

"Aye, aye, sir," Jameson yielded. "Four knots."

We had another look when the stop watch read twenty minutes. They were drawing ahead rapidly now.

"All tubes ready for firing," Captain Jameson ordered.

I thought for a minute he was going to take the bit in his teeth and bore on in anyway. But he was only preparing for any chance that might come his way.

At twenty-five minutes they were dead ahead of us. The range was only thirty-five hundred yards. The nearest screening destroyer was only fifteen hundred yards away. We could try a long-range shot under the screen, but they would be almost certain to sight the torpedo wake and avoid it by maneuvering. Our presence would be disclosed and we might never get our precious message on the air.

Cautiously we poked up only a foot of periscope. "There they are, dead ahead, commander," Captain Jameson reported, and stepped back from the periscope eyepiece.

Commander Dryden gripped the round steel handles. He swung the periscope slowly from bow to stern and back again. I could see his lips mumble as he counted.

"Take it, Wade," he said, "and check our observation."

There in the clear morning light was a long column of battleships, like the pictured silhouettes from Jane's; familiar, though I had never before gazed upon them. I counted. Nine! Nine battleships majestically proceeding on their own appointed business, with pomp and deliberate purpose, the power and confidence of a nation behind them.

The light forces we had seen were hull-down ahead. We were almost directly abeam of the center of the column, less than four thousand yards away. Over on the other side of the column I could faintly make out the crazy top hamper of the plane carriers.

"Down periscope! A hundred feet!" Captain Jameson ordered. . . . "I can still get in an attack on the last ship in column, commander," he pleaded.

"Let's get the hell out of here," Commander Dryden ordered. "Come around to reverse of their course and bend on all the speed you've got."

"Come right to course zero three zero. Eight knots," Jameson ordered.

"A half of eighteen is nine, and four makes thirteen," the division commander computed. "Thirteen miles. A half hour ought to do it. In half an hour they will be thirteen miles away, and we can come up and transmit."

"We can't keep up this speed very long, commander," Jameson warned.

"I know! I know!" the division commander replied irritably, as he bent over a message blank at the little chart desk. . . . "Here, Wade. Code this and get it down to the radio room to release as soon as we surface."

I glanced at the message: "Six-thirty enemy position: Square sixty-three. Nine battleships in column. Light forces concentrated fifteen thousand yards in the van. Four carriers four thousand yards to the right of main body. Course: Two one zero. Speed: Eighteen."

I met the engineer officer at the top of the ladder and stood aside for him to gain the conning tower. His eyes questioned the captain.

"Half an hour, Scotty," the captain answered his unspoken question. "Then we surface to get that message off."

"It will pull the pants right off the can," the engineer protested.

"I know that, Scotty," the captain replied, "but it's got to be done. Pull that battery right down to the bottom if you have to, but hang on like grim death."

I coded the message and took it to the radioman. The minutes wore on. The lights grew dim. In each bulb the filaments burned red and visible. The main motors were sucking the life out of the battery. Sucking out the life and energy that we might need to pull us out of tight places we would be sure to encounter before daylight was gone. The engineering officer stood at the diving controls and anxiously watched the voltmeter as the voltage dropped lower and lower. The electricians hurried through the ship with their little lead-lined hydrometer boxes and confided the specific gravity of the battery electrolyte to the engineer in whispers. We hung on!

The captain called the engineer to the conning-tower hatch. "When we surface, get the forward engines on the battery charge and the main engines on the screws. We will be safer with a little distance behind us."

The engineer nodded in understanding.

"Two knots!" the order came. "Fifty-five feet." The dim filament grew suddenly brighter. "Up periscope! All clear, commander! Surface!"

I jumped down to the radio room to get my message on the air. The chief radioman bent over the key and hammered it out. He listened a moment and grinned. "Message sent and acknowledged," he reported.

As I came through the control room I could hear the forward engines clattering away as they bit into the long battery charge. The big main engines wheezed as they were jacked over against the chance that water might have leaked into the cylinders during the dive.

I climbed into the conning tower and shouted to the bridge, "Message sent and acknowledged, sir!"

As though my report had released an alarm, the bridge personnel tumbled through the hatch. The diving alarm blared.

"Planes! Planes on the port beam!"

"Did they see us?" Commander Dryden asked.

The captain was already at the periscope, turning it hurriedly to the bearing. "Yes, I think so," he said. "They have headed this way. Take her down! Down to a hundred feet!"

We were under water again before the planes could get over us. But the depths held no safety for us now. With an exhausted battery and no bottom at all beneath us, it would be only a matter of minutes before we would have to come up again. Needed no longer in the conning tower, I dropped down into the control room to watch my colleagues struggle with a desperate situation.

"Two knots," the diving officer ordered in a voice that hinted no lack of confidence. "Shift to hand power on bow and stern planes."

He knew he must conserve his little remaining battery power at all costs, and he didn't dare risk jamming his planes when the inevitable failure came.

To the great brass wheels the planesmen now stood, straining every muscle to accomplish a task at which their flicking thumbs had a few minutes before directed a distant motor. Their faces were bathed in sweat. Their breath came in gasps. Ten minutes passed. Two other men replaced the planesmen. We were using emergency lights now. The shapes of the men were shadowy in the dim light.

The maneuvering room reported: "Main motor stopped, sir." The battery had been played out to the bitter end.

The diving officer reported that the main motors would turn over no longer.

"Try to balance her for a few minutes longer, Scotty," Captain Jameson ordered.

The planesmen stood back from the controls and rested. Bow and stern planes and rudder were all useless now. The Ocelot lay as dead as a log in the water. A few extra pounds of weight and she would sink—sink until she found bottom more than a thousand fathoms down. Long before she reached there her bones would be cracked by the tremendous pressure, her rivets sheared and her hull twisted and crushed. And we would all be dead. If she were only a hundred pounds too light, she would rise—rise until she reached the surface, where the airplanes hovered like hawks waiting for a rabbit to leave the cover of a thicket.

The depth-gauge needle quivered as the diving officer tapped it lightly to keep it from sticking. It started down.

"Pump from auxiliary to sea!"

The pump groaned once and stalled.

"No power on the pump motor," the manifold man reported.

"Put a hundred pounds pressure on Number One Auxiliary. Blow from Number One Auxiliary to sea," Scotty directed.

The water gurgled as it hurried through the manifold, but we were going down—going down slowly at first, then more rapidly. Two hundred feet, two hundred and fifty feet.

"Blow safety!"

The air whistled in the blow valve. The depth-gauge needle checked. We started up.

"Flood safety!"

We were coming up faster than we went down.

"Secure Number One Auxiliary! Flood Number Two Auxiliary from sea!"

The orders came thick and fast. Hurrying hands spun valve wheels to obey. Still she came up.

She was at a hundred feet, then fifty, before he could check her. We knew she was heavy, but still she came up. It was easy to adjust the dead weight of the ship with the greatest exactness, but the momentum was a dynamic force. Before the depth-gauge needle could portray a movement, twenty-five hundred tons of ship and ballast water had gained so much momentum that only a radical change of weight could check her. Then she went just as hard, just as stubbornly in the opposite direction.

First she plunged toward the bottom. Then she shot toward the equally dangerous surface. She was coming up fast now. The sweat ran in rivulets from the diving officer's face. Impatiently he tapped the glass of the depth gauge. Unnoticed, the glass shattered and gashed his drumming fingers. Still she came up. Fifty feet. Now thirty feet. The top of the bridge would be out of water now, advertising our presence to all the world. Slowly, very slowly, he got her under again.

The division commander called me up to the conning tower. "There were no planes in sight when we broached that time," he told me. "We are going to go battle surface. Tell Scott to get a charge started as soon as the hatch is open, and be ready to put his mains on the screws. Tell him to get all hands in life preservers. We will abandon ship if we have to. You take your men from the Otter and get the gratings off the boat islands. We will open the main-engine-room hatch and get all the idlers top-side."

The preparations took only a minute.

"All hands, battle surface! Blow main ballast!"

We broke the surface with a rush. The gun crew scrambled up the gun-access hatch. The quartermasters wrestled two machine guns up to the bridge. Like a cornered rat baring her teeth, the Ocelot mustered and manned her puny surface armament. I waited for word to open the engine-room hatch and hurried to the boat islands.

In frantic haste we took off the gratings. The forward engines were already started on the charge. The main engines coughed and added their heavy bass notes to the clamor below.

The minutes passed and every minute brought greater security. In an hour we could put in enough of a charge for a short dive again in case of necessity. Every turn of the screws took us farther from danger. But it was not to be.

From high out of the sky above us, an airplane motor screamed in tortured anguish. Straight down out of the blue they dove at us.

"Commence firing!" I heard the captain order.

The ship heeled over to the rudder as he attempted to zigzag away from the diving planes.

The deck gun spoke. It was a futile bark of pure defiance. By no possible twisting and turning could it be brought to bear on the attacking planes. The machine guns added their clatter to the din. The planes came straight at us, as though they meant to dive into our deck. I could see the bombs leave the racks. The planes pulled out of the dive. Straight over the top of the bridge they flew, their spitting machine guns spreading death and destruction on our crowded decks.

For a few seconds my eyes followed the silver shape of the bombs. The blast of the explosion threw me to my knees. A great column of water rose up from the sea on her port side and drenched the forward deck. I scrambled to my feet and hurried up the ladder to the bridge.

Captain Jameson lay crumpled on the deck of the bridge. Commander Dryden hung on to the bridge rail, his face contorted with pain. Blood stained his trouser leg.

"Take charge of her, Wade," he told me as I reached the bridge. Unhurt, but dazed by the fury of the attack and the burst of the bomb close aboard, the quartermaster clung to the steering control. The ship was still swinging to full right rudder. I wrenched the control away from the quartermaster and I eased the rudder to straighten her out on her course.

Over the bridge rail I shouted for my men from the Otter

to come help me. My own quartermaster took the wheel. With difficulty we lowered Captain Jameson down the hatch and helped the division commander below.

The planes were circling now, gaining altitude and position for another attack. The deck gun boomed again—almost under my feet, it seemed. I could see the white burst of shrapnel far to the right and below the planes. We had survived the first attack, but in a few minutes now, another one, just as vicious, just as dangerous, would be upon us. The end was almost a foregone conclusion.

They had reached their proper altitude now. Any second we might expect them to commence the dive. I changed course sharply to the left to make them attack cross wind. Suddenly they straightened out their flight and streaked away to the south. Helpless as we were, they had abandoned the attack!

Far on the southern horizon we could see that the air was filled with planes. Our own planes, we hoped, in the first air raid that was to lift the curtain for the mighty battle that was to come. Our adversaries had been recalled to counter a thrust far more dangerous than any we could threaten.

The air above and the sea beneath grew quiet again. At least we were to be afforded a short respite. Several of the men on deck had been wounded by machine-gun bullets. We got them below as quickly as possible.

One bomb had exploded very close to the port side. Astern of us spread a wide oil slick from a punctured fuel tank. It would betray our course, on surface or submerged. The ship listed to port. A ballast tank had been shattered by the explosion. The forward engine room reported that the circulating water hull fitting had been fractured by the blast. Water poured into the engine room, but by emergency connection to the engine circulating water pump, they would soon be able to control the flood. Scotty brought the ship back to an even keel by counter flooding.

Word came to me that the division commander would like

to see Scotty and me. I turned over the bridge to the Ocelot's torpedo officer and went below to his cabin. Scotty was already there.

Commander Dryden lay stretched on his bunk. The hospital corpsman had done what he could to relieve his pain. A machine-gun bullet had shattered his knee. It was obvious that he would be unable to get about.

"Wade," he addressed me, "you are senior to Scott, I believe."

"By a few numbers, commander," I replied. "But this is Scotty's ship. I would be very glad to act as his engineer, if he is to take command."

"Very generous of you, I'm sure, Wade," the division commander said, "but Scott reports that the forward engine room has a sizable leak. If we have to dive, the diving officer is going to have a tough time. Scott knows his own boat and his own men better than you do. I think it would be better for him to continue at the diving station. He has turned in an excellent performance today. No one could have done better. You take command, Wade, and, Scott, you continue as diving officer and engineer."

"That arrangement suits me perfectly," Scotty said. "I'm sure we can work together." We shook hands on it and hurried back to our stations.

There was nothing at all in sight when I got back to the bridge. I stopped the engines. We were in as good a position as any we might achieve. We might as well concentrate on the battery charge and such emergency repairs as we had facilities to make. The charge went merrily on. We crammed amperes into the battery until the connections were hot to touch and the electrolyte boiled with the gassing. Until we had some sort of a charge in the battery, we were helpless.

We were still far from out of the woods. With a discharged battery, we were unable to dive. It would be an hour or two before we had any charge worth considering in the battery. For the next couple of hours we would be helpless on the surface, easy pickings for any light bomber that happened our way. We were overmatched in gun power by any type of ship we could possibly encounter, and we didn't have the speed to escape or the ability to conceal ourselves by submergence.

An hour passed. Our chances of escape increased as time went on. There wasn't much we could hope to do now but limp back to port. The division had shot its bolt. The Orcus was too far to the eastward to have much hope of making contact again. Crippled and almost helpless, the Ocelot certainly constituted no great threat. The enemy had disappeared to the southwest at a speed we couldn't match. It looked as though we were out of the battle.

Two hundred men had died, for the most part drowned like rats in a trap. Fifteen million dollars' worth of ships and equipment lay rusting in the ooze of the ocean bottom. Not a single torpedo had been fired. Perhaps some of the Ocelot's machine-gun bullets had found their targets. If they had, then a few holes in a plane's fabric was the only damage we had assessed against the enemy.

But our mission had been accomplished. If we listened closely, we could hear the thunder of the big guns beyond the southern horizon. We had delivered the enemy battle fleet into waiting hands, ready and competent to deal with them. Guided by our contact reports, Admiral Barston had found out his adversary in the vast reaches of the ocean.

Of course, it was weeks before we could piece together even the bare outline of what happened. But all during the past night there had been sporadic cruiser contacts. Convinced that major forces were at sea, the enemy admiral had concentrated his light forces and increased speed to eighteen knots at dawn. Admiral Barston had put his full air force in the air before daybreak. That last contact report of the Ocelot's, for which we had paid so dearly, had guided our bombers to the enemy's aircraft carriers.

The carriers had been caught with most of their planes on

deck. Light demolition bombs had ripped up the vulnerable flight decks and piled them high with the wreckage of planes that never had time to get into the air before the attack was upon them. A few minutes after that vicious light-bomber patrol had left the crippled Ocelot, they were homeless birds, destined to flutter for awhile through the bright sky before they settled forever on the sea beneath.

Before the enemy could fully recover from the blow, his main battle line was engaged. The battle thundered away to the southward of us. The sound of guns seemed to be coming closer. Nearly two hours had passed since we had surfaced. We breathed more easily. We could dive again now and, perhaps, our oil slick would escape notice.

Soon we could see the masts of big ships coming up from the south. Without stopping the charge on the forward engines, I got under way on the mains. I wanted to get a little closer to the oncoming ships. Perhaps the Ocelot wasn't completely beaten yet.

As their fighting tops reared above the horizon, I was sure they were enemy battleships. Down we went. Down to fifty-five feet. We couldn't afford the chance of being sighted, even though submergence greatly increased the difficulty of controlling the leak in the forward engine room.

Through the periscope I could barely make out the tips of the masts. I called down through the voice tube to Scotty, "Enemy battleships standing this way. Get the tubes ready for firing."

I could hear a spontaneous cheer go through the ship. Poor devils. More than two weeks now they had stood up under an almost unbearable strain. They knew that three of our five ships were gone forever. They had never had the satisfaction of dealing an effective blow against the enemy. The officers could understand the necessity for the strategic information, but the men in the engine rooms and torpedo rooms only wanted to get in there and shoot.

Captain Jameson, who had pleaded so urgently for a chance

to attack, lay dead in his bunk below. The last of our skippers who could have done justice to the occasion was gone. Upon me the mantle fell. I had once commanded a smaller ship than the Ocelot. I knew what to do and what was expected of me, but I had no illusions that I was worthy to stand in Jameson's shoes.

When I heard the cheer of the men below, my throat constricted with emotion. The ship was leaking like a sieve. The fuel oil oozed out of her in a telltale stream astern. We had but half a battery charge. They knew the danger, but there never was any doubt but what they supported me in my decision to attack. I offered a silent prayer to all the gods of battle. My hands shook as I grasped the periscope handles.

"Bearing: Three four zero!" I called out to Peterson. "She's hull down! Range: Twenty thousand yards! Can't estimate her speed!"

"The collision course is zero seven zero, captain," he answered promptly.

His calm assurance, his easy competence, calmed my jangled nerves. The greater part of the credit for what happened ought to go to Peterson. He never was the least perturbed about anything that happened. He never seemed the least bit in a hurry. He sat on the deck in the conning tower with his plotting sheets, instruments and tables scattered about him in seeming disarray, but his hand seemed always to find the right one. Somehow he was able to carry the whole picture of the attack in his mind's eye from the scanty information I slung at him from the periscope. I never asked him a question but what the answer was ready. He had all the information at his finger tips.

"Down periscope! Come left to course zero seven zero. Speed: Four knots!"

"I'd like to go a little faster," I confided to Pete, "but I'd hate to get into attack position with a spent battery."

Peterson looked up from his plotting sheet and nodded in agreement.

"How are you making out in the forward engine room?" I called down the voice tube to Scotty.

"We'll make it all right, captain," he replied. "But don't go to a hundred feet unless you have to. If you have to go down deep, I'll hold her somehow, but it will be hard going."

"I'll remember," I promised. Ten minutes flew by. "Two knots. Up periscope!"

She was closer now. I could make out her upper works and funnels. The whole battle line stretched away behind her. I could see the puffs of yellowish-brown smoke as their turrets fired. I gave Peterson the data he needed.

We should stand a good chance if we could get within range. The anti-submarine screen had been withdrawn. The destroyers of that screen now had their hands full elsewhere. The enemy battleships were fully engaged and we were on their disengaged bow. In the confusion of battle, we could, in all probability, make an undetected approach despite our oil slick.

But our position was against us. The enemy was still fourteen thousand yards away. Reasoning and the rapid change of bearing both told us that he was making close to top speed. He wouldn't pass within ten thousand yards of our position—far outside of effective torpedo range. If we attempted to use our highest speed to close the range, we were certain to exhaust the battery before the attack was finished. If we continued at four knots, the battery would last, but our closest range would be seven thousand yards. I went to six knots over Scotty's protests. I intended to get in for at least a long-range shot.

Five minutes later I had to have another look. The listeners could hear the propellers now. I could see the decks; I could see the guns belching smoke at every salvo. The third in line was afire aft. Great sheets of flame spurted as high as the masthead. They were taking a beating, but they were standing up well under punishment. We could only hope that our battle line was doing at least as well. I watched them with fascination. I could see the spotting planes overhead. No need of taking any chances of being sighted.

"Down periscope!"

The next time I looked, I could see them well. It was heart-rending to know that after all the Ocelot had been through, we would miss making an effective attack by a few thousand yards. Pete gave me their course. He estimated their speed at twenty knots. Five thousand yards would be the closest I could come to them.

"I'm going to make a straight bow attack," I told Peterson. "I'll reserve my stern tubes for what might happen afterward."

He simply nodded and gave me my firing-periscope angle.

The sound operator was checking off the bearings for me now. I should have kept my periscope down and waited, but I couldn't control my impatience. I had to have a look. It was a good thing that I did. The battleships had made a big change of course to the left. They were coming down almost straight at me now, in three parallel columns of three ships each. I was in perfect position. I took a quick look around the horizon. Over to the eastward I could see the black clouds of a smoke screen. That was the reason for the change of course. The destroyers were attacking on the other bow.

"Two knots!" I called. "Stand by all tubes! Down periscope! . . . I'll fire the bow tubes on the first ship in column, Pete," I told him. "Seventy track. That should give me plenty of time to catch the leader of the second column on about a hundred and ten track with my stern tubes."

Peterson gave me the periscope angle for both setups.

I stood by my lowered periscope, listening to the sound man sing out the bearings, waiting for my targets to approach the firing bearing, so that I could make a short periscope exposure when I fired. An icy calmness descended upon me. The enemy's battleship columns were about two thousand yards apart. I intended to get in between their right and center columns and pick off a ship from each, one with my bow tubes and one with my stern tubes.

"Coming on the bearing, captain."

"Up periscope! Stand by! Fire one!" The range wasn't more than a thousand yards. I felt sure of a hit. "Fire two!" I hadn't been sighted. "Fire three!" I could see the white track of the first two torpedoes speeding hot and true to their target. "Fire four! Stand by the after tubes!" I swung my periscope around, deliberately turning my back on my first target. A shell splash rose in front of my periscope. I'd been sighted. The second target was coming into the cross wires. "Fire five!" Shells rained all around me. "Fire six!"

I heard the thud of an explosion ahead. My first torpedo had scored a hit. Let them shoot at me. They would have to be good if they could hit a periscope! I swung my periscope around to have a look at my first target. I heard the dull boom of the second torpedo explosion while the periscope was swinging. As the battleship slid into my field of vision, I saw a great column of water arise abreast her forecastle. A huge cloud of steam and smoke enveloped her amidships. Almost immediately, another great white fountain of water leaped up by her quarterdeck. Four hits! Four clean hits! She was a gone goose or I never saw one.

Spellbound by the sight, I could hardly tear my eyes away to have a look at my second target. I brought the periscope around. I could see her mammoth bows headed directly toward me. My stop watch told me it was only a little over a minute since I had fired my first shot. She had probably had her rudder over before I fired my stern tubes. I could see the white wake of my two torpedoes passing ahead of her. She had turned toward me both to avoid the torpedoes and to ram.

"A hundred feet," I ordered. "Right hard over rudder. Eight knots."

Scotty would have to do his best with the forward engine room. We had to dive under the enemy battle line to safety.

Her bulk grew in the periscope until it seemed a solid wall of gray bearing down upon us.

"Sound the collision alarm!"

The siren screamed the alarm. The submarine was going down with maddening deliberation.

I could see her starboard side. We were pulling clear of that awful bow. The secondary-battery guns were spitting flame in my direction. I could plainly see the gun crews at the guns. We were so close now that the gun could not be depressed sufficiently to hit us.

The periscope ducked under. Sixty-five feet. Seventy feet. My fingers found the button to lower the periscope.

"Abandon the conning tower!"

Too late! I heard the lower hatch bang shut. The peremptory commands of the collision sirens had to be obeyed without regard to consequences. Peterson, the steersman and I were locked in the conning tower.

The periscope was coming down. Suddenly it jammed and stopped. The periscope motor spat fire and sparks. The submarine heeled way over to port. I was thrown off my feet and landed on my knees on the conning-tower deck. Through the little conning-tower eye ports I could actually see the great bulk of the underwater hull of the battleship as she rolled us along her keel.

Eighty feet. The ship rolled back to an even keel. In my ears I could hear the loud thump of the screws. She had passed.

"Four knots! Rudder amidships." I could hear the hiss of air as Scotty fought against the incoming sea in the forward engine room. We were at a hundred feet. In a few minutes we could hear the left column of battleships, following in the wake of the center, passing directly over us.

"I can't control her much longer at this depth, captain," Scotty reported by voice tube from the control room.

We had to hold on a couple of more minutes. The noise of the screws receded.

"Fifty-five feet."

I jumped to my second periscope. It vibrated and wobbled, but it went up. Scotty was at his wit's end trying to keep her under control. The forward engine room was half flooded.

When I finally did get a look, I couldn't understand at first what had happened. My first target, I knew, was done for. She was limping along to the northward, but already her quarter-deck was awash and she had a bad list to port. She wouldn't limp far.

My stern-tube shots had missed. The center column of ships had turned right to avoid them. The left column had followed in their wake. And both columns had steamed smack into the torpedo fire of the destroyers.

They had jumped out of the frying pan into the fire. They found themselves in a sea alive with torpedoes. A hundred and fifty torpedoes were in the water. Their courses crisscrossed and interlaced in a mad pattern. It was impossible to dodge. Into the melee our battleships poured heavy shells in an unrelenting hail.

It was a confused picture that met my eyes. The enemy fleet had lost all semblance of a formation. Only a few ships could manage to continue firing their main batteries. In the mix-up, many ships masked the fire of the others. I watched in fascination.

I saw one salvo land three hits on a big battleship, well bunched up near the bridge. There was a rose-red bloom of shell bursts against heavy armor. The ship seemed to stagger under the blow. Then a great column of smoke arose from her deck, completely obscuring her from my eyes. It rose higher and higher; above her masts, two hundred feet in the air, the pillar of smoke and dust arose, before it spread out in a great mushroom. One of the ship's boats, the size of a small yacht, tumbled slowly over and over in the smoke.

The smoke clouds slowly disappeared. Beneath it was a boiling sea. Forty thousand tons of ship had disappeared from the face of the earth. High-explosive shells must have found her magazines. Strangely, I had no feeling of exhilaration at this success we so greatly needed. Rather I felt depressed at seeing more than a thousand men meet such a sudden death. A ship that seamen had cherished and served, and that they had so valiantly fought to the last bitter end, was now junk at the bottom of the sea.

The destroyers' torpedoes had found targets in no less than three of the enemy's battleships. No one ever knew exactly how many hits had actually been scored. But all organized resistance had been broken. A beaten fleet scattered and retreated on northerly courses. Admiral Barston was right after them in pursuit. He needed not only victory but annihilation.

As the battle receded a safe distance to the northward, I surfaced. The battery was about done for again. There would be no enemy ships to the southward, but our own ships were nearly as dangerous to me. All submarines look alike to a hard-pressed battleship in action. It would be the irony of fate to bring the Ocelot through all her trials and tribulations, only to have her sunk by one of our own ships.

I steamed on south. From the periscope shears I flew the largest set of colors I could find. Number One Periscope lay bent over at right angles over the bridge. The bridge rail was dented and torn where it had rubbed along the side of the battleship. Slowly Scotty got the upper hand of the flood in the forward engine room.

A couple of destroyers limped past me, northward bound. They were the cripples of the destroyer attack, still vainly trying to keep up with the battle after shell fire had ripped them nearly to pieces and reduced their speed to a crawl.

Soon I found one destroyer that was unable to steam at all.

I moved over close to her and established my identification. She would welcome my proximity because it didn't seem likely she could float much longer, and I felt much safer standing by her. Passing ships wouldn't be so likely to open fire on us by mistake.

Steadily we charged our batteries. Daylight darkened into dusk. Late in the evening our listening radio picked up what is probably one of the shortest battle reports on record:

"Enemy battle fleet has been annihilated."

We are back at the Seven Islands anchorage now. Some of

us are back. There are yawning gaps in the ordered ranks of our anchorage. We lost three great battleships, and half of the remaining eight had to be withdrawn to navy yards for extensive repairs. Scores of destroyers and cruisers limped into the nearest ports, days late, their crews exhausted by the unremitting fight against the sea. There is not an arm of the fleet but has suffered losses almost overwhelming.

The repair ships bustle with activity. The tankers hurry about refueling the fleet. The fleet is preparing again to take up the intolerable burden. Soon we will sail again to draw tight the net of a relentless blockade. A blockade that will cut the enemy's expeditionary force until failing munitions and supplies drive them back again into the sea from whence they came; a blockade that will bring the pinch of starvation to a whole nation, that will cut off her raw materials until, one by one, the wheels of her industries stop turning. Defeat for her is certain now. I only hope that she will see it so while, in the flush of a quickly won victory, we are disposed to grant a generous peace.

The wardroom radio is turned on the short wave from home. Already the air is filled with the yammering and bombast of the politicians—boasting men who never saw a ship go down with all her crew, who never committed the naked body of a comrade to the cold waters of the sea. They are building up barriers of hate that will leave the task to do all over again for another generation.

The whole nation is hysterical with joy. Only here in the victorious fleet there is no rejoicing. The colors hang dejectedly at half mast for those who sailed out with us, but did not return. Nearly every ship bears plainly the scars of battle.

I have just been over to the flagship to see my admiral. The whole world resounds with his praise. He has aged ten years in the past month, bowed down by the long nights of ceaseless vigilance and the weight of great responsibility. Sadly he inquired for news of his son. No man in either fleet had died more bravely. It was small comfort.

NIGHT ACTION

THE AFTERNOON I reported on board the Dodger my morale reached its all-time low. I hadn't wanted to leave the Armstown. I didn't consider that going from assistant gunnery officer of a new light cruiser to executive officer of a twenty-year-old destroyer was any step up in the world. Besides, the Armstown would be headed back home in a few days. Port Nelson was to her, and the other two light cruisers of her division, just a port of call. The Dodger was a part of the permanent squadron there. When I was ordered to the destroyer I faced a two-year tour of duty on the station, and I wasn't pleased at the prospect.

Now that I look back on it I can understand that there were more subtle reasons for my disgruntlement. When the word leaked out that an officer was to be detached from the Armstown to relieve someone being invalided home from one of the destroyers I hadn't any suspicion that it would affect me in the slightest. I suppose every member of a smooth-running organization, sooner or later, gets the feeling that he is an indispensable part of it. I had been a couple of years in the Armstown, and gradually I had come to feel a proprietary interest in everything that went on aboard her. It came as a shock and a surprise that she was going to get along very well without me. I suppose subconsciously I had expected at least a minor upheaval at my detachment. Nothing of the sort had happened. Both the gunnery officer and the executive officer had been genuinely sorry to see me go, but there was no glossing over the fact that the ship's routine continued to go along without any discernible hitch.

It was late in the afternoon when I got aboard the Dodger. The captain wasn't on board. Welles, the gunnery officer, had the duty, and he showed me my room and made me welcome on board. I had had duty in destroyers some years before. All of the old wartime destroyers are pretty much alike, and I had a good general idea of the layout of the ship. A few of the officers from the Armstown had tentative plans for dinner together that evening at the club, so I didn't stay aboard much longer than necessary to stow a portion of my outfit. I caught the five o'clock boat to the beach. Welles had told me that we were going down the bay at seven-thirty in the morning to fuel from the Emma Johnson, the station tanker. I intended to get back to the ship early.

A number of the officers from the Armstown were already in the club when I arrived. I ordered a drink and joined them, feeling more at home than I had all day.

"Did you see the selection board list, Steve?" someone inquired.

"No," I answered in surprise. "Is it out? Tell me all the hot dope."

"Mr. Durfee made it," the assistant engineer announced with a grin.

I got up and walked over to my old gunnery officer and shook his hand. "Congratulations, Commander," I told him. "Never any doubt about it of course, but it must be nice to have it behind you."

"Thanks a lot, Steve," Mr. Durfee acknowledged, "but save the 'commander' until I put on the stripes. There are still a few formalities to go through before I get them."

"Funny no one on board the Dodger mentioned the selection list," I remarked, resuming my seat.

"Probably isn't considered a fit topic of conversation in the Dodger," someone volunteered.

I looked up in surprise.

"Your new skipper, Lieutenant Commander Shears, was passed over," Durfee informed me.

There was a moment's strained silence, and then the conversation flowed on. The selection board was naturally the major topic, and I joined in as best I could. I couldn't rise to the defense of my new captain. I hadn't met the man. I didn't know anything about the reason for his pass-over and I didn't feel I could inquire too closely, but I kept my ears open. Mr. Durfee came over and sat beside me.

"How do you like your new skipper?" he asked.

"I haven't met him yet," I admitted. "He wasn't aboard when I reported, and I came ashore as soon as I had my things stowed."

"Shears is a fine officer," Durfee stated emphatically. "He's a classmate of mine, and I know. It's too bad that he has a knack of getting into trouble on the beach, but I am sorry to see him passed over. There he is right over there at that table in the corner. I'll take you over and introduce you in a minute."

While Durfee was finishing his drink I had an opportunity to look over my new commanding officer at long range. He was a big man in a white linen suit that fitted him just a little too quick, as though it had been tailored when he was about fifteen pounds lighter. His light-colored hair was getting a little thin on top. His face was round like a full moon, and there was a sort of puffy look under his eyes. They were doing a lot of talking at his table, and the skipper had a flushed appearance as though he had been drinking a little too much. I wasn't impressed.

After a little while Mr. Durfee and I got up and moved over to the other table. The skipper saw us coming and rose to meet us.

"Hello, Shears," Mr. Durfee greeted him. "How has the world been treating you these past three or four years?"

"No complaints," Shears answered. "Sit down and have a drink. And by the way, Commander, let me congratulate you on your selection. It's no more than you deserved, but it must be a comfortable feeling to have it over with."

Mr. Durfee shook his proffered hand and said simply, "Thanks, Doug." I could see that he was embarrassed. He hesitated an instant and then added: "I was sorry to see that your name was not on the list. It takes all the joy out of selection to see good men like yourself passed over. The board has to make some mistakes, and there will always be another board next year."

"Think nothing of it," Shears replied. "We can't all be admirals. The selection board has to let the ax fall somewhere, and this wasn't exactly unexpected, you know."

"I haven't time to stay long," Mr. Durfee said. "I just wanted to say hello and introduce your new exec. This is Lieutenant Wiston, Captain. He has been my assistant gunnery officer for two years. I would like to keep him with me, but I've just been telling him how lucky he is to get ordered to the Dodger with you."

"You would have to be a fast talker to charm a man off a homeward-bound cruiser and make him like it," Shears laughed, shaking hands with me.

"Sorry I wasn't aboard to meet you this afternoon," he continued, addressing me. "I hope you made out all right."

"Yes, sir," I answered. "No trouble at all. I had a little unfinished business on the beach, so I came ashore as soon as I had moved in."

"Pull up a chair and let the boy have your order," Captain Shears invited. "You're just in time to join the feast of the 'pass-over.' "

I asked to be excused, pleading that I had a dinner party all arranged. That was that. I was glad to get away. I didn't like the looks of the party that seemed to be building up around the skipper, and under the circumstances I felt just a mite uncomfortable in his presence.

Our dinner party turned out to be a quiet affair. I suppose I wouldn't have been good company that evening anyway, but the news about the selection board further dampened my spirits. There was no way of telling how his pass-over would affect my new skipper. Some take it philosophically and some take it hard, but any way you figure it, it's a fearful jolt to a man's pride to be passed over. The selection up to commander is always a pretty severe elimination. There just isn't room on the commanders' list for all the good lieutenant commanders, but I suppose that anyone with any gumption always figures that he, at least, is deserving of promotion. It's a trying time for all concerned. You never know whether to offer your sympathy or just keep quiet about the whole affair.

The victim must know that everybody in the service is holding post-mortems on the list. For everyone who thinks an injustice has been done, there will be three who adopt a superior air and profess to find ample reason for the board's action. Every skipper who has been passed over must be aware that his junior officers are discussing the selection behind his back. It would take a good man to maintain a happy, taut ship under the circumstances.

I didn't have much to say all evening but I kept my eyes and ears open, and I wasn't very long in finding out what I wanted to know. It seems that my new skipper had a wide reputation for being a hell raiser on the beach. His wife tried to keep him down, but she wasn't always around and she wasn't always successful when she was. At no time did I hear anyone say anything reflecting on his ability as an officer; but he seemed to have a talent for getting into trouble when he was ashore. In a way that was reassuring, but I wasn't too happy about it.

I got back to the ship at midnight and turned in. I was up early in the morning to supervise getting the ship ready to get under way. The gunnery officer reported that there was one absentee in the deck force, but I was mainly concerned with the continued absence of the skipper. I hadn't met the division commander as yet, and I didn't want the job of reporting to him, at our first meeting, that the skipper was not aboard at sailing time. None of the other officers seemed at all concerned. They seemed to have every confidence in the skipper despite all the stories I had heard the night before.

Captain Shears got back at about seven. He came out in a shore boat looking none the worse for wear. I don't know where he could have spent the night in Port Nelson, but wherever it was it didn't seem to have affected him much. He went below, and I suppose he must have bathed and shaved because he came up on the bridge about five minutes before we were to get under way looking as fresh as a daisy.

The turbines had been warmed up. We had steam up to the throttles and the crew was all at its stations. I reported to him that we were ready to get under way. He put his finger in the collar of his white uniform blouse and pulled out hard, stretching and craning his neck as though his collar was too tight. Then he looked casually around the bridge and walked over to each bridge wing to assure himself that the destroyers on either side were standing by the lines.

"Very well, Wiston," he said. "I'll handle her today. Take in all lines."

The lines came snaking in and I reported all clear.

"Rudder amidships, all engines back one-third." He walked back and forth across the bridge, watching both sides as the ship slid out of the nest. The mud started churning up astern. The bow was hardly clear of the nest before he swung her neatly on her heel. By the time we hit the breakwater entrance we were making ten knots.

He had nothing to say to anyone on the bridge. I suspect he was harboring a hang-over, but he didn't seem to be grouchy and the bridge personnel worked as smooth as silk. Handy, the chief quartermaster, had the wheel. Half the time the skipper didn't bother to give his orders to the engine order telegraph man. He just walked by and gave the handles a flip to where he wanted them, saying nothing to anyone, with the apparent assumption that the ship would do exactly what he wanted her to.

It didn't take us long to get down the bay. The Emma Johnson was lying head to the wind, and there was plenty of clear water astern of her. The captain took the Dodger around in a wide sweep. It seemed to me that he held his speed on the approach overlong. We weren't more than two hundred yards astern of her when he stopped his engines. We came coasting in at a good clip, the sides of the Emma seemed to be sliding by like the view out of an express train window. The skipper walked over to the engine order telegraphs and flipped them back to Full Astern. It was like putting the brakes on a speeding automobile. He stood there, watching the deck of the tanker. At just the right moment he flipped up the handles to Stop. On the deck the lines were already going over.

The captain leaned over the bridge rail and shouted down to the chief engineer on deck.

"How are we lined up for the fueling hose, Chief?"

"That's just right," the chief engineer called back.

The captain walked off the bridge. I could see Handy grinning at me over the wheel. Everybody seemed to be in a good humor. There is nothing a crew appreciates more than a good piece of ship handling, and we had just seen one of those "one bell landings" you hear about and seldom see.

"This ship would jump through a hoop for the old man," Handy confided to me with an obvious feeling of pride.

We were fueled in a few hours. The trip back to the harbor was just like the one out except that we had a difficult landing to make to get tied up again with the division. There was a mud bank close under the stern by our buoy, and the ship had to be spun around in her own length to get alongside. By the time we were secured I could appreciate that Handy was right about the "Old Man's" ability to handle the ship, and I commenced to feel a little glow of pride in the Dodger and her performance.

As soon as we got back in the nest the man who had been absent in the morning reported on board. He was a second-class boatswain's mate by the name of Lewis, and of course I had never seen him before and knew nothing of him. He looked pretty disheveled and shamefaced, and I thought his explanation was weak. Welles, the gunnery officer, seemed quite concerned about the man and the trouble he had gotten himself into. There wasn't anything I could do but hold him over for captain's mast in the morning.

The skipper went ashore before dinner. He was the only officer who did, and I was glad to stay aboard and get acquainted with my new shipmates. There was Welles, who was quite talkative and gay, and Marley, the chief engineer, who was quite the opposite. The torpedo officer and the communication officer were both young ensigns, and so was the assistant engineer. I could sense that they were sizing up their new executive officer, but they didn't have much to say.

We steered shy of the subject of selection boards as a topic of conversation but I wasn't long in sensing that, to a man, they liked and admired their skipper. Of course they were bound not to say a word against him, but the feeling was deeper than that. They had the repeated evidence of their own observation that he was the best ship handler in the squadron. They evidently also considered him the best destroyer commander, and I didn't know who would have a better opportunity to judge.

I still entertained some doubts. Everybody knew why Douglas R. Shears was passed over, but everyone I had heard express an opinion seemed sorry to have it happen. The Navy certainly has a right to expect reasonably good conduct from its officers no matter where they may be, but on the other hand officers with the ability of the captain are hard to come by in any Navy. After all, if promotion had always been made on the basis of conduct on the beach Nelson would never have been more than a post captain.

The skipper held mast in the morning. Welles went up to mast along with Lewis and me. The gunnery officer had told me the night before that Lewis was one of his gun captains. He was interested in the case because he was worried about what the captain would do at mast. According to Welles, Lewis was a good man aboard ship, but about every three months or so he went off on a bender. He had been rated second class only a few months before, and Welles was afraid that this little incident would be enough to bust him.

The captain held mast in his cabin. Lewis appeared spick-and-span in a white uniform with a couple of blue hash marks on his sleeve. I read the charge and presented the service record to the captain. The captain asked Lewis if he had anything to say for himself.

"Nothing worth saying, Captain," he replied. "I must have just overslept, that's all. I missed the liberty boat and I didn't have any money. The beach guard staked me to the price of a shore boat. By the time I got out here you had already gone down the bay to fuel."

The gunnery officer tried to say a few words in the man's favor. The skipper listened attentively. I liked the idea of Welles going to bat for his man, but there wasn't an awful lot he could say and I suspect the skipper already knew more about Lewis and his troubles than Welles did.

"Drunk?" the captain asked.

"Yes, sir," Lewis answered. "The night before. I was sober when I came down to the dock in the morning, sir."

Knowing the skipper's reputation and remembering my own worry about him that same morning, I just didn't know what to expect then. Technically I suppose the man was guilty of "missing ship" although we had only moved down the bay and back.

"Lewis," the captain said to him, "you know and I know what liquor will do to a man. You are certainly old enough to manage your own affairs. Your conduct on the beach is your own business so long as you do not bring disgrace on the uniform you wear. There is no evidence of that. Not being ready for duty is something else again. That I will not stand for."

I felt as though the captain had expressed his own code of conduct. Lewis must have understood. He stood there without one word in answer.

"Five days solitary confinement on bread and water with a full ration the third day," the captain pronounced sentence.

"Make out a letter of committal and send him over to the Deneb for execution of the sentence," he directed me, and mast was over.

I was a little dubious about the sentence, but it was legal enough. In the fleet they didn't give petty officers sentences of bread and water. If a rated man turned out to be unreliable he was disrated. I didn't say anything. It wasn't any of my business if they ran things differently in this squadron. I had a feeling that Captain Shears had his own ideas about how to maintain discipline, and that it would take pretty strong pressure to make him alter them.

Welles must have sensed my disapproval. I went down to the little cubbyhole of an office to get the yeoman started on the necessary paper work. After it was finished I dropped into the wardroom for a midmorning cup of coffee. Welles found me there.

"That's just the kind of a sentence Lewis needed," he said to me. "Lord knows I had hard enough time making him keep his record clean long enough to make second class. I didn't want to see him busted right away. He is one of my best gun captains."

I didn't say anything.

"When his five days are up he'll come back aboard and do the work of three men. He will take his punishment without a grumble, and that will be the last trouble we will have with him for a long time," he explained.

The discussion didn't get very far because the torpedo officer came into the wardroom just then to announce that the Regina was standing in. That effectively changed the subject of our conversation. The Regina, a modern light cruiser, was station flagship. The Admiral's mission was almost as much diplomatic as it was military, and the Regina rarely operated with the rest of the squadron. She hadn't been expected in Port Nelson for another two weeks.

"I hope that doesn't mean there is going to be trouble," Welles remarked wistfully.

I hoped so too, but I knew enough of the situation to be apprehensive. International politics had been in a state of turmoil for a long time. It had seemed for a while that things were rapidly coming to a head, but lately there had been a quiet spell. Perhaps it had been the lull before the storm. There had been endless wardroom discussions in the Armstown, but for the past few days I had been so concerned with my personal affairs that I hadn't been following the trend of events.

A few of the officers of the Armstown had professed to be concerned over the position of the light-cruiser division with the international situation being what it was. It would be extremely easy for the enemy to interpose any force he chose between Port Nelson and the fleet based on Hastings. Torcas, the only port between Hastings and Port Nelson, was weakly defended. If it fell the squadron out here would be effectively cut off until the fleet could capture new bases and consolidate its position. Under the circumstances, they contended, a light-cruiser division was too weak to do anything effective and still too valuable to risk away from any possibility of support. The fleet would badly need all its light cruisers if it had to fight its way to the relief of Port Nelson.

The great majority of the Armstown officers pooh-poohed the fears of the "nervous Nellies." They had seen worse situations build up, blow over and be forgotten. Anyway the light cruisers could outrun anything they couldn't outshoot, so why worry about it? It was difficult to imagine those superb ships getting into a situation they could not deal with effectively. My own views were those of the majority, but lately I had made a few disquieting observations.

When the cruiser division first dropped anchor in Port Nelson we had been surprised to find so many of the destroyers tied up to the buoys in the harbor. There were two destroyer divisions, twelve old four-stackers on the station. We discov-

ered immediately that they were all in port. That looked as
though there was no excitement at Port Nelson, but as soon
as I had joined the Dodger I learned that the opposite view
could be taken. For weeks the destroyers had been maintaining a patrol of the northern approaches. Suddenly they had
been recalled. All their operation orders had been canceled,
and new ones had been issued in their place. No one in the
destroyers knew what was going to happen next. The submarines continued their patrol, returning occasionally for fuel,
provisions and overhaul. There was a squadron of patrol
planes at Port Nelson. Some of them seemed to be constantly
in the air.

The Regina came right on in and dropped anchor inside
the breakwater. As soon as her hook was down there was a
traffic jam of small boats off her gangway. Admiral Thompson
from my old cruiser division went aboard to pay his official
call on the Commander in Chief of the station, and all the
division commanders of the destroyers and submarines followed right behind him. From what happened immediately
afterward I gathered their calls were not social.

Our own division commander was back within an hour. He
apparently didn't lose much time in passing the dope to the
commanding officers. The skipper came back from his conference with the division commander with fire in his eye and
about as conversational as a clam. As soon as he was aboard
we began to strip ship.

You would have thought there wasn't much to be done on
the Dodger. For the past couple of months she had been cruising with war heads on her torpedoes, detonators in her depth
charges and service ammunition ready at the guns. Nevertheless we still had a lot of stuff to get off her. It's surprising
what a ship carries in peacetimes that you can really get along
without. We pulled out everything that was inflammable and
that we didn't really need.

The next day the work of stripping ship went merrily on.
We were getting rid of everything that did not contribute

directly to the fighting efficiency of the ship: the boats, boxes of filed correspondence, wooden furniture, the movie projector, all the paint out of the paint lockers, everything we didn't need immediately. About noontime the Navy Yard sent over a string of barges, and we piled the accumulation aboard them. With some misgivings I watched the trunk with my dress uniforms go with the rest. Weighed in the scales of war they were not of any great value; but they represented a considerable investment to me. I hope nobody accidentally dropped them over the side.

The maelstrom of work into which we were all flung gave me an opportunity to get better acquainted with the skipper. Because of my unfamiliarity with the ship and everything in her, I am afraid that I wasn't very much help to him. He was patience itself with me. He was all over the ship at once, taking on my job as well as his own, laughing and joking with the men as well as the officers. I went along with him because it was the easiest way of learning my new job. He knew every man on board, and what his job was. There was very little that he found to censure and much that he found to praise. His intimate knowledge of every inch of the ship was something to marvel at. He made a point of introducing me to all the key men, and I found that I was glad to be back in a small ship where an officer can learn to know every man in her. Slowly it dawned on me that the men as well as the officers practically worshiped the skipper.

At dinner that night we had our first real opportunity to discuss the situation. The skipper sat at the head of the table, amused at our wild conjectures, but carefully volunteering no information. Speculation ran all the way from it being just another drill to the possibility of an all-out attack on the enemy bases. The cruisers had spent the day fueling. I was of the opinion that our fate was inevitably bound up with theirs. If anything was going to break, those cruisers would dash back to rejoin the battle fleet. In event of war, they would need an anti-submarine screen whenever they put to sea. I felt sure that we would escort them back at least as far as Torcas.

Marley, the chief engineer, was a dyed-in-the-wool pessimist. He always took the darkest view of everything. I don't know if he was born that way or if the attitude had slowly grown upon him through his job of keeping the old can running. The skipper evidently enjoyed drawing him out. The chief was always predicting calamity yet somehow always managing to keep the engineering plant running at the peak of efficiency. It was easy to see that there was a deep-seated affection between the captain and the chief engineer, but even Marley was unable to worm any information out of the skipper.

Early the next morning the Commander in Chief shifted his flag to the submarine tender Deneb. That was the most ominous note of all. The Deneb was an old tub, whose only military value lay in the spare parts and Diesel fuel she carried for the submarines. Shifting the flag to her meant inconveniences for the staff, and staffs don't like inconveniences. The hope that it was to be just another drill was ended. The Regina went down the bay to fuel.

Toward noon we got a signal from the Deneb, now flying the big flag: "Cruiser division seven plus Regina and destroyer divisions nine and ten will depart for Hastings by way of Torcas at seventeen hundred."

After that there was no more communication with the beach. What we needed to finish out our wardroom stores we drew off the Deneb, so even the stewards didn't get ashore again. The news went through the ship like wildfire. I think everybody felt glad to be leaving Port Nelson behind.

About two o'clock in the afternoon a boat from the Deneb pulled up to the gangway, and out jumped my old friend Lewis.

"Reporting for duty, sir," he said to me with a snappy salute.

I had been talking with the gunnery officer on deck. When

I looked a little uncertain, Welles pleaded, "We need him, Mr. Wiston."

"That's something for the captain to decide," I told them. "Let's get it over with right now."

The skipper was up in the charthouse, so the three of us marched right up to the bridge.

"It's you again, Lewis," the skipper said, looking up from the charts. "What are you doing here? By my count you've got three more days to do on your sentence."

"Yes, sir," Lewis answered. "I talked them into letting me come over to see you, sir. I heard you were going to sail."

"What has that got to do with it?" the captain snapped back at him.

"Nothing, sir," the boatswain's mate replied. "I'd like to sail with you."

"You haven't got good sense, Lewis," Captain Shears told him. "Nobody in his right mind would give up a good clean cell in the brig with plenty of bread and water three times a day to make a destroyer trip like we are going on."

"No, sir," Lewis agreed.

"All right," the captain yielded. "Put him to work. But remember this, Lewis, the first port we hit, back in the brig you go to finish out your sentence."

"Yes, sir," Lewis accepted.

I could see that he was anxious to let it go at that, so I got him out of the charthouse as fast as I could.

There wasn't any fuss about getting under way. It was all done very quietly. As far as anyone on the beach might be aware we were just stepping out for a little target practice, but we left the harbor pretty empty after we pulled out. The Deneb was still there, bravely flying an admiral's flag but an old tub for all that. A little farther down the bay was the old Emma Johnson, now riding high after fueling the cruisers and destroyers. She has been due for the junk pile for a long time. The patrol planes and the submarines were out operating, so that the base had been denuded of anything of military value.

We steamed down the bay toward the sunset over Mount Tabor. It was beautiful. The fortified heights of Pearl Island loomed across the entrance to the bay. To the northward the red light of the Nun flashed in the gathering darkness, and to the south we could see the steady white light of the Monk. I felt wonderfully elated to leave them all behind.

I wonder how the Commander in Chief felt, watching us go. We were stripping him of the major part of his naval force. Nearly all his mobile gun power went with us. If war came he could only hold on as long as possible and wait for the fleet to come out. The coast forts were strong enough to discourage direct attack. The submarines and planes could keep him from being closely invested. As long as he held on, the fleet would have a base from which they could operate when they did arrive. The enemy would be certain to try to wrest it from him. Without the fleet he couldn't hold out forever. Rarely has an outlying base, without active fleet support, been able to hold out long against a determined attack.

As soon as we cleared the bay, Admiral Thompson, the commander of the cruiser division, took charge of the detachment. The cruisers were in column. My division and two destroyers from the other division were in the close anti-submarine screen. The four other destroyers formed a line sweeping the path of the detachment far up ahead. The Dodger was second ship in the starboard screen, and before long she was living up to her name. The whole force zigzagged, and on top of the zigzags the destroyers wove in and out, ahead and back, patrolling their stations. Just before sunset we received orders that all ships would be darkened and that the close anti-submarine screen would stay in position until the moon set.

We went to general quarters shortly before the end of evening twilight. After that it was watch and watch for the rest of the night, and we settled down to the routine that we would follow for the rest of the trip. Half the ship's company turned in. Half the battery was manned. Half the engineers force stayed on watch. The cold boiler room was manned, ready to work up to full steam on short notice. I was to stand the night watches on the bridge with the communication officer as my relief. The gunnery officer and the torpedo officer split the watch at the fire control station on top of the bridge. The chief engineer and his assistant relieved each other in the engineroom. There wasn't much light from the moon, but evidently Admiral Thompson considered that there might be enough to enable a submarine to sneak in. We kept our close anti-submarine screen as long as the moon was up.

I hoped that the men off watch slept well. I confess I dozed off only now and then when it came my turn to go below. When you are in a close screen, zigzagging, with darkened ship, it takes a lot of faith in the people on the bridge to let a man do much sound sleeping. All the deck force sleep up forward. The wardroom country is up there too. Outside the thin steel plates you can hear the rush of the sea. Up in the forward "Guinea Pullman" the ship's sides slope in and forward, conforming to the shape of the bow. A dozen men sleep there in close-packed bunks, one above another. It's two decks up to get out on deck and a long haul aft to the first hatch. You can't avoid a feeling that you are being rammed through the water and that your life depends on that sharp bow meeting nothing solid. It isn't much better for the men back aft, with the bunks vibrating and shaking with the rhythm of the pounding screws. There is just as much danger of being cut down by the next stern as there is in ramming the next ahead.

Up on the bridge in the uncertain light you can make out the bulk of the cruiser on the port beam. You can see a dark blur three or four hundred yards ahead. It's the destroyer ahead of you in the screen. The next astern you hope will take care of herself. No lights. No stadimeter now to help you keep in position. It's all a matter of judgment on the part of the officer of the deck. You glance up at the luminous dial of the clock. A little over a minute to go for the next zig. You dare not take your eyes off the cruiser and the destroyer ahead for more than a second. Your eyes must stay focused to the uncertain light.

"Thirty seconds to go, sir," the quartermaster warns.

The second hand crawls up toward the vertical.

"Left standard rudder." The ship heels to the rudder. Down below in their bunks the men will roll slightly to port. They will half awaken, wondering if this is a standard zigzag turn or if the ship is sheering out to avoid collision. Dreamily they will count off the seconds. No collision alarm. They doze off to sleep again.

You watch the cruiser to see if she will start her swing on time. If she doesn't you will be pulling across her bows in another minute. She is just a dark blur. It's hard to see when she starts to change her course. Then you can see the angle between her masts closing. She is swinging. Every ship in the formation is coming around to the new zigzag course. No signals. It's all on time. And if a single ship misses her cue there will be chaos, confusion and possibly worse.

"Ease the rudder. Steady as you go."

The turn will bring you in toward the cruiser. You will have to steer a slightly diverging course for a while until you have regained your position about a thousand yards out on her beam. The shadow ahead appears fainter and farther away. You have lost distance on the turn. You call for ten more turns from the engineroom to catch up. Now you are safely off on the new leg of the zig. You have only to hold your position for another five or six minutes and then it will be time for the next zig. And so it goes as the watch drags slowly on.

The skipper sits on a high-backed stool on the port side of the bridge. He hasn't left the bridge since we got under way. The mess boy brought him his dinner on a tray. He hasn't much to say. He watches the officer of the deck maneuver the ship. He is there to take over any second that he thinks things aren't going just right. Occasionally he tells the officer of the deck to take off a few turns if he thinks we are getting too close to the next ahead, or he orders him to sheer in a little farther if it appears we are getting outside our station. Sometimes I think he dozes a little, but any unusual move or motion will bring him up sharply. The skipper of a ship is like the mother of a very young baby. Nothing can ever relieve him of the certainty of his responsibilities. Even when he sleeps his vigilance never relaxes.

When the moon set we stopped zigzagging and changed our formation. The screen from our side pulled up and prolonged the line ahead. The port screen dropped back into column astern. It was too dark then to make out a ship at a thousand yards and there was too much danger that a screening vessel might be mistaken for an enemy. It was a relief not to have to change course so frequently, but we closed up the destroyer formation three hundred yards, and even then it was hard to make out the next ahead. I went off watch at midnight. I was tired enough to sleep no matter what happened topside.

At four o'clock when I came back on watch we were still in a long column formation. The skipper was still in his seat as I had left him.

"Good morning, Wiston," he greeted me.

I couldn't see much of anything good about it until the bridge messenger brought me a bowl of steaming coffee. It took some minutes for my eyes to get accustomed to the darkness. When I could make out the next ahead and the next astern I relieved the communication officer, and he seemed glad enough to leave the bridge. In two more hours he would have to be up again for general quarters.

At the first gray light of dawn we skipped back into our screening position. As the sea grew light you could feel the bridge personnel relax. How grateful you can be for such a small thing as enough light to see by!

There is something mystical about a dawn at sea, on a group of ships steaming in formation. Slowly the shadowy monsters that have been crowding around you in the darkness are changed by the dawn light into friendly familiar ships. You recognize each vessel in turn as the increasing visibility discloses it. Through the long night you have been able to see but dimly your nearest neighbor. Somehow it seems surprising to see the formation again intact, each ship where it should be and the whole equal to the sum of its parts. There is a sense of newness about familiar things. The big cruisers seem grayer and cleaner. They stand out sharply against the dark blue of the sea. The immensity of the great ocean, suddenly again reaching from horizon to horizon, dwarfs the little ships creeping slowly across it.

We went to general quarters just before dawn. My own battle station was on the bridge. Half the crew were already at their stations. The rest roused out sleepy-eyed from bunks they had hardly had a chance to warm since they came off the midwatch. We didn't keep them long at their stations. As soon as we were sure there were no strange ships in the vicinity of our formation, we secured. The men had to get some rest during the day, and the never-ending business of a ship's life had to keep going on.

After we were all buttoned up and steadied down on the daylight routine, the skipper paced up and down the bridge for a while to stretch his legs after the long night's vigil.

"I think I'll go below for a minute," he said to me, "and have breakfast like a gentleman in the wardroom. If I have time I'll get a hot bath before I come up again. Give me a shout over the voice tube if there is anything interesting happening."

We had had comparatively little conversation all the watch. That night was the first time I had stood a watch on a destroyer in quite a few years. Naturally I was a little nervous at first, but it seemed to come back to me easily enough. I felt a glow of satisfaction that he was willing to leave me alone on the bridge so soon. He must have liked the way I had been handling the ship. Life can be just bearable for a destroyer skipper if he has an executive officer he can trust.

Without that confidence he never has a moment's rest. I felt we were going to get along all right.

He was back in about an hour. The mess boy came up and made up the folding bunk over the chart desk in the chart-house. The skipper took off his shoes, shucked his blouse, and turned in. From there he could hear everything that was happening on the bridge, and he could be out and in charge in a matter of seconds. That way he could get a little rest, but it would be too much to say that he could be comfortable. The accommodations would be a disgrace to a first-class county jail. I'd have to be in and out to get the charts as soon as I was relieved, and the listener stood a constant watch in there listening for submarines.

After I came off watch I worked out the star sights I had caught while I had been on watch. I hadn't been navigating lately, and it took me longer than it should. By the time I was through, it was time to get a shot at the sun, so it was nearly ten o'clock before I had had my breakfast and had a chance to lie down a little while myself.

A short time after I came off watch, and while I was still on the bridge working out my navigation, the flagship signaled over to expect contact with our patrol planes. It wasn't long after the message came in that one of the planes came over, coming up from astern and passing right over the formation to disappear again ahead. It was the only one we saw, but I suppose it was one of a scouting line, sweeping the area to seaward of us.

Nothing much happened all day. I had the four-to-eight watch in the afternoon. The cruisers catapulted four planes in the late afternoon, and they scouted ahead over the sea area we should pass through during the night. We picked up the planes again just before evening general quarters. As long as the weather stayed calm enough to permit recovery operations, we should be able to keep reasonably good security against surprise by surface ships. That wouldn't stop submarines from getting in, but it was the destroyers' business to attend to them.

For the first couple of days I felt as though I shouldn't be able to last out the trip. After that I dropped into the old routine of catching a moment's sleep, any time, anywhere I could. The main trouble was that there wasn't enough time available. It got so I didn't think of the end of the voyage at all. I set my mind on the completion of each watch, each hour. After all, what I had to put up with was nothing alongside what the skipper had to endure. He was never off the bridge more than an hour or so each day, and the rest he was able to get in the charthouse must have been pretty sketchy. As long as he could stand it, there wasn't much reason for the rest of us to complain.

The third night out we had a little excitement in the Dodger. I suppose something like it was bound to occur sooner or later. After it was all over I had a little more confidence in my ability to handle an emergency. Also I had a better appreciation of what it was to work with a man like Captain Shears.

We were still in close screened formation when it happened, but a cloud had momentarily obscured the moon and it was dark as the inside of your hat. It had to be just then that the time came to change course to the new leg of a zig. It was a pretty wide change too. I knew it was coming and I closed up on the next ahead as far as I dared, so I would be sure to see him as he came around. Everybody started the turn on time and it looked as though everything was going to come out all right. The next ahead of us was but a dark blot, and the course change had put him up on my port bow. I had just gotten around to my new course and eased the rudder when I could see that something had gone wrong. The next ahead kept coming right around and before you could say Jack Robinson she was right across my bow. I think the rudder jammed. She snapped on her dimmed running lights and gave me five toots on her whistle.

By that time I had my hands full. I threw the rudder hard left, backed full on my port screw and went ahead on the starboard, intending to pass astern of her. That must have been the right thing to do, for the skipper was on his toes right beside me and the only thing he did was to tell the quartermaster to turn on our dimmed running lights. We passed under her stern so close I could see the white water boiling around her stern as she tried to check her swing with the screws.

By that time we were under the bow of one of the cruisers. It had to be my luck that it was the flagship. Her great sharp bow loomed right over us. I called for full ahead on both screws. Even then I thought for a minute that she would cut through our stern. I suppose she was doing everything she could to avoid us but it seemed she was coming right in toward us as inevitable as death itself. My heart was in my mouth.

The skipper, standing at my elbow, as cool as ice, said: "I'll relieve you, Wiston. Left full rudder." We heeled way over under the rudder and it seemed to me that the stern walked sideways away from the looming bows of the cruiser.

She missed us by inches. The skipper checked her swing with the engines and rudder, and we passed down the port side of the flagship so close I could have tossed a spud onto her quarter-deck. Then there was the port screen to worry about. If we overran too much we should be right into them. But Captain Shears brought the Dodger sharp around the flagship's stern, and at full speed ahead brought her right back through the cruiser line and back into position.

As soon as we were back in position all ships snapped off the running lights. I was still in a cold sweat. The moon came out again and we could see a little more. Down at the forecastle gun I could see a knot of men standing together looking questioningly up at the bridge. I think quite a few men had jumped out of their bunks and made it up on the deck in time to see the final maneuver.

The captain put his hand on my shoulder. "You were doing all right, Wiston," he told me. "I didn't take her over because I'd lost confidence in you. But those cruisers get worried if it looks as though you are going to scratch up their paint work and you can never be certain how they will react. Anyway, if anyone gets huffy it would be better if I had the deck."

Just then we caught a blinker-tube message from the flagship: "Report signal number of your officer of the deck."

I don't suppose the Admiral had been able to see how it all started. You couldn't blame him for being mad enough to start looking around with a noose to slip over someone's neck. I felt that I should be able to justify my conduct in any investigation. I just started to tell the quartermaster my signal number when the skipper spoke up.

"Send the flagship my signal number," he directed the signalman.

"I've been expecting that signal," he said to me. "Now you can relieve me and take over the watch again."

He climbed back on his high stool as though he was satisfied with how that had been settled. "And when we get in I'll tell Admiral Thompson that if he has anyone over there he thinks could have handled it any better I'd like to meet him."

You can go to town for a guy like Douglas R. Shears. I don't give a damn what was on his record that made the selection board pass him over. There was an officer and a gentleman. I felt that I was becoming a part of the Dodger. She was a part of me, and the thing that welded us all together, ship and crew, in one strong and elastic whole, was the personality of the skipper. Quick to punish any dereliction of duty as he had proved himself in the Lewis case, I knew then that he stood ready to take on his own broad shoulders the entire responsibility for the actions of his subordinates. That fracas hadn't been my fault or his. The responsibility for the ship was his in any case, but it takes a man to stand up foursquare to criticism without trying to shift at least a portion of the blame to others. Moreover his handling of the ship had been a beautiful thing to witness. The Navy will search a long time before they find a more competent destroyer commander.

When I came off watch I met Marley in the wardroom. He had just been relieved in the engineroom.

"What was that tune you were trying to play on the engine order telegraph a while back?" he asked.

"That wasn't engine bells you heard," I told him. "That was the sound of harps at the pearly gates."

"I thought as much," Marley admitted. "I could tell the minute the Old Man grabbed the telegraph handles, and I knew you must have been in a tight spot."

It must be a nice feeling to be battened down in the engine and fire rooms, working like the very devil, and wondering all the time when the crash is coming and where it's going to be.

Late the next afternoon the blow fell. In the Dodger we intercepted a message from one of our submarines to our flagship, the Hastings.

"Enemy force consisting of transports, three heavy ships, cruisers and many destroyers, course one six five, speed fourteen."

We knew the position of the reporting submarine. That put an enemy expeditionary force seven hundred and fifty miles from Torcas and heading in its general direction. There was a possibility that he was going about his own peaceful business, but in the light of his past record it was much more probable that he had the intention of pinching off Torcas by way of a declaration of war. That's about all the declaration you get nowadays.

The message came in while I was off watch. After I had decoded it I took it up to the captain on the bridge. He pondered it awhile, cutting in the enemy's reported position and measuring off the distances on the chart.

"Humph!" he said at last. "Looks like we are going to have even more excitement than we bargained for, this trip."

"Maybe not, sir," I suggested. "There have been no hostile moves made yet. Maybe this is just some routine maneuver."

"That fellow's on the prowl, Wiston," the captain answered emphatically. "He has no business down here if he isn't. He's headed for Torcas, and there is no use closing our eyes to it."

I had to admit to myself that I was guilty of wishful thinking, trying to reason it out otherwise.

"The main question," he continued, "is, What are we going to do about it? You've been in Admiral Thompson's division long enough to know him, Wiston. What is he going to do, fight or run away?"

I didn't like his way of putting it. It sounded as though the Admiral had a reasonable choice. I didn't think that he had.

"I guess he would like to fight all right," I answered. "But what can he do? If he engages with the force he has he will only be throwing it away. I think he will avoid action and carry out his orders to join the battle fleet."

"His orders to join the battle fleet might salve his conscience, but I wouldn't be too happy about it if it was me," the skipper replied.

"I don't suppose Admiral Thompson is too happy about it either," I said; "but he can't be expected to accomplish the impossible."

"Convoys have been raided by inferior forces before," he reminded me. "With a fast mobile force like ours we ought to be able to drive the enemy admiral to distraction. If we just sneak off, Torcas is doomed within forty-eight hours."

"I still think it's too big a risk to take," I maintained.

"No risk, no gain," the skipper retorted. "Nobody ever won a battle keeping out of gun range. But neither you nor I will be consulted about the decision, so why should we argue about it?"

The captain had me convinced that we were in for trouble.

I spent the rest of my time off watch looking over the charts and reviewing what I knew of the situation. We had a battalion of Marines on Torcas. If the enemy was coming down on Torcas he was coming down in plenty of force. It looked as though they intended to sweep over the defenses before they could develop any effective resistance. It was like trying to drive a tack with a sledge hammer, but I don't know as I could blame him much for that. He would want to establish himself in an impregnable position as soon as he could, and he probably already knew that if he started to push the Marines around somebody was going to get hurt.

I was sorry for the Marines. For the past decade they had been sitting out there like a bump on a log, everybody knowing they would be the first to get it. They could have taken that as part of the hazards of their trade if they had been given the equipment to put up a decent fight. Instead they had only their field equipment and no planes. Their advice as to what was necessary to defend the place had been carefully disregarded for years. Now, exactly what they had foretold seemed about to take place. We have always been afraid to build up the defenses of Torcas for fear someone would put up a squawk. The Marines were going to pay for our indecision. I had a momentary feeling of unreasonable indignation. If we couldn't make up our minds to defend the place why couldn't we have had the grace to abandon it?

I didn't see what Admiral Thompson could do with the force he had. He was under orders to join the battle fleet as soon as he could. Those orders, of course, weren't absolutely binding now that there had been an unexpected development, but what else could he do? If he attacked the strong force now bearing down on Torcas he would only be wiped out, and no good whatever accomplished. Fortunately our force was compact and fast. He wouldn't have any difficulty avoiding action. The enemy was tied down to his convoy. Even if he found out we were in the vicinity there wasn't much doubt that we could get away from him. He didn't dare send too big a detachment against us for fear we might slip around him and chew up his convoy.

Our urgent problem was fuel. The destroyers had to be refueled at Torcas. At six o'clock that evening we were only four hundred and fifty miles from there. We could beat the enemy in, but whether we should have time to fuel and get out before he came down upon us was another question. It was a foregone conclusion that they had the entrance to the port under submarine observation. If we appeared there the enemy was bound to find out all about us. We could refuel at sea and continue on to Hastings by a circuitous route. We might be in for a bit of bombing if we were discovered, but if we cleared out during darkness we might avoid discovery. A force like ours could weather some severe bombing but damaged ships would be an awful embarrassment on the long haul to Hastings.

The message didn't make any immediate change in our disposition. We kept plodding right along toward Torcas. I had some misgivings that Admiral Thompson, too, was doing some wishful thinking. The evening flight of observation planes from the cruisers evidently got back without sighting anything. I rather expected the Admiral to change course to the southward during the night, but in the morning we were plugging right along toward Torcas, still making good our fleet speed of twelve knots. That brought the destroyers' average up to fourteen. If we went much faster we ran the risk of the destroyers running out of fuel before we got there.

By morning we had only three hundred miles to go. I thought the Admiral was holding on, hoping the enemy might turn back or we would get some kind of break. After all, there had yet been no open hostilities. We got no more reports from the submarines and we had no knowledge whatever of the enemy's movements during the night.

As soon as it was light in the morning we began fueling the

destroyers from the cruisers. Each cruiser fueled one destroyer at a time, and the rest of us formed a circular zigzagging screen around the fueling group. It was a pretty ticklish operation in view of the fact that we might expect some kind of enemy submarine activity against us. During the fueling each ship had to steer a straight course into the wind at dead slow speed. That made an ideal set-up for a raiding submarine, and everybody was pretty nervous until it was all over. It took most of the day to fuel all the destroyers.

I took the refueling to mean that we were going to avoid by running south, but the skipper pointed out that the destroyers would have to refuel anyway if we were going to attempt anything against the convoy. We had headed south after the refueling was over, but we didn't cover much ground in any direction that day. We steered a northerly course while fueling and the short run in the afternoon brought us back to just about where we were in the morning.

All that night we continued running south. A little before midnight Admiral Thompson broke radio silence to order the patrol planes at Torcas to be prepared to locate and trail the enemy at daylight. That was the first we had heard of the patrol planes being there. They must have continued right on out after passing over us that first day out of Port Nelson. He gave the enemy's most probable daylight position as three hundred miles from Torcas and in the northerly sector.

I still thought I could guess the Admiral's intentions. By daybreak there would be five or six hundred miles between opposing forces. We were running south, which was a good course to take us clear of all involvement. If he located the enemy with the patrol planes he would have the initiative, and we were almost certain that we hadn't been sighted. I was still sure he intended to avoid action. My deductions couldn't have led me any further from the truth. I don't believe that Admiral Thompson ever had the slightest idea of leaving Torcas in the lurch. He was just biding his time, waiting to strike when the enemy least expected it. If a favorable opportunity hadn't presented itself he would have created one. The skipper had him sized up better than I had.

At seven o'clock in the morning of the 7th we got our first patrol plane report. The enemy was two hundred and ninety miles due north of Torcas. We were then about three hundred miles to the southwest of the port. There was no longer any doubt about the enemy's intention. Soon after the contact report came in, even I could no longer doubt what Admiral Thompson intended to do. We changed course directly for Torcas. He had had his best opportunity to avoid and he was deliberately throwing it away.

We kept plowing along at twelve knots. There wasn't much of anything to do all day. The Dodger was prepared for action to the last rivet. We were filled up with fuel. The ready ammunition was in its racks at the guns. The torpedoes were topped off with air in the morning and the torpedo men went over them all adjusting the detonators and getting them all set for a run. The four destroyers in the van moved in and formed with the anti-submarine screen so that we had a complete division on each side in a compact formation, ready to deploy in any direction. The cruisers' observation planes took over the scouting in the van, and we had at least two of them in the air all day. Every few hours a cruiser would have to haul out of formation to recover her planes for refueling and a couple of destroyers would drop out with her to screen her during the operation. We never saw an enemy submarine. They may have been there, but I think it more likely that they were lying submerged off Torcas, keeping the port under observation.

We were getting reports on the enemy position every half-hour. At ten o'clock the report failed to come in. It was an hour before the relief shadowing plane picked them up again. Then he reported that the first plane had been shot down by enemy fighters, and that he had barely escaped the same fate. That was the first intimation we had that the enemy had a carrier with him. It made the task of the patrol planes doubly hazardous. The day was fine but there were a few low-hanging cumulus clouds for the patrol planes to hide behind. At any rate they did a fine job of shadowing. The reports kept coming in, and we were able to plot every move the enemy made.

When he shot down the first plane the enemy drew first blood in what will probably be a long and exhausting war. By now he knows for sure that he has bitten into something, and he may have commenced to have some faint misgivings then, when he realized that our patrol planes were keeping him under surveillance. Those boys in the planes were good. I don't suppose their complete story is known yet; but they turned in a bang-up job of shadowing, and they were Johnny on the spot later when we needed them most. We lost another plane in the afternoon, and through it all we kept plodding slowly along toward Torcas.

At sunset we were a hundred and fifty miles from Torcas. The enemy was then one hundred and sixty miles to the north of there and about three hundred miles from us. I had a few misgivings that maybe Admiral Thompson couldn't make up his mind whether to fight or run, and so was doing neither.

Since we had changed course toward Torcas in the morning the skipper had grown more talkative. We spent a great deal of time discussing what we thought the next move would be, and very often we found ourselves in disagreement.

"If he is going in, let's get going and get it over with," I remarked to the skipper. "He's so far away now that it will take us all night to catch him, and if we have any kind of a search problem it might be dawn before we concentrate for attack."

"Take your time, take your time," the skipper cautioned. "The old boy knows exactly what he's doing. He's giving the enemy credit for as much sense as he has himself. Right now he is trying to outguess him and predict his plans. If you were in command of an enemy expeditionary force coming down on Torcas now, just how would you go about it?"

I hadn't given that much thought. My main concern was what our own forces expected to do. I had somehow figured that the enemy would arrive when he got there, do a little long-range bombardment, land his troops and carry the place by assault. He had plenty of power to do it without trying any fancy stuff.

"If I was doing it I wouldn't be so precipitate," Captain Shears lectured. "Remember, an amphibian operation is the trickiest of all operations in war. Any little miscalculations are apt to throw the whole thing off balance. While they are unloading, the transports are as vulnerable as a pup on his back with his feet in the air. Once the troops are in the boats they are almost impossible to protect until they have established a beach head. You can't afford to be surprised. Give the enemy admiral credit for some sense."

"How do you think he's going to go about it?" I asked. I commenced to see that a correct estimate of the enemy's plan was going to have a tremendous effect upon what we would do.

"If it was me," the skipper explained, "I'd figure on being at least a hundred and fifty miles away from Torcas by dusk this evening. The enemy probably knows that there are no motor torpedo boats there and that the defense is weak, but I give him credit for realizing that there is no use in taking any chances. He will close the islands during darkness and be in a position to bombard by dawn. Tomorrow he will bombard all the likely landing places with his heavy ships so that no one will know which one he will decide on. His planes will conduct a complete reconnaissance and test out all the beach defenses. The cruisers and destroyers will guard the convoy during the bombardment and keep them well offshore out of harm's way. Then at dawn, the morning following, he will land under cover of heavy fire from the ships and a full-scale air attack."

"That gives us two nights for counterattack," I figured.

"Perhaps Admiral Thompson will wait until tomorrow and see if anything develops."

"No, Wiston, I don't think he will," Captain Shears continued. "Admiral Thompson figures that the enemy will make a complete air search of the area between him and Torcas late this afternoon. So far we have been lucky enough to remain undiscovered. We are killing time now, staying outside that search area. If he gives the enemy another day we are bound to lose some more patrol planes, and I don't see that we will gain very much by delay. Tonight is the night, my lad, or I am greatly mistaken."

Well, as usual the skipper proved to be right in his estimate. About sunset the Admiral broke his radio silence again to order the patrol planes to concentrate over the enemy. Right after that the cruisers catapulted all their planes. They made a flight of thirty planes, and when they were all assembled they flew off in the direction of Torcas. That made it certain that Admiral Thompson intended to fight before another daybreak. Those planes wouldn't be of much use in a night action. With our own patrol planes overhead there would be too much risk of mistaken identity. From Torcas, in the morning, they would be available for whatever service presented itself.

As soon as the planes were gone we went to thirty knots. The formation stayed closed up, with a destroyer division on either flank and the cruiser column in the center. Our course would bring us within thirty miles of Torcas in passing. That was the most probable enemy submarine area, but at the speed we were making and with the visibility what it was a submarine wouldn't stand a chance of getting in. Luck would play a large part in the night's operations anyway, and the Admiral evidently intended to shoot the works. We didn't put out a searching force. The planes were doing all our contact work. We stayed concentrated for attack.

If I ever get any decorations for that night's work you

can accept my assurance now that they will be undeserved. Frankly I was scared to death from the time it was certain that there was going to be no holding back. The darkness multiplied my fears. I could imagine enemies on every side. It seemed certain that we were steaming into a trap. There was only three hundred yards between destroyers, and at thirty knots, darkened ship, that doesn't allow much leeway. That was fortunate in a way because it didn't allow me much time for cogitation. As it was I could heartily wish myself elsewhere.

There wasn't any zigzagging now. We went boring straight in, depending on our speed to carry us through. In the dim moonlight what I could see of the formation made a pretty picture. The destroyer squatted down to her business and the white water boiled up astern of us. She bucked and reared over the low swells like a skittish colt, and at the least touch of the wheel heeled way over and swung her bow in a dizzy arc as though she resented the restraint and control. The blowers whined in fiendish glee and the wind swept through the rigging in a gale. It could have been exhilarating under any other circumstances.

We were all at general quarters from the time we increased speed. The guns were fully loaded, and the guns' crews standing by. As we heeled a little to the rudder or caught a large swell just right, a shower of spray swept over the men at the torpedo tubes. Down below in the fireroom, deafened by the roar of the blowers, men stood before the boilers, revealed to each other by the flashing light through the slots in the air registers of the oil burners. In the engineroom the chief machinist's mates stood alert to the throttles, and the oilers wandered to and fro intent on the lubrication of each bearing, listening to the familiar whir of the turbines and the sob of the air pumps. The ship was a live thing, and a hundred men tended solicitously to her every need.

In the gloom of the bridge I was suddenly conscious of Marley, the chief engineer, standing at my elbow.

"How's everything going below, Chief?" the captain asked.

"Doing all right, I guess," Marley answered as though he momentarily expected the worst. Then his pride in his plant must have gotten the better of him, for he added, "Making thirty-one knots by revolutions, and she's got another knot or two left in her if you want it."

"She ought to have," the captain bantered. "She made over thirty-two on her trials twenty-three years ago, and she's had time enough to wear in her bearings and settle down since then."

"She may be over age, but there's plenty of life left in the old girl yet," Marley commented, with an obvious glow of pride.

"That's right, Chief," Captain Shears agreed. "She may be short on gadgets, but she still has twelve torpedoes and speed enough to get us where we want to go."

The chief engineer left the bridge. I more than ever appreciated the privilege of my own job. I could at least see what was going on. I had a feeling of having some control over my own destiny. Down in the enginerooms and the firerooms the men saw only the familiar gauges and controls. For all they knew, any second might bring a salvo of high explosive shells down into that labyrinth of steam lines and whirring machinery. Steam! Steam that was now the servant, hastening to do their bidding, might at any instant turn and snuff out all their lives. They must have the feeling of working in a trap, from which there was no escape. Every heel of the ship might mean the turn to the deployment course or a frantic effort to avoid collision. The thin steel sides and the deck of the ship offered no protection to them. They only served to confine the men and to hold the machinery that was at once their servant and their master.

For seven hours we held her nose down to the track of the next ahead. For seven hours we hurried through the darkness. The communication officer brought an occasional message to the captain, contact reports from the patrol planes, now concentrated and hovering above the enemy convoy. Only once did we make a slight change to the right. There were no signals. The moon set a little before one o'clock. There were no lights. Only the cruiser on our beam and the destroyer ahead could be seen from the bridge.

It was some time after moonset before anything happened. Suddenly away out on the port bow there was the flash of gunfire. It seemed a long time before we could hear the roar of the guns. We steamed on in the darkness and in silence. We were drawing ahead of the cruisers. They were dropping back to give the destroyers room to deploy and attack. The roles of the destroyers and the cruisers now were reversed. All during the voyage we had dodged and frisked around the outskirts of their formation, guarding them from the submarine menace. It was their job now to support us as we pushed home our attack. They lurked in the darkness right astern of us, ready to counter the enemy cruisers that would steam out to meet us, ready to smother in gunfire any opposition we might meet before we achieved our objective.

A star shell burned high in the air well astern of our formation. The gun flashes to the left were repeated at rhythmic intervals. Now star shells burst right over our formation. The left-flank destroyers opened up in reply. Almost immediately the whole arc of the sea to port broke into flickering gun flashes as the enemy fleet picked up the target and opened up on us. Shell splashes arose in a forest between us and the port line of destroyers. Star shells weirdly illuminated scattered patches of the night's black void. The cruisers astern of us were firing steadily, rapidly. The long slim length of the Dodger seemed to crouch to the surface of the sea as she sped on through a bedlam of noise and fire.

"Shall I open up, Captain?" the gunnery officer yelled down the voice tube.

"Not yet," the captain replied quite calmly. "Follow the action of the Division Commander unless you get a target close aboard. I don't believe the enemy has seen our division yet."

I don't know whether the Admiral ordered the planes to illuminate, or whether they acted on their own initiative as soon as the action opened up. Over to port a new bright star appeared in the blackness between the sea and sky. It seemed to waver and grow. Then it was a great bright white light held high above the sea by an invisible thread. There was another and another until there was a long line of bright luminous, flickering lights above the sea. At first we could see nothing on the sea beneath them, but as the flares sank lower we could make out the ghostlike shapes of the transports. The long line of flares looked like a fiery dragon in the sky, the ships beneath unreal and motionless on an invisible sea.

The transports were six or eight thousand yards away. Between them and us we could occasionally see the futuristic shape of an enemy destroyer. The left-flank destroyers were under heavy fire. We could see the red flare of occasional hits. Star shells burst over the enemy cruisers in the van, helping the flashes of the gunfire to reveal their position. Astern of us our cruiser line was one long flame of gun flashes. It was no longer possible to hear anything. The action was rapidly degenerating into the melee that is the usual course of a night action. In it anything might happen.

In we steamed, still silent, still undiscovered. The other division was taking terrific punishment. There was a heavy blast and an explosion that could only mean the end of one good ship. From our line it appeared that there was a solid wall of gun splashes ahead of the left flank. It didn't seem possible that any of them could steam through and live. Enemy cruisers were laying down a curtain barrage between the destroyers and the transports.

"There they go!" the captain shouted above the din. "They are peeling off now!"

For a brief second I took my eyes off the next ahead to

look. The port line seemed broken and shattered. No longer did it bear any resemblance to a close-order attack group of destroyers. In the fitful illumination of gun flashes and star shells the black ships blended with the black sea. Only by the silhouettes of the masts and funnels and by the bright flashes of the guns could you see them. I saw one turn sharply to port away from us and right into that barrage of shell fire. She had fired her port tubes and was turning to bring her starboard ones to bear. The others were following her, more in a huddle than in any distinct formation.

Still we steamed on toward the transports. Nothing ahead of us but enemy now. The great ships seemed bigger. They had appeared to grow up out of the surface of the sea. Above them the airplane flares glowed and flickered like our guiding stars. Occasionally I could see great fountains of water spring up among them. The planes were unloading their bombs in coordination with our attack. On board the Dodger not a gun had been fired. In the uncertain illumination I could make out that the transports were attempting a simultaneous course change. Warned of the torpedoes coming down at them from the attack of our left flank, they were attempting to avoid. They appeared to be in confusion. Their formation was breaking up.

"Stand by to fire the port tubes!" I heard the captain shout to the torpedo officer.

"Hold her on her course now, Wiston," he ordered.

I could see the next ahead turn sharply to port. There was nothing now between us and the enemy line. I never heard the order to fire the port tubes. The captain must have moved over until he was at the torpedo officer's elbow. I felt the repeated thud and jar as the tubes fired in succession, and I knew we had successfully launched half our torpedoes.

"Now bring her left, Wiston," the captain commanded, "and bear right down for the center of that group of transports."

"Left standard rudder." The quartermaster spun the wheel.

For an instant I thought the ship was going to turn over. She lay over on her side and hung there. Great sheets of spray flew over her decks. The inboard rail was awash. The sound of the sea tearing at her fittings was more insistent than the distant sound of gunfire.

"Six tubes fired following the action of the Division Commander!" Captain Shears was shouting in my ears. "But I'm going to carry the message right home to Garcia with the starboard battery. I'll take them in so close we can't miss and they won't have time to dodge."

"Rudder amidships, steady as you go," he ordered with more calmness than I should ever have been able to muster just then. The ship came back to an even keel. The captain was charging straight on in, holding the fire of his starboard tubes until he was within killing range. There was no longer any semblance of a formation. We had lost all contact with our own division. We were on our own. Behind us the booming roll of the cruisers' gunfire had momentarily ceased.

Suddenly on our starboard bow there was the apparition of a huge shape looming over us.

"Cruiser to starboard!" I yelled. "Right full rudder!" The ship lay over on her side again. I saw the captain jump to the telegraphs and pull the starboard handle down to full astern. We were almost right under her bow. The Dodger was coming around, skidding and heeling on the turn like an ice skater.

There was a blinding flash of gunfire—almost right in my face, it seemed. I was aware that our forecastle gun was firing in return. The whole port battery of the cruiser opened up on us in a roar and flash that blotted out everything else. There was a crash and a shock that threw us all off our feet. As I went down I was aware of our bow folding up like an accordion. We lay over on our starboard side, and I tumbled across the deck trying to grab something to pull me to my feet.

We came rolling back and I heard a rending crash of boat

davits and tubes and guns being torn out by their roots as we wiped our port side clean along the length of the cruiser.

Somehow I got to my knees. Instantly I was knocked flat again by the blast of one of the cruiser's guns. She couldn't depress her guns to hull us but her fire was wiping us off almost level with the bridge. I heard the mast come down on top of the bridge and then I think I must have lost consciousness. I probably picked up this splinter in my leg then, and some time during the night I got an awful whack on my head. If it hadn't been for that I wouldn't be alive to tell the tale, for I was lying senseless on the deck through what must have been the worst of the holocaust.

When I again became conscious of what I was doing I found myself trying to struggle to my feet in the mass of rubbish that had been the bridge. There was the blinding glare of a searchlight right on us, so intense that I could almost feel the light rays beat against me. I couldn't see a thing outside that beam of light. The round glaring orb of the searchlight seemed to tower almost directly over the Dodger. The cruiser was pouring shells into us at the range of a few hundred yards. She couldn't miss, and her searchlight showed us up as a beautiful target. Only the gun on our after deckhouse was returning the fire. It couldn't last more than a few seconds, and in my confused half-conscious state I didn't greatly care.

It was the searchlight that I cursed that saved us. In its light the enemy cruiser was pounding us to pieces, but by its use she also made a perfect target of herself. Off in the gloom one of our own cruisers had been following nearly in our wake. Suddenly presented with an illuminated target, she opened up with her full battery. It was magnificent. Checking back, I think it was the Armstown that came to our rescue, but there never will be any way of knowing who actually fired on whom that night.

If it was the Armstown I drew dividends then for the months I had spent on her gunnery training. There didn't seem to be any break in her firing. At the first blast the searchlight went out and the enemy frantically trained her guns on her new opponent.

Then there occurred an inspired and unpremeditated bit of cooperation such as can occur only in a perfectly disciplined organization in which each individual has been trained to act on his own initiative. The electrician on our own searchlight opened up and illuminated the enemy. There hadn't been any orders. He knew that his action would bring a rain of shells down again on his crippled ship. But for the brief instant that it lasted the enemy stood out perfectly illuminated.

The Armstown made the most of her opportunity. Her guns rolled on in a continuous eruption. The enemy made a feeble attempt to return the fire. We could see splinters flying out of her in all directions. In the first salvos her gunnery organization must have been wiped out. I could see some of her secondary battery guns trained on us in an effort to blast out our searchlight. She was afire midships. Her stack came down. Our searchlight died out as our generators gasped their last. All was darkness again except for the glow of the fire on the enemy cruiser. There was a heavy internal explosion as though her boilers had been hit. I could see the bulk of her bow rising high in the air. She was gone. In what must have been only a minute or two of concentrated fire the Armstown had literally sawed her off at the water line.

After the Armstown ceased firing, it was quiet. There was the flickering of gun flashes off in the distance. I commenced to take stock of the situation. The bridge was wrecked. First I must look for the captain. In the darkness I could only feel my way about. I bumped into someone crawling around on his hands and knees. It was Handy, the quartermaster.

"Have you seen the skipper?" I asked him. He rolled his head in a dizzy sort of way. I shouted my question at him again.

"Over there," he muttered, pointing to a tangle of wreckage where the mast had fallen over the bridge.

It was there I found him, and there I left him lying. He was beyond any help from me, and no selection board would ever again pass on his merits. For a moment I had an overwhelming desire to lie down beside him. It would have been so easy to quit. Life itself wasn't worth the struggle. My leg hurt me, and there was a confused ringing in my head. The ship was a shambles. It was useless to try to carry on. There wasn't a possibility that we should survive the next few minutes.

No one would ever know how perfectly Captain Shears had led his ship into attack. No one would ever realize how dissatisfied he had been with less than perfection, how his determination and his alone had willed that the Dodger should carry her remaining torpedoes into the very heart of the enemy formation. If survivors ever told the Dodger's story, old fuddy-duddies and bright young squirts fancying themselves as naval tacticians would read only mistakes into his action. The life of a destroyer, once she arrives at decisive range, they would argue in the light of after events, is so short that she makes a mistake in holding her fire. Events would bear them out, for the Dodger still had six unexpended torpedoes in her tubes and I was abruptly aware that we were lying dead in the water.

It slowly dawned on me that the ship and those torpedoes were my responsibility now. I had succeeded to my first command. Whatever Shears would have done, I should do now. We were still afloat. We had torpedoes. The battle was still on. There might still be an opportunity to be of some use. I wasn't a free agent. I had Captain Shears' ship to fight the way he would have fought her. The old destroyer dictum never to get sunk with torpedoes unexpended forced me to carry on.

I began to take stock of the situation. I threw the engine order telegraphs over to Stop and then back to Ahead and got no answer. The wheel was equally useless. Handy had come to his senses and was helping me. Of all the bridge personnel we seemed to be the only ones left alive.

"We will have to try the after steering station, Mr. Wiston," he suggested.

I assented, and we picked our way down off the bridge in the darkness. At the foot of the bridge ladder we ran into the gun captain from the forward gun. He was helping the pharmacist's mate dress the wounds of some of the men of his gun crew.

"The forward gun is washed out, Mr. Wiston," he reported as soon as he recognized me in the darkness, "and the forecastle just ain't no more."

I went forward to have a look. The bow was crushed nearly all the way back to the gun, and the gun itself was canted at a crazy angle. She was just a mass of wreckage forward, and the sea sloshed and sighed in among the twisted plates. All the deck force had berthed in those forward compartments, but fortunately they had all been at general quarters stations. I couldn't be sure but she had been wrecked far back into the officers' country. I hoped the bulkhead was holding. If it wasn't we might yet have trouble keeping her afloat.

"Get a couple of your men, and go below to shore up the bulkhead," I directed the gun captain. The assistant engineer was the damage control officer, but he was nowhere to be found. Probably he was having his hands full elsewhere. So far I hadn't located a single officer, but the crew was carrying on, doing what could be done.

We went aft along the starboard side. It would have been impossible to climb over the wreckage to port. The top of the galley deckhouse was a shambles. The cruiser's gunfire had swept it clean. Broken ammunition cases lay scattered on the deck. If any men had survived that storm of shells they had been carried to the main deck below, where the ammunition parties were trying frantically to render first aid to the wounded. A minute's inspection told me that both those guns would be unserviceable.

As we made our way aft along the main deck I found the starboard tubes trained out and the crew still standing by. The chief torpedo man almost tearfully explained to me that he had never been able to bring the tubes to bear on the cruiser. It was those unexpended torpedoes that weighed heaviest on my mind.

We climbed up to the top of the after deckhouse, and I was surprised and pleased to find that station practically unharmed. The gun's crew still stood by the gun. My old friend Lewis was gun captain of that gun. Under his command each man was as steady as a rock, although for all they knew the ship might be going down beneath their feet. I spun the wheel and there was no response. I pulled the engineroom bell pulls and nothing happened.

I saw a man in dungarees with an officer's cap heave himself heavily up the ladder to the deckhouse.

"Is that you, Chief?" I asked.

"I think so," Marley replied. "Where's the captain?"

"The captain is gone, Marley," I told him, feeling a sinking sensation inside me as I said it. "How did you make out below?"

"Not so well," he admitted. "We took a shell in the after condenser, and the after fireroom is a wreck. We lost steam pressure, and we had to stop. The telegraphs have both swung down to Stop."

"Cables shot away, I guess," I told him. "The wheel rope seems to have gone too."

"Where's Jonas?" I asked, inquiring for his assistant engineer.

"He had the repair party mustered on the port side abreast the galley the last I knew," he answered. "If he was still there when we hit whatever we hit I think there is no use looking further for him."

I had seen the galley deckhouse, and I could agree without discussion.

"Can we still steam?" I asked.

"Forward engine only, on the forward boilers," he answered shortly.

"Good!" I shouted at him. "Let's get going!"

Marley dropped back to the ladder and made his way forward to the engineroom.

"Handy," I said to the quartermaster, "get two men from somewhere and go down to the steering-engine room. I'll conn through the voice tube. If you've still got steam back there use the trick wheel. If not we'll steer by hand. It's up to you to steer her, and I don't give a damn how you do it."

"Aye, aye, sir," Handy answered.

I think he was glad to have a definite task again. The tour of the wrecked ship he had made with me seemed to have depressed him, and I think he mourned his ship more than the shipmates of whose loss he couldn't yet be certain.

"Did I hear you say the captain is dead, Mr. Wiston?" Lewis asked me out of the darkness by the gun.

"Yes, Lewis," I answered. "His body is up on the bridge in the wreckage."

Lewis made no reply.

Over the voice tube Marley reported that he was ready. I gave him three bells, and it seemed strange to feel the ship moving through the water again. I ordered the rudder amidships. The steering engine commenced to grind and wheeze, and I knew we still had steam back there. Until then I hadn't given a thought as to where we were going.

The sea was covered with a pall of smoke. Not a ship was in sight. Overhead I could hear the roar of a plane's motors. Ahead I could see nothing. The smashed bow threw spray high in the air. My forward gun's captain came aft to report that the wardroom bulkhead was holding. I sent him forward to the bridge to act as lookout.

Off on the starboard bow there was the flash of gunfire. Something was in that direction. I could head over that way and trust to luck to run into something.

"Destroyer on the starboard quarter, sir," Lewis suddenly sang out.

I could see her dark mass steadily overtaking us. We had no lights on board. There was no way of making a recognition signal. Instantly I was glad there wasn't. In the light of a gun flash I made out that she had two stacks. Enemy!

"Open fire," I ordered.

Wham! The gun let loose right at my elbow. I couldn't see a thing after the flash. I was conscious of men in rhythmic movement, like a dance in which each motion has been rehearsed again and again.

"Bore clear!" I heard the breech slam shut.

"Ready two!"

"Wham!"

"Up one double oh!" Lewis shouted, spotting his own shots.

"Steady down, you punk," he cursed at his gun pointer.

"Bore clear! Ready three!" I could see her now. She was sheering off. The third shot was slow getting off but I could see it burst on the enemy's forecastle.

"Hit! Hit! No change! Rapid fire!" Lewis ordered. "Pour it into them, you lazy bastards," he exhorted his gun crew. "One more hit! One more hit for Captain Shears!"

There was the flash of at least three guns from the enemy's deck. Short. The splashes rose between her and us. She was obscured for a moment. She was drawing away in the murk. We had scared her off. If she could have known how pitiful our condition was she could have blasted us out of the ocean. She was firing but her fire was wild and uncontrolled. I lost sight of her. The pointer could no longer see his target. Our gun was silent.

From out of the darkness she let fly a ragged salvo. By all the miracles of luck it landed well bunched amidships. Instantly there was a flash of flame from the galley deckhouse.

It carried higher than the mast had been. That lucky parting shot of the enemy's had found the broken ammunition cases still up there by the wrecked guns on the galley deckhouse. The whole surface of the sea must have been lit up. I was blinded and seared by the torch the burning powder made amidships.

It died down as quickly as it had flared up, but there was still a flicker of flame from burning life rafts on top of the galley. In its light I could see that men were fighting the fire with whatever they could lay their hands on.

High above us I could hear the roar of a plane's motors reach a screaming pitch. In the light of the fire we must have stood out plainly to the planes that hovered above us. I could see the blue flashes of his exhaust as he dove straight down at us. It seemed he would dive into our deck but it must have been hundreds of feet above us that he pulled out.

To starboard a column of water was slowly arising from the surface of the sea. The ship seemed to lift clear out of the water to shake herself before she fell back. Tons of water cascaded down upon our decks.

From the engineroom I could hear a bedlam of noise and again we groaned to a stop. The water that had come aboard had put out the fire. We could hear the motors of the retreating plane. For an instant all around us was quiet again. Then up ahead there was the roaring boom of gunfire to remind us that the battle still went on.

Marley found his way to the after deckhouse again. He sat on the deck with his head in his hands. In the darkness he looked as if all hope had left him.

"Right down through the after fireroom it went," he lamented bitterly. "What was it anyway?"

"Dive bomber," I told him. "But it didn't hit us. The bomb must have exploded at least fifty feet to starboard."

"Maybe one did," he admitted, "but one went right through the after fireroom, right down through the bottom of the ship. Good thing it didn't explode there, or we would have been blown in two. The after fireroom is flooded, but it was all shot to pieces anyway."

"Something exploded," I reminded him.

"You're right. It did," he agreed. "The forward turbines lifted right off the bed plates. When they came down again they stripped every blade in their rotors, from the sounds. Maybe it was the bomb exploding under us, but it might have been the near miss you talk about. Anyway that's that."

"Are you all washed up below?" I asked.

"Let me think," he answered. "The forward boilers can still steam. I think the steam lines are still holding together. The forward engineroom is finished and we can cross that off. Only the condenser and the exhaust trunk is wrecked in the after engineroom. Let me think, what can I do with that?"

I wasn't much help to him. I had been aboard such a short time that the maze of pipe lines and machinery in which he dwelt was a mystery to me.

"I think it will work!" he shouted, pounding his fist in his hand. "We will steam with the after engine on the forward fireroom and exhaust into the engineroom. I'll open up the throttle wide and control her with the bulkhead stop valve from the deck. How's that?"

"It sounds fine if you can do it," I answered. "We can try anything, and if it doesn't work we won't be any worse off than we are now."

"We will be able to steam ahead only," he cautioned. "No back bells, and it's good only for an hour or so. By that time we will be out of fresh water and we'll be through."

"An hour is better than nothing," I encouraged. "Get ready. We will stay here until I see something promising."

It must have been fifteen or twenty minutes before he reported ready. All around the horizon to the northward there were fitful flashes of gunfire. The enemy was retiring the way he had come. The action had broken up into private fights as ship met ship in the darkness. It was all a confused melee, but the general trend seemed to be away from us as the enemy retreated.

When Marley reported all in readiness we tried it out. There was a billowing cloud of steam up out of the after engineroom grating. The only control I had was to shout down to Marley on deck to go ahead and to stop. But it worked. It wasn't much, but it gave us a glimmer of hope and something to do.

We must have been waiting nearly an hour. The battle receded from us until we could only hear the rumble of occasional gunfire. We lay still, rolling in the swell, creaking painfully with each roll. Like a wounded animal we waited, husbanding our strength for one final effort.

In the darkness above we could hear planes circling and watching. It seemed that their number was increasing. On the starboard bow, back in the general direction of Torcas, I picked up a light, then a dim glow. It was moving toward us.

"Here we go, boy!" I shouted down to Marley. "Open her up wide!"

We were under way again. But no longer were we in a proud and swift destroyer, knifing our way through the water. She was a clumsy leaking wreck beneath us, pushing up the water ahead of the wreckage that hung across her bow, crawling painfully over the sea.

I conned the steering-engine room on until we were on a course that I estimated would intercept. She came up rapidly. In a minute or two I could make out what it was. It was an aircraft carrier! From the activity in the air above and from the lights she dared to show I knew she was busy flying on planes. I knew then that she would be steaming into the wind at high speed.

There was no time to ponder on the reasons that brought her there. I suppose she had been on a detached mission far in advance of her fleet when the battle opened. Now she was attempting to follow her consorts in retreat. Her fighter planes must be nearly out of fuel. Their need must have been desperate, or she never would have risked the lights necessary to guide them in their flying on operations. Unless she could recover them, all the enemy's fighters would be down in the sea long before dawn. The battle receded into the distance, and she must have decided to accept the risk.

It was over in a few minutes. She came charging through the night and painfully we crawled toward her. Fortunately her course would bring her near us. We couldn't do much to close. I brought the Dodger lumbering around until we were steaming parallel to her estimated course. I watched her coming up swiftly from astern of us and over a deck stanchion I checked her bearing. The tubes were trained out on the beam.

"All right at the tubes. Stand by." I could only guess at the offset angle. All our fire control instruments were gone, but we were close in and the torpedoes were set for a spread.

"Fire!" I felt a thud and heard the splash of a torpedo hitting the water. I looked down to the deck below in time to see a torpedo man swing a mallet at the firing mechanism of the last tube to fire. The torpedoes were on their way. A load was off my mind. The skipper had been vindicated.

"Right standard rudder." The Dodger came slowly around in answer to her rudder, a tired and beaten old ship that had started out the night so handily. I could think now of saving what remained of her. My obligation to the captain was ended.

"Everything you've got, Marley!" I shouted down to him. "Let's get out of here and give us some smoke to hide her!"

There wasn't any communication with the fireroom except by messenger, so the smoke was a little while in coming.

I heard a heavy rolling explosion. Even above the billowing clouds of steam and smoke that rolled out over the sea aft of us, the flames leapt high. There was a wild burst of gunfire. Occasionally I could see splashes ahead of us and around us. It lasted only a little while. Then they lost sight of us in the darkness. Overhead the planes buzzed angrily, like wasps whose nest has been destroyed.

Through the thick black cloud of smoke I headed her in the general direction of Torcas. The light breeze from aft kept us hid in our own smoke screen. The greasy soot descended on everything. She couldn't have been making more than six or seven knots at the most.

Long after I heard the last of the planes I called down to Marley to cease making smoke. As the black sooty clouds thinned out a little I could see the first faint light of the gray dawn in the east. I knew then that Marley had kept steaming much longer than his promised hour. Suddenly there was again a rending noise from the engineroom. Again we came to a halt.

"Keep her going!" I yelled frantically to Marley. "Keep her going until we have light enough to see!"

"That's all finished now, my lad," said Marley, coming up the ladder. "No more water."

"Feed your damn boilers salt water!" I shouted angrily at him.

"Hell, Steve!" he countered. "I've been feeding them salt water for twenty minutes. The boilers are salted up tight. That noise you just heard was water coming over and taking the guts of the turbine along with it. And that's all for the night, I guess."

We lay there unable to move a wheel as the dawn broke. I had lived through a lifetime in a few short hours of darkness. Planes were coming toward us from Torcas. In desperation we manned the machine guns. A little knot of men stood by the three-inch antiaircraft gun on the fantail. With it we could make a loud noise that might scare a timid enemy; but effective defense against an air attack, we had none.

It was with profound relief that we recognized them as the cruisers' planes. They came right over us in a fast and compact formation. Before dawn they had left Torcas, sweeping out to bomb what they could find of the transports before the scattered enemy forces could be organized in their defense. We cheered feebly as they flew over.

For a long while after it was light we couldn't see anything but wreckage. The sea was covered with oil. Through it all at last the Armstown and two destroyers came steaming. The Armstown towed us in to Torcas. It was only fifty miles away. So the Dodger came to Torcas at last, came in stern first, but the skipper was on the bridge when we made port.

We buried Captain Shears that afternoon, in a grave in the white coral ground. The doctor relented enough to let me ride out in a car to the ceremony at the graveside. The firing party was from the Dodger, and Marley commanded it. When we came back we hauled down the Dodger's commission pennant. They have decided that she is beyond hope of salvage. I shall keep that commission pennant until I can deliver it to Mrs. Shears.

They transferred the remnant of the Dodger's crew to the Armstown. Soon after we came aboard Lewis came up to my room to see me. He stood in the doorway with his hat in his hand, with that embarrassed and apologetic air of his.

"Mr. Wiston," he addressed me, "I've got three days b. and w. coming to me and I'd like to start them now if I may, sir."

Despite the pain in my leg I found myself on my feet.

"Lewis," I told him, "every man who was in the Dodger with me can have anything I've got, any time, anywhere. That sentence is all over and forgotten, and I won't have it otherwise."

"Yes, sir," he answered, fumbling with his hat. "I know. But Captain Shears told me that I would have to finish out that sentence the first time we hit port. It was Captain Shears' orders, sir, and only the captain can rescind them."

I could see that his face was working violently, and I knew

he wished the interview over. I couldn't stand much more of it myself.

"I'll see Captain Reed of the Armstown and ask his permission," I conceded, and limped away.

When I went into Captain Reed's cabin he was seated at his desk.

"Captain," I requested, "I have a man from the Dodger that I'd like to have committed to three days' solitary confinement on bread and water."

"What!" he shouted at me, slapping both hands down on his desk in surprise.

"It's an unfinished sentence for an offense committed back in Port Nelson before we sailed, sir," I tried to explain.

The captain jumped to his feet and walked over to me so belligerently that for a moment I thought he was going to throw me bodily out of the cabin without waiting to hear any more.

"Young man," he thundered at me, shaking his finger in my face, "your lack of loyalty to your men is a disgrace to the service." He was so mad he was choking.

"It's the man's own request, sir," I added, "that he be permitted to finish the sentence. Captain Shears told him that he would have the three days coming to him in the first port we got in. I tried to tell him how I feel about it, but he says that Captain Shears sentenced him and he wants to carry it out."

I guess then that Captain Reed could see something in my face that I had seen in Lewis's. Suddenly he relaxed.

"Very well, Wiston," he told me sadly, "I'll issue the orders."

"Shears must have been a man!" he said to me as I left his cabin.

So Lewis is turned in, in the brig tonight. I hope he is easier in his mind down there than I am in mine in my room up here. I wish there was some way I too could demonstrate what I think of my old captain. The doctor keeps me sitting here with my leg propped up on a pillow. After the manner of doctors he advises that I relax and give the wound in my leg a chance to heal. I wish I could follow his advice.

The Regina and the Hastings both made port a few hours after the Armstown towed us in. Eight destroyers have limped in during the day, some of them pretty badly crippled. The whole force is busy at emergency repairs, getting ready to sail for Hastings to join the fleet. The Admiral seems to think I've done something special, but I have tried to make it clear that it was Douglas R. Shears' ship and I only fought for him a part of the night.

The Naval Institute Press is the book-publishing arm of the U.S. Naval Institute, a private, nonprofit professional society for members of the sea services and civilians who share an interest in naval and maritime affairs. Established in 1873 at the U.S. Naval Academy in Annapolis, Maryland, where its offices remain today, the Naval Institute has more than 100,000 members worldwide.

Members of the Naval Institute receive the influential monthly magazine *Proceedings* and discounts on fine nautical prints, ship and aircraft photos, and subscriptions to the quarterly *Naval History* magazine. They also have access to the transcripts of the Institute's Oral History Program and get discounted admission to any of the Institute-sponsored seminars offered around the country.

The Naval Institute's book-publishing program, begun in 1898 with basic guides to naval practices, has broadened its scope in recent years to include books of more general interest. Now the Naval Institute Press publishes more than sixty new titles each year, ranging from how-to books on boating and navigation to battle histories, biographies, ship and aircraft guides, and novels. Institute members receive discounts on the Press's nearly 400 books in print.

Full-time students are eligible for special half-price membership rates. Life memberships are also available.

For a catalog describing the Naval Institute Press books currently available, and for further information about U.S. Naval Institute membership, please write to:

Membership & Communications Department
U.S. Naval Institute
118 Maryland Avenue
Annapolis, Maryland 21402-5035

Or call, toll-free, (800)233-8764.